"Nice to see you're still in one piece."

Lindsay didn't wait for an invitation to come in.

Mitchell was sitting at the kitchen table, and the sight of him caused a pain in her heart.

"What the hell are you doing here?" he demanded.

She took a purposeful look around. "Cleaning up, from the looks of it. This place is a pigsty."

She was facing the back of his head, but he never turned to her. She wanted to go to him, to tell him that she knew how he felt. But that approach wouldn't work yet. She had to fan a spark before she could get a steady flame.

"Don't bother."

She was already unbuttoning her sleeves and rolling them up. "Might as well see what the rest of the place looks like before I tackle this," she said instead. "After all, this could be the cleanest room. Now, is there an extra bedroom, or do I throw you out of yours?"

Dear Reader,

When two people fall in love, the world is suddenly new and exciting, and it's that same excitement we bring to you in Silhouette Intimate Moments. These are stories with scope and grandeur. The characters lead lives we all dream of, and everything they do reflects the wonder of being in love.

Longer and more sensuous than most romances, Silhouette Intimate Moments novels take you away from everyday life and let you share the magic of love. Adventure, glamour, drama, even suspense— these are the passwords that let you into a world where love has a power beyond the ordinary, where the best authors in the field today create stories of love and commitment that will stay with you always.

In coming months look for novels by your favorite authors: Kathleen Eagle, Heather Graham Pozzessere, Nora Roberts and Marilyn Pappano, to name just a few. And whenever you buy books, look for all the Silhouette Intimate Moments, love stories *for* today's woman *by* today's woman.

Leslie J. Wainger
Senior Editor
Silhouette Books

Kathleen Korbel

Perchance to Dream

Silhouette Intimate Moments

Published by Silhouette Books New York

America's Publisher of Contemporary Romance

To sleep, perchance to dream.
Aye, there's the rub.

Shakespeare
Hamlet, Act 3 Scene 1

SILHOUETTE BOOKS
300 East 42nd St., New York, N.Y. 10017

ISBN: 0-373-07276-7

First Silhouette Books printing February 1989

All the characters in this book are fictitious. Any
resemblance to actual persons, living or dead, is
purely coincidental.

®: Trademark used under license and
registered in the United States Patent and
Trademark Office and in other countries.

Printed in the U.S.A.

Books by Kathleen Korbel

Silhouette Desire

Playing the Game #286
A Prince of a Guy #389
The Princess and the Pea #455

Silhouette Intimate Moments

A Stranger's Smile #163
Worth Any Risk #191
Edge of the World #222
Perchance to Dream #276

KATHLEEN KORBEL

blames her writing on an Irish heritage that gave her the desire and a supportive husband who gave her the ultimatum, "Do something productive or knock it off." Kathleen's hard work has more than paid off, and she was named "Best New Category Romance Author of 1987" by *Romantic Times*. An R.N. from St. Louis, she also counts traveling and music as addictions and is working on yet another career in screen writing.

To my family,
too numerous to name,
who told me I'd better dedicate something to them.
And to Rocky J.,
the life of the party.

Prologue

Look up. See what's waiting for you.

He looked up, his head back so far he was afraid he would fall, even though he was standing on the ground. He saw.

A great skeleton consumed the night. Black on black, geometric bones set one upon the other, this was a beast that could challenge the sky. A storm stalked the beast's heels. Gathering its strength from the mountains beyond, it flickered across the roiling clouds at the skeleton's head and swirled through the debris at its feet. Thunder muttered at its edges.

He stood below, eyes to the top, to where lightning lanced through parallels that lit like hollow eye sockets. To where the beast waited. Beckoning, threatening.

It was so high. A person could fall to his death from its heights.

A building, you idiot, he thought, already sweating. *It's nothing more than a forty-story frame, and you have to get your rear end up there.*

The skeleton summoned with the whisper of approaching thunder. The night watched. He saw that the elevator waited for him. Still he hesitated, his heart hammering. The wind plucked impatiently at his hair, picked through his clothes. A newspaper tumbled across the hard dirt and slapped against his pants leg. He didn't notice.

Mitchell knew it was his job to follow the men who had just climbed to their clandestine meeting. He just didn't realize when they'd told him the address that the building had already grown. He envisioned an empty lot and followed willingly. Now he watched his worst nightmare loom in the dark.

He didn't remember moving. He didn't know that he'd stopped staring at the building's height. Suddenly, though, he stood in the cage, the mesh cold against his slick fingers. The skeleton still waited, high, lethal. It seemed to chuckle in anticipation. But there wasn't anyone else to go up. Maggie wasn't there yet. She would have gone up instead, leaving Mitchell in peace on the ground, but she was too late. He had to climb into space in that open cage.

He could see the button, red against the yellow mesh. He hit it, and the car jerked upward. Weaving his fingers into the metal gridwork, he locked his jaw against the nausea. He couldn't close his eyes. He had to be ready. He had to see what was happening. But he couldn't watch the earth fall away from him, either, because he knew he would fall away with it.

One story, ten, twenty. The floors passed in mute succession, mocking him with the emptiness of their edges. He struggled to keep his eyes level, to ignore the wind that tugged at him for attention. Sweat collected beneath his arms and trickled down his back. He didn't notice. If he looked away, he would fall. He would tumble into space, over and over until the ground rushed up and struck him like a clap of thunder.

He kept his eyes on the passing concrete, looking for signs of life, trying his damnedest to ignore the gravity that pulled ever harder at him.

The altitude clawed at him, twirled him so he couldn't find his balance. But there was something else. Something ... prescient. There was a gnawing in his chest, a rat trying to get out. Something he knew, but couldn't remember. Something that was about to happen.

He found them at the top. They were shadows beyond the illumination of a single bulb, their movements jerky in the shudders of lightning. Thirty-nine floors into space. Thunder reverberated around them. The wind howled. The storm shook the floor in a hollow rush of wind and rain. Beyond, the city winked in silence.

There had been two going up. Now he spotted four. The man they were going to meet had already arrived. If only Maggie had made it, they could have nailed them all together. She could have witnessed the deal and they both could have put them out of action back on the ground—or trapped them all together in the sky until the reinforcements came. Alone, he was useless. He could only watch, the fire in his chest closing off speech and watering his eyes.

I'm acrophobic, Maggie. Only you and I and the boss know that. I can't go above the third floor without bringing up my lunch. I'm not going to bore you with explanations. You just have to know that when it comes to any high stuff, that's yours. I can handle the rest.

We're not the ski patrol, Mitchell. I don't think it's a problem to worry about.

It is now. Where the hell are you, Maggie?

They're fighting. Yelling and shoving. He should get out there. Stop them. They've dragged someone to the edge of the floor. It looks as if they're getting ready to throw him off. There can't be a worse fate.

The car shuddered to a stop and he tried to drag in a lungful of storm-tossed air. *Get over there. Stop them. They're screaming at him, but the words aren't clear.* The thunder was too close, the air too thin. He strained against the paralysis, his hands talons around the protective mesh, the wind snaking around him with cold fingers. *Go out there and stop what's going to happen.* The rat worried at him, too, his teeth sharper, his bite quick. You can stop it. You can prevent it, just this once.

I can't.
I'll fall.
He never knew how close he was to moving. The lightning struck first. A sharp, pronged slash of it, so close he could hear the sizzle, smell the ozone as it flooded the concrete and steel space with a fearsome blue-white light that froze time.

He saw them then. All of them.

Maggie!

How could she be here? How had she made it ahead of him? His hand came away from the cage. He lunged with a terrible cry....

It was Maggie, balanced at the edge of her life, bowed at the brink of the storm. Mitchell saw her and his heart died. He saw her face, her beautiful young face that had never betrayed fear, and she knew. She knew he was there. He understood, because the last he saw of her, she reached out her hand. She reached out to him.

To him. And he could never get to her in time.

"No!"

His heart clamored. His chest was on fire. Coming bolt upright in bed, Jason Mitchell screamed at the end of the dream. The end of his memory. The beginning of his nightmare.

Chapter 1

Lindsay McDonough pulled off her glasses and rubbed gently at the bridge of her nose. There had to be something she could do about the situation, some way she could convince the director she was right. She'd been holed up in her office for two days, interviewing, analyzing, conferring, and she was still facing a blank wall.

No one wanted to deal with Jason Mitchell.

His face stared up at her from the opened dossier on her desk, his strong, angular features pleasantly blurred before her myopic eyes. A tantalizing cleft in his chin softened the crystal green of his eyes, the granite edges of his cheeks. In the picture, he'd pushed his thick chestnut hair impatiently out of the way as his only concession to the banalities of procedure.

Stern, hard, Mitchell had a streak of the loner in him, a touch of the iconoclast. He hated authority, and because of it he did his job well. He also suffered more when it didn't go well. And he was suffering now.

"Do you really think it's that bad, Lindsay?"

Slipping her glasses back into place, Lindsay faced her boss. The rest of the room's occupants slipped into focus, as well—a group of five, gathered around the battered old conference table they used for brainstorming. The window beyond revealed the smog that the summer storm had failed to dispel the night before.

"He didn't even go to Maggie's funeral," Lindsay said. "He walked out of the hospital three days after surgery, and disappeared into the woods. From what Al said, Mitchell hasn't been out of his cabin for a solid two weeks. Yeah, Bob, I'd almost classify that as bad."

Bob Peterson nodded his silvering head reflectively. The top member of the Special Assignment Crime Task Force, Bob was as much father figure and camp counselor as senior officer. The task force had been set up under his tutelage seven years ago, and molded by his values and pragmatism. The well-being of his agents was a serious matter for him.

"Mitchell's taken off for the cabin like this before," he said. "He'd rather recover there than at a hospital. Mitchell likes to heal his own wounds. Besides, he just lost his partner—and not very pleasantly. We still don't know everything that went on up there. Do you really think a couple of weeks is so out of line to recover from all that?"

Lindsay overcame an urge to rub at her tired face again. "This department has a mandatory policy of counseling when an agent is involved in *any* shooting, much less one which results in the loss of a partner. One way or another, I think we have to get Mitchell to comply."

"Comply?" Al Amato echoed from the other side of the table. "Are you kidding? You know how fond Mitchell is of shrinks. Seems to me the last time you had him in to talk about a shooting, he told you that the day you fired a piece in the field was the day you could counsel him about it."

The round of chuckles that met the lame joke was just a little uncomfortable. It was one thing for a psychologist to do consulting on criminal mind-sets or hand out multiple choice tests to potential employees. It was altogether another to accept the idea that a member of the elite little band would actually need to unload on one. That kind of stuff was done privately, as if in a confessional. No one else really wanted to know about the details.

The idea that it could be Jason Mitchell needing that help was tantamount to sacrilege. Mitchell was the dalai lama of law enforcement around here. However he handled it, it worked. Whatever he said was carved in stone. Dalai lamas did not suffer breakdowns.

Nobody here understood the paralysis of guilt. But Lindsay did.

"Do *you* think he's handling this well?" Lindsay challenged, swinging on the diminutive man. Al had been up to the cabin a number of times over the past weeks.

Al hedged, running a hand over the shining surface of his head. Even at thirty Al bore an uncomfortable resemblance to an onion dome. Below the pate a set of open blue eyes now betrayed his real fear for his friend.

"You can't expect him to get over this according to some timetable. He and Mag were pretty tight."

Lindsay nodded, understanding. It was her job to understand. She'd been the one to pair up the partners in the first place, insisting that Mitchell temper his ferocity with the more steadfast nature of Margaret O'Brian. She'd seen the initial resentment, the hesitant jockeying for position between the two and then the bond begin to form.

Maggie had once admitted that it had never extended to the bedroom. But she and Mitchell had developed the special rapport that sometimes grew between two people who needed to trust each other implicitly. They had been the best team the task force had fielded.

"What was he doing the last time you were there?" Lindsay asked, not about to back down.

Again Al hesitated, worrying at the pencil he held as if he could produce conviction like friction. "He . . . well, he was just kind of sitting there. You know how it is. Sometimes you just don't feel like talking. Give him some more time, Lindsay. That's all he needs."

Lindsay shook her head. "I don't think so." She wished she could make these men see what they didn't want to. "Everyone has his breaking point," she said. "Even Jason Mitchell."

Al stiffened at that, his blue eyes suddenly hot with animosity. "You'd just love to shove him into a locked room to prove a point, wouldn't you? Or is it just that the idea of seeing him squirm appeals to you so much?"

The words echoed in the suddenly silent room. Five pairs of eyes avoided Lindsay's. Five well-groomed heads bent a little. Lindsay knew it wasn't venom that had propelled Al's words, but fear for his friend. Even so, it hurt, almost as much as the fact that the other men looked away rather than speak up in her defense.

It was no secret that Lindsay and Mitchell didn't get along. From the first day Lindsay had walked into the threadbare utilitarian offices of the task force in her designer suit, Jason Mitchell had labeled and discarded her as just another paper pusher come to interfere with the already overburdened life of a special cop. She was an outsider in a closely knit and exclusive club. He resented her exalted education, her profession, and most of all, her suggestions. And he made his opinions known in no uncertain terms.

Lindsay considered Mitchell a hotshot with a taste for the dramatic and a loner's disregard of convention. In her opinion, he was also suspicious of change—especially the kinds Lindsay had proposed.

Lindsay had made him take personality tests, sit in on reviews of his cases, and submit evaluations to her. Worst of all, she'd made him partner with a woman. Jason Mitchell partnered with no one. And he most certainly wasn't going to trust his life to someone of Lindsay McDonough's choosing.

In the end they had negotiated a truce. Lindsay recognized Jason for the brilliant field man he was, and he grudgingly acknowledged her instincts when it came to the criminal mind, whether she had field experience or not. He had also grown to depend on the partner he'd sworn he would never have.

"Yes," she agreed with a nod, her tawny eyes just a little chilly. "I do consider Mitchell to have the personality of a rattler with a sore tail. I also consider him to be the best agent this department has. And to lose him—especially like this—would be a disaster."

"Then what do you want to do?" Bob asked from his end of the table.

Pulling her attention away from Al, Lindsay leaned back in her chair to lessen the intensity of the discussion a little. She knew just what kind of image her carefully groomed blond looks projected, and she knew how best to utilize it. She shrugged. "I'm not completely sure."

But she was. She had been for more than two days. It was just that no one in this room would understand her motivation.

"Number one," she suggested, studying her pen, "I don't think Mitchell should be left alone like this, no matter what his usual preference is. I also think we should consider forcing him to see someone."

"Force Mitchell?" One of the other men almost smiled. "That would be one for the books."

Lindsay looked up. "Do you want him back?"

It was Bob who answered, nodding almost contemplatively. "I'll get him back."

"How?" Lindsay and Al asked almost simultaneously.

Bob considered them for a moment, sitting very still, as was his way with conclusions. "In his own time, I think. I've known Mitch longer than anybody. That cabin's worked for him before. Besides, until this mess is completely cleared up, I'd much rather he be as inaccessible as he is. Nobody but us knows where that cabin is."

"If you pay for the services of a psychologist," Lindsay suggested dryly, "don't you think you might as well use her?"

"I do use her," Bob countered with a knowing grin. "She handles more work than any other five people in the force.

I don't think she should hold it against me that I don't always take her advice. Brent," he said, turning to his left and effectively ending the argument, "anything new on the case?"

The agent shrugged. "Cold stone zeros. Al and I were trying to pick up the trail, but we're not having much luck. We got one buyer and two of Wilson's midlevel sellers, and the case of coke in the elevator with Mitchell." A small smile of appreciation lighted Brent's features as he shook his head. "That must have been a hell of a firefight. I'd love to know how it went down."

"Mitchell any help?"

Another shrug. "Maggie was the only one with an in to Wilson's people. Mitchell had hunches, not much more. And how all those dead bodies got there is one of the things he doesn't remember."

Bob sighed, closing the folder in front of him. "So, we're no closer to Esperanza."

"Not unless you'd consider a leap of faith," Brent suggested sarcastically. "*I* sure as hell believe it's his game."

"Yeah, well, that's fine for us," Bob agreed. "Let me know when you have something to take to court. If we don't get a connection between Wilson and Esperanza, we can't nail him for anything more than high living."

Lindsay didn't notice that folders were snapped shut all around her. Her own gaze had strayed back to Mitchell's likeness. He looked up at her as he always did, slightly accusing, eyes hard and challenging. Lindsay couldn't shake the feeling that she was somehow letting him down.

"You really are worried about this, aren't you?"

Lindsay looked up to see Bob standing over her. They were the only two left in the room.

"He might not be as safe in that cabin as you think," she said. "His acrophobia is a wild card, Bob. I think it's costing him more than any of us think."

Bob nodded, his own eyes falling to the image of his best agent. "Okay, how about this? I'll go on up after work. How 'bout if I give you a reading on things tomorrow?"

"I'd rather go with you."

Bob just shook his head. "Mitchell won't throw things at me if I show up unannounced. He just might if you're on my heels."

It was the best Lindsay could hope for. Maybe once Bob saw for himself what Lindsay instinctively knew waited up at that cabin, he would be ready to entertain her suggestion. Until then, the best she could do was get caught up on her other work. Giving Bob one last nod, she gathered her paraphernalia together and left.

Lindsay's office wasn't much more than a converted broom closet at the end of the hall that had been installed four years ago when Bob Peterson garnered the funds for a full-time psychologist. It had been his contention that not only would a house psychologist benefit his employees' screening and team matchups, but one with a background in criminal psychology, like Lindsay, could offer unique insight into the people they were investigating.

Born in the days when all investigative agencies in the U.S. had come under severe scrutiny, the task force dealt with only the elite of crime: syndicates, drug dealing, gunrunning. Given a free hand and universal support, the task force went after the big boys. So far, their track record had been impeccable.

Alone once again at her tiny, meticulously organized desk, Lindsay finally gave in to frustration and raked impatient hands through the shoulder-length, sun-bleached hair that no one in the office had ever seen out of place. Her decision already weighed heavily on her, and she wouldn't be able to put it into practice until tomorrow, at least.

Lindsay loved her work, even the challenge of dealing with someone as stubborn as Mitchell. It had never occurred to her in the four years she had walked these halls that she would ever be the one fighting for him. But then she'd never realized until the moment she'd seen Jason Mitchell looking like a lost child in that hospital bed that he and she had anything in common.

This wouldn't have happened if she'd stayed on at the University of Chicago, she thought blackly. But after the task force, going back to the university now would be a crashing bore. Thinking ahead to what she was going to have to do to pull Jason Mitchell back from the brink, Lindsay briefly wondered if something boring might not be the better option.

"Lindsay?"

She looked up to see Brent leaning in her doorway. "Yeah, Brent, what can I do for you?"

He edged inside almost shyly. "I just wanted to suggest that you don't pay any attention to all that macho garbage we dished out today. Al's worried. So am I. If you can help, then go for it."

Doing her best to keep the shock out of her voice, Lindsay smiled. "Thanks, Brent. I'll do my best."

Maybe she'd hang around, after all.

Bob didn't make it in to work until well after noon of the next day. Pacing off the hours in her office, Lindsay went over her plan again and again until it started to actually make sense. None of her professors would agree with her. She wasn't even sure anyone with common sense would. But then, this was a situation where common sense didn't stand a chance. So the minute Bob's secretary buzzed her, Lindsay headed down to his office.

The truth was there in his eyes before he said a word. It wasn't merely concern Lindsay saw there. It was distress. Helplessness. Whatever he had found when he'd gone to meet Mitchell had been far worse than he'd anticipated.

"He wants to be left alone," Bob said without preamble, never quite meeting Lindsay's eyes.

Lindsay merely nodded, calling upon all her training to keep from saying the wrong thing as she settled into a chair across from Bob's desk. "He told you that?"

Bob nodded, concentrating on the pencil he ran through his fingers. "He said . . ."

Lindsay waited, knowing exactly what Mitchell had said, but needing to hear it from Bob.

With a painful shrug, Bob finally raised his eyes to his associate. "He said he'd shoot the first person who tried to drag him out of that cabin. I don't know what to do, Lindsay. He's…I don't know, lost. I really didn't have any idea."

Lindsay leaned back in her chair and took her time rearranging the skirt of her windowpane check suit over her knees. "I think you're probably right. It won't do us any good to try and force him out of that cabin."

"Then what do we do?"

Lindsay was sure now that her answer was correct. But she also realized that if Bob knew what she had in mind, he would cart her off long before she went after Mitchell. A feeling of dreadful anticipation had begun to slip its cold tendrils around her chest.

"Give him the time," she said. "Let him sit up there and stare at the mountains and commune with nature. You can look in on him later."

Bob betrayed his surprise. "That's it?"

"I'd like to take the week's vacation I have coming to me, if you don't mind."

"You…"

Lindsay got to her feet. Without waiting to hear the objection Bob was trying to frame, she turned for the door. "As a matter of fact, I also have a week left over from last year I never took. I may tack that on, too. Since the Esperanza case is already assigned, you won't need me for a while."

Bob's eyes narrowed suspiciously. "Just where the hell are you going?"

Flashing Bob a four-point smile, Lindsay took hold of the doorknob. "Remember. Don't bother with Mitchell until you hear from me."

She was halfway down the hall by the time Bob recovered himself enough to react. "You're crazier than he is, McDonough!"

Probably, Lindsay silently acknowledged. But she had a gut feeling that this was the way to go. And there was only one way to find out for sure.

In the light of an early summer afternoon, Denver looked as if it had collected all the pollution east of the Rockies. The brown foothills beyond the city were blurred and indistinct in the haze, the beautiful blue Colorado sky a miserable ocher. Lindsay was glad to be getting away from it all, even for such dubious pleasure.

She stopped at her house long enough to pack and change out of office attire and into country casuals. Lindsay had no idea how long she was going to be welcome, but she was going to be prepared for it. Down came the carefully groomed hairstyle that she affected for the office, and up went the French braid. Off came the very proper suit in favor of jeans, sneakers and cotton shirt. No one in the task force would recognize her without her work persona. But then no one at the task force ever followed Lindsay around on her off hours to see what a completely different person she became.

She had been trained to always present a carefully professional image, and never had reason to change it, even in the mostly informal atmosphere of the task force. But on the other hand, Lindsay had been born and raised hardy in Portland, not more than a couple of hours away from every form of recreation one could want. As a result, her personality had become permanently and irrevocably split, and she'd never once regretted it.

When Lindsay came upon Mitchell's cabin it was in shadow. Tucked into a narrow valley up by Winter Park, it was the perfect hideaway, a mile beyond the maps and isolated enough to warrant extra directions from the local grocer.

As Lindsay made the last turn, the sun had just slipped behind the far peaks, leaving the valley in a soft green twilight gilded by the blue-gray spirals of wood smoke. There were other cabins just out of sight in the thick woods that carpeted the valley, and any number of animals rustling amid the underbrush.

Lindsay immediately liked the place. She could see how Mitchell would choose to escape here. A stream chattered nearby, and the air was crisp and clean, even at the edge of summer. Pulling in next to a Jeep at the edge of the small clearing, Lindsay took a coward's breath and stepped out of the car.

The cabin itself was rough-hewn and simple, a ranch-style building with an excess of windows and a screened-in porch that overlooked the morning. A pile of cut wood huddled next to the front door, and an empty clothesline hung between two trees. No smoke issued from the chimney. Gathering the bag of groceries she'd collected into her arms—as much out of defense as helpfulness—Lindsay made the final approach.

She immediately discarded the idea of entering the front door. If she was right, the kitchen would be the testing ground, and there was no reason to lose the element of surprise. Lindsay circled around the porchless side in search of the back door.

The sight that met her at the rear of the house brought her to a halt. Beyond the cabin, the clearing opened into a pasture, now nodding in columbine and daisies. The evening breeze whispered through the bordering pines. Farther into the shadows, the stream she'd heard sped by, fed by the snows that still burned away from the high mountains beyond and choreographed by the tumble of boulders that littered its way. Its echo chuckled and sang in the twilight. Blue spruce and quivering aspen crowded its far bank.

It was a magical place, all music and soft color—a place to restore peace. Lindsay knew now why Mitchell had thought he would find his here.

She didn't wait for an invitation to enter.

"Nice to see you're still in one piece." The screen door banged shut behind her as Lindsay stepped into the gloom of the kitchen. She didn't wait for Mitchell's reaction, but walked over to the counter and set down the bag.

Lindsay was amazed she got a reaction at all. He was sitting, as she'd thought he would, hunched over the kitchen table, his eyes focused beyond the beautiful scenery, his expression blank. He hadn't shaved in days, probably hadn't even changed his clothes from the looks of him. The kitchen was a disaster, tin cans piled up where he'd left them, the plates he'd bothered to use spilling over the sink, the vestiges of any number of meals caked on the edges of the counter. The whole room stank of despair.

Bob had been right to be afraid. Lindsay took one look at Mitchell and almost turned away. How could she possibly think this would work? He looked so lost, like a child without hope, a man without a future. His eyes were red-rimmed and empty, even the challenge in them dead. Lindsay saw the slump to his shoulders, the apathy in his face, and wanted to cry for him.

She knew. She saw him sitting at that table, all alone and desperate—and saw another picture from six years ago. And because she saw that picture, because the sight of him startled the pain in her again, she knew she had to at least try.

"What the hell are you doing here?" he demanded, even his voice no more than a shadow. He didn't move.

Lindsay took a purposeful look around. "Cleaning up, from the looks of it. This place is a pigsty."

She was facing the back of his head. Mitchell never turned to her. Lindsay wanted to go to him, to ease to her knees next to him and put her arms around him. She wanted to tell him that she knew how he felt. But if anyone knew, it was she. That approach wouldn't work yet. She had to fan a spark before she'd get a steady flame.

"Don't bother."

She was already unbuttoning her sleeves and rolling them up. "Might as well see what the rest of the place looks like before I tackle this," she said instead, ignoring him. "After all, this could be the cleanest room. Where do you want me to store my things?"

That got a certain reaction. He turned his head, just a little. "What things?"

"Clothes, my dear Jason. I'm not leaving here until you do."

Lindsay wasn't sure what she expected. She tensed for attack. All she got was a slow turning of his head until his eyes, so cold and empty, fastened on her. "Get out."

It took all the courage she had to counter his animosity with a broad smile. "I told you. When you do. Now, is there an extra bedroom, or do I throw you out of yours?"

That brought him to his feet.

He was tall. Lindsay had never appreciated just how tall until he leaned over her in that small pine and gingham kitchen. Six foot three, his dossier said. More like seven foot three, she thought with a dry mouth, thinking suddenly of a grizzly. Huge, strong, unpredictable. What had she gotten herself into?

"I said get out!"

Looking up at him, Lindsay did her best to draw herself to her full five inches over five foot. It didn't seem to help much. Well, she'd been looking for a spark. She might just have gotten it.

"I heard you the first time," she countered with deliberate ease. "And I told you. I leave here when you do. Now, where's the cleaner?"

He never moved. "Why are you doing this to me? I don't even like you."

"And I like you even less. But all this time you're spending here staring at your belly button has Bob and the boys all crazy. And, typical men, they can't think what to do about it."

"I already told them," he retorted, leaning much too close. "Leave—me—alone!"

Lindsay flashed him one more grin before turning back to her task. "No."

She was furiously scrubbing at the dishes when she heard the door slam.

Lindsay's shoulders slumped. A heartfelt sigh escaped. That had been close. She turned to the window and made sure he was still within sight.

Mitchell had gone no farther than the edge of the stream. He stood there, head bent, hands in his pockets, stiller than Lindsay had ever seen him. She wondered yet again at her coming up here. He was right. The minute he started getting his steam back, they would bicker like in-laws. From that point on, she wasn't sure just what kind of staying power she was going to have. But after seeing the emptiness in him, a man who had more energy and drive than any six she'd ever known, she knew it was too late to change her mind.

Lindsay nodded to herself. Then she turned to putting her decision into practice.

The nearest neighbor wasn't as far away as Lindsay might have thought. A vacation cabin rented out for the better part of the year by its distant owners, it sat no more than a quarter of a mile up the stream. The two men who were renting it now hadn't been seen in town, or frequented any of the fishing spots. It didn't matter much to the locals, who usually had all they could do to handle overeager tourists. They gladly left the men in peace to enjoy the solitude of the valley and the beauty of the mountains.

Those men stood now in the living room of their cabin, clad in slacks and blue shirts. Empty cigarette packs clogged the trash and TV dinners filled the freezer. One, an older man with a lumpy, ex-fighter's face, lowered a pair of binoculars and then turned to his companion for a consultation. The other, slimmer and quicker, paced alongside him.

"What are we going to do?" the fighter asked.

"I don't know. I thought for sure it was fixed that he'd be left alone."

"Well, he ain't."

The walker shrugged, took a long drag from his cigarette and a pull from his fourth bottle of beer that day. "I don't know. She's probably just come to cheer him up, you know, chicken soup an' stuff. It'll be okay as long as she doesn't try and drag him back outta there.''

"I still say we should just take him out."

The younger man snorted and lifted the bottle again. "And have two cops killed in two weeks? That's the last thing we need. Everybody's happy right now. Kill him, and they're gonna start askin' questions all over again. We got ten days, and then it doesn't matter what he remembers." Making it a point to check his watch, he patted his friend on his massive back. "Gimme a half hour and I'll relieve you. It'll be time for *Wheel of Fortune* then, anyway."

"You don't mind?"

"Hell, no. Just do me a favor and figure the puzzles to yourself. All that yellin' makes me jumpy."

Nodding sheepishly at his partner, the big man grinned and turned back to see if he could see anything else at the neighboring cabin. When the time came, though, he hoped they'd let him be the one to nail that cop. He had a score to settle, and he wanted to do it in the worst way.

Across the valley, a shadowy figure slipped into the twilight. Swinging the glasses after it, the big man began to think how satisfying it would be to put a bullet through that head, even at this distance. It'd be better than a date with Vanna. The idea appealed to him so much, he laughed.

Chapter 2

It could have been worse. In her search through the house, Lindsay found that the kitchen had taken the lion's share of abuse. There was another pocket of beer cans and debris on the porch, and newspapers were heaped like cordwood in the living room. What had once been the garage had evidently been transformed into a workshop. Lathes and saws and carpentry tools lay coldly silent beneath a coating of dust and sawdust. Other than that, there was little to clean.

Lindsay was surprised by the cabin's decor. She had fully expected early rustic, old beat up couches and secondhand armchairs. This didn't seem to be the average weekend home, though. The furniture was in modern Danish style, all teak and glass. Handmade, probably on the dusty workbench, and beautifully crafted. The only decoration was the view from the huge windows.

Lindsay remembered that Mitchell had rented a studio in town for the last assignment. Other than that, he was on the road so much, that when he was home, he just came here, to the cabin he'd bought from his uncle some years back. Now Lindsay could see that Mitchell had been fitting this place together into a home. Until the last few weeks, it had been a comfortable one.

She was relieved to find that there were two bedrooms. Well, one was a den with a fold-out couch in it. Lindsay immediately staked claim and carried in her overnighter, all the while keeping an eye on Mitchell's rigid back down by the stream.

His room looked much more like the kitchen. The bedclothes were haphazard and stale, a residue of sleepless nights and bad dreams that Lindsay recognized. A few clothes lay huddled in limp masses across the floor, and beer cans were scattered like fallen darts around the trash can across from the bed.

Alcohol doesn't help, Lindsay thought with a sad smile. It doesn't help you get to sleep or stop the dreams. But he wouldn't believe her just yet. He would have to trust her first, and there were several steps she'd have to take before reaching even that objective. Squaring her shoulders like Hercules before the Augean stables, Lindsay waded in to begin her task.

Why the hell had she come?

Mitchell stood at the edge of the clearing, his eyes on the soothing rush of water, his right hand kneading the painful spot in his leg. It had been bad enough when Al had come, or Bob. Their concern had been annoying, an itch at the edge of his perception. He'd seen the sympathy in their eyes and wanted them to get the hell away from him.

And they'd gone, uncomfortable, shifting on their feet and unable to meet his eyes, leaving him to the quiet of his isolation. Leaving him to crumble as he saw fit. They hadn't warned him that they were sending a bloodhound after him.

If he'd had the energy, he would have been amazed. For the first time in two weeks, he'd felt anger. A blue flash of it, the moment he'd locked in on the face of that smarmy, office-bound pencil pusher. But it had died just as suddenly, drowned in the apathy that seemed to swamp him these days.

Dragging his hand from one ache to another, Mitchell rubbed absently at his unshaven face. He was so tired, so old, all of a sudden. Caught between what he couldn't remember and what he'd never forget. Responsible. Guilty. Sentenced to spend the rest of his life reliving the flash of mortal fear in Maggie's eyes when she'd seen him, close enough to save her, too frozen to move.

And then... and then, what? What had she screamed at him in those last moments, as she'd toppled over the edge? What was it that followed him so closely, taunting him, accusing him?

Why couldn't he remember?

When he couldn't stand in the gathering dusk any longer, Mitchell turned back to his house.

Lindsay greeted him without turning from the sink. "Just in time for dinner."

The kitchen was clean, the trash raked, collected and consigned to the outside cans. The stains on the counter had been scrubbed away and the floor swept. For the first time in weeks, the room was warmed by the smell of good food. Mitchell blinked as if he'd stepped into some kind of a time warp.

"I'm not hungry."

He limped slowly toward the living room, not sure where he was going or why. Lindsay refused to let him. As he passed within reach, she turned from the sink and in one movement had him into a chair. There was a place mat before him, a plate and flatware. A small bunch of columbine had been stuffed into a peanut butter glass and stood in the center of the table.

"I know you've been eating," Lindsay was saying, already back at her work. "I've been cleaning up the evidence for the last two hours. Oh, and the cockroaches of Colorado thank you for supplying their needs for the summer and ensuing winter. I had to evict several families."

"I told you. I'm not hungry."

"Probably because I'm not scooping anything out of a can. Sorry, I like the majority of my food heated."

Bent over the salad she was finishing, Lindsay listened to the monotone of Mitchell's voice and wondered just how far she was going to have to push him before she would hear it change. The idea of sitting across from him for a simple meal was almost the least appealing thing she'd ever contemplated, but she knew that she couldn't let him back down. Face-to-face confrontation was still the quickest, the most dramatic way to get action. It was just the dramatic part that set her stomach to lurching again.

He never moved while she set a baked chicken breast, potato and salad before him. Everything was ready to eat and savory enough, she hoped, to at least attract his attention.

He looked at his plate and then up at her. Lindsay took that moment to ease into her own chair. There was such a frightening silence about him, such an emptiness. Lindsay remembered the day she'd told him she was partnering him with a woman. He'd stormed into her office and threatened her. Ranted, raved, taken up the whole room with his energy. When he'd leaned over her desk, she'd actually backed away, stunned by the ferocity in those hot green eyes. All she saw in them now was suspicion.

"You're damn near the last person I want here," he said, not moving.

Lindsay chose to attack her salad. "I'm not any happier about it than you are."

"Then why come?"

"I told you. No one else knew what to do."

Now she got a sneer out of him. "And you do?"

"As it happens, I do."

"That's what I've always liked about you, McDonough. Your exaggerated sense of your abilities."

Lindsay did everything but hold her breath. This was more like it. "How's your leg?"

"What difference does it make?"

She shrugged. "You walked out of the hospital after three days. According to the doctor who excavated for the bullet, not the brightest of moves. I have the feeling that if you've been taking care of your leg as well as you have your house, it's about due to fall off. Which reminds me. Did you ever remember how it happened?''

Mitchell's head came up, the first flashes of emotion dancing across his eyes. ''Want to finish filling out your paperwork?''

It took all the strength Lindsay had to do it, but she met his gaze with an unconcerned one of her own. ''Yes.''

It cost him the first real meal he'd had since yanking out the IV and walking out of the hospital, but Mitchell reared himself to his feet. ''Listen, you bloodsucking paper pusher. I don't know what you expect to get by coming up here, but you're not getting it.'' With a powerful swipe of his hand, he swept the carefully prepared dinner onto the floor. ''Now get the hell out of my house!''

Lindsay sat alone in the kitchen for a long while, her eyes on the door into the living room rather than on the mess on the newly cleaned floor. Well, she supposed it was a trade-off. He wasn't going to get any nutrition tonight, but she'd made the first break beneath the ice of his despair.

The night sighed and rustled around the cabin. Shadows danced across the valley, and the moon silvered the little glade beyond the porch. Lindsay sat in a wicker chair, her feet up, looking out at the peacefulness of midnight, trying to concentrate on the coolness of the dark. Trying to ignore the stifled mutterings that Mitchell had locked in with him behind his bedroom door.

She hadn't seen him since dinner. He had stormed through to his room and slammed the door behind him, reappearing only about an hour ago to pull some beer from the refrigerator. By then Lindsay had been safely out of sight on the porch.

Sighing a little, she tapped absently at the latest pile of debris she'd unearthed—news clippings and a bank statement. When she gathered the energy to get to her feet, she'd have to add it to the stack already in the living room. It was so quiet here, though. So washed in moonlight and silence.

She could almost pretend that Mitchell wasn't waiting behind that door to test her.

Tomorrow would be soon enough to start her campaign. For now she would give Mitchell the room he needed, the illusion of solitude. She knew the nights were the worst, not cool like she saw them, but hot. Hot and long and full of ghosts. She would give him tonight, and then force him to face his ghosts.

Her brother Alex had been the one to force Lindsay to face hers. He had moved into her house and bullied her, pulling her back from the brink with the sheer force of his love. Listening to the echoes of her own nightmares, Lindsay knew now just how close to the edge she'd been. And how lucky that Alex had been there.

Six years. Six long years. Now she could welcome the night, drink in its flavors and float contentedly in its peace. Her ghosts had become dear friends to sit alongside her. It would be her job to teach Mitchell how to help his do the same. She just hoped she could.

Mitchell woke with a sore leg and a sore head. His mouth tasted like tin cans, and he could smell beer on the sheets. Another fun night in old Colorado. Another nightmare, ending short of Maggie's strangled cry.

Damn, he couldn't live like this. But he couldn't seem to pull himself beyond it, either.

Dragging himself to the edge of the bed, he swung his injured leg gingerly over the side. It was almost two weeks. It shouldn't still hurt so much. The thought occurred to him briefly that he couldn't remember the last time he'd changed the dressing. He couldn't remember the last time he'd *seen* the dressing. He supposed the wound could be infected.

Maybe he should shuck his jeans and find out.

Maybe he should crawl into the shower. A little hot water might rinse some of that brackish taste from him.

Mitchell raised his head in the direction of the suspiciously tidy bathroom and considered the energy involved. Just the thought was tiring. Then again, Peterson's pet bulldog was out there. A shower would put off facing her a little longer.

"Oh, what the hell."

He managed to wait until he got into the bathroom to re-decorate the floor with another layer of clothes. The old dressing lasted as long as the first five minutes under a steady stream of hot water, and the vague aches in the rest of his body somehow dissipated like the gauze that finally slid from his leg.

Mitchell stayed under the water longer than he'd in-tended. He'd forgotten how hot water soothed, especially when you turned your face to it, taking the full force of it right on your closed eyes, forcing out bad tastes and bad dreams. The water exploded against him, slicing along muscles and tendons, and traversed his thigh.

The water numbed him. It deafened him. It loosened something in him that felt like tears against his cheeks.

He never heard the pounding outside the door.

Mitchell would never had considered dressing in the bathroom. He never would have anticipated finding a woman in his bedroom, either. He pulled open the door—and came to a sudden halt.

Lindsay had been sitting in a chair, flipping a roll of gauze into the air. When Mitchell appeared, stark naked and wreathed in the steam escaping from the bathroom, she dropped it. Then she almost dropped her teeth.

Lindsay had never considered Jason Mitchell attractive enough to turn around for. His features, so mesmerizing to other women, had always seemed to taunt rather than at-tract her. Suddenly Lindsay saw how wrong she'd been.

She'd never seen a more impressive-looking man in her life. It didn't matter that he was unshaven and red-eyed, still stooped beneath the weight of his grief. Or that he was patched together and hung over. He was taut and well mus-cled and graceful, standing on the balls of his feet as if ready to move.

Wet hair curled across his forehead and along his neck. Sunbaked skin met a tan line just shy of his navel. The gold-tipped hair fanning his chest trailed off into a tantalizing line that begged for exploration. His hips were slim, his arms and legs powerful.

Powerful. That was it. He radiated a strength that sapped hers. It made her understand better why other men feared him. Why other women sought him.

"I was right," she managed to announce, amazed at how hearty her voice sounded. She felt like a Victorian virgin, ready to swoon. "Your leg *is* about ready to fall off. Ever occur to you that you should have had those stitches out about a week ago?"

"That door was locked," he accused, not bothering to move.

With some effort, Lindsay raised her eyes to meet his and shrugged. "You're not the only one who knows how to pick a lock. I do more than fill our Social Security forms while I'm at work."

She didn't tell him how she'd rattled at that lock for a good five minutes, fingers shaking, heart hammering, afraid of what she'd find. She'd heard the water running and running and running, and hadn't been able to get an answer from him when she'd yelled. And Lindsay remembered a time when she had stood alone in a bathroom staring into her mirror, trying to work up the energy to act while her brother had pounded on the door.

It simply hadn't occurred to her that Mitchell would be taking a shower.

"Am I supposed to be amused?" he asked, frowning.

With deliberate calm, Lindsay reached over and retrieved the gauze. "You can be anything you want. But I promised Bob I'd bring you back in one piece. Since I assumed that meant with a full complement of legs, I thought I'd make sure you took care of that one there."

There was more than a hint of rancor in his voice. "You didn't tell me you were also a nurse."

"I'm not. But a twelve-year-old Boy Scout would be able to do a better job of that than you have."

For the first time, Mitchell looked down. The suture line *was* inflamed. And she was right about the stitches. Any other time he would have taken care of that. It just hadn't seemed to matter.

Letting the first smile in two weeks touch his lips, Mitchell turned back to his intruder. "In that case, I'm sure you won't mind taking the stitches out yourself." There was no humor in his eyes.

Lindsay caught his challenge, and knew that she could just as well walk back out the door if she didn't meet it. Answering his cold, goading smile with an indifferent one of her own, she nodded her head. "Fine. I brought up some equipment with me, but I'm not sure these scissors are the right size."

The scissors she held up would have been suitable for shearing a sheep.

Shrugging his shoulders, Mitchell just walked up to her. Lindsay felt his approach like the opening of a hot oven door, the air suddenly stifling and close. He padded across the wood floor, stopping in front of her before she could manage to get to her feet, before she could minimize his position of power. There was nowhere to go. Nothing to do but what she'd suggested in the first place.

Suddenly the reasons she'd first come up to the cabin became lost. She couldn't think past the very distracting field of vision that presented itself. Mitchell was awesome. Just the very intimate sight of him sent Lindsay's pulse rocketing. Damn him for forcing the situation like this.

But Lindsay knew that she'd been the one to force it. She had just never considered these particular consequences.

"Well?"

Mitchell looked down at the top of Lindsay's head. The morning sun glinted in her hair. A stray curl had managed to work its way loose from her braid and swept the side of her cheek. He could see her sooty lashes lay against her cheeks, and the press of her wide lips. She was at a real disadvantage, and he should have felt a sense of victory. He should have felt something. He hadn't been able to abide this transplanted yuppie from the first day she'd walked in to dictate procedure to him. He'd resented her sleek clothes, meticulously styled hair and her cool, perfectly modulated voice.

Looking down on her now, though, he couldn't define what he felt.

"All right," Lindsay breathed, picking up the scissors. "Don't move, or you'll never see your grandchildren."

The stitches weren't plastic surgery quality. Even so, it took some concentration to get beneath the tiny knots and snip them. Lindsay placed a steadying hand against the solid plane of Mitchell's right thigh and slid the scissors upward. It was all she could do to keep her eyes on her task, with such an obvious distraction so close.

His skin was still warm. It rippled a bit beneath her touch, the beads of moisture running down alongside her fingers. Lindsay ran a nervous tongue across her lips and started snipping, trying her very best to keep her hands from shaking. There wasn't a damn thing she could do about the fireworks that had begun to detonate throughout her. Pinwheels of exhilaration had suddenly been let loose along her limbs, frissons of anticipation that dangerously tested her dexterity.

"I don't suppose you've cleaned this since you've been here."

Mitchell couldn't take his eyes from the top of her head. "I spilled some beer on it."

Lindsay snorted and pulled another of the threads free. Mitchell flinched at the movement, and she looked up to see his discomfort reflected in the tightened crease of his forehead.

"Next time, try doing this the right way," she suggested with a perfectly straight face, glad he couldn't tell that she was sweating.

"Are you about finished?" Her eyes were like warm brandy, he thought, golden at the centers. A cat's eyes. A witch's eyes. Suddenly he couldn't take his gaze from them.

"The stitches are out," she answered, not dropping her eyes a millimeter. "I just have to clean it and rewrap the wound."

"Any small amount of pain you can inflict." Why did he sound like he'd been running, damn it? Why did he suddenly feel the chill of the room, the soft pressure of her fingers, the whisper of her breath against his thigh?

Where the hell had that knot of desire come from?

When Lindsay smiled, it was with a fair amount of satisfaction. "Exactly."

Mitchell didn't realize he'd lifted his hand, but suddenly he was tucking that stray piece of hair behind her ear. Her knees were against his, her jeans rough and warm against his bare skin. Her breasts, so close to his legs, strained against the coarse cotton material of her blouse.

Lindsay started at his touch.

"What did you do?" he demanded. "Buy out L. L. Bean to come up here and impress the locals?"

His voice didn't match his words, Lindsay thought distractedly. Where was the rancor, the acid? And why couldn't she suddenly seem to draw a decent breath? Green was such a cool color, such a peaceful, reflective sea. Why did his eyes suddenly spark like heat lightning?

"I keep a stock just for occasions like this," she managed, finally dragging her own eyes away.

That only made things worse. The evidence of a completely unanticipated problem presented itself without disguise, not more than five inches from her nose.

Oh, God, she thought, her hand still against his skin, her eyes riveted on a spot a little to the right of his thigh, her heart pounding. What have I gotten myself into?

"You were the one who wouldn't leave," he accused, noticing where her attention had focused, his hand still against the silk of her hair. His voice was raspy, his touch hesitant. He began to slide his fingers along to Lindsay's neck.

Lindsay defended herself instinctively. With a bottle of alcohol. Uncapping it, she poured.

The minute the cold liquid hit the suture line, Mitchell leaped back like a scalded cat, howling mightily.

"What the hell did you do that for?" he grated, bending over the shrieking wound.

Lindsay smiled with a great deal more self-confidence than she really possessed. "It was the next step, remember? Clean and rewrap. And here I thought you agents were so stoic."

"*I'll* rewrap," he snarled, physically picking her up from the chair and turning her toward the door. "Otherwise I could lose some very cherished body parts."

Slamming the door behind her, Mitchell locked it and turned back into the bathroom. Before resuming the care of his wound, he took a moment to cast a stunned look at the once again docile, cherished part that had so surprisingly betrayed him. Who would have thought it? The glacial Ms. McDonough couldn't have been any more surprised than he that he'd still been able to react at all, much less to her.

Rubbing once again at the fire that gnawed at his wound, Mitchell shook his head. He guessed he wasn't quite as numb as he'd thought.

Standing outside the door, Lindsay couldn't help but shake her own head. She'd sure gotten her spark this time. It had probably been a stroke of brilliance to have settled into that chair after she'd realized that Jason was all right in his shower. She just didn't know whether it was going to do her any good.

Good God, reacting to Jason Mitchell like a teen in heat. Jason Mitchell! It was ludicrous, as if Marie Antoinette were making eyes at Robespierre. Her fingers were still tingling. Her stomach carried a hot nugget of desire that surprised her. Well, she thought, giving her head another shake and heading toward the kitchen, it just proved once and for all that sex didn't necessarily have anything to do with love.

"She still there?"

The heavy man shrugged, his attention on the mist-wreathed cabin across the valley. "Haven't seen her leave yet. Car's still there."

"Fair enough. I'll let 'em know when I call in. Maybe they'll let us tap the phone now."

"I've just about had a bellyful of waitin', Artie," the big man complained, turning to his partner. "Ain't there nothin' else we can do?"

The thin man took a last bite of his toast, smearing butter across his chin. "We can sit here and watch the cabin, Mick. We see that cop head out, we let the man know. Otherwise, we wait."

"Nobody comin' to relieve us, Artie?"

Artie shook his head. "Not for the money we're pullin' in on this. Boss don't want too many people involved. Give me the glasses. I'm goin' out."

Mick lifted the field glasses. "Where?"

"Get a number on her plate. I wanna know who she is." When he reached the door, Artie turned to see the ex-boxer bend back over the gun he was meticulously cleaning. "And, Mick. You don't use that until I say so. Hear?"

Mick's smile lighted his eyes with real delight. "As long as I get to use it when you say so."

Artie nodded. "He's all yours."

"Be back by ten, Artie. My show..."

Lindsay had to go out to the porch to find Mitchell for breakfast. His hair was still wet, curling at the back of his neck and glinting darkly in the soft sun. He'd donned a T-shirt and jeans, his bare feet up on the same porch railing that had held Lindsay's the night before. Taking a moment to assess him fully clothed, she realized that he hadn't sacrificed much of his magnetism by covering up. The clothes simply molded to him, enhancing his sleek lines.

They were the same clothes he'd worn into the office a thousand times, a coat thrown over them to add an air of respectability when necessary. Why should he suddenly seem so different? Possibly, she thought, because before she hadn't seen his—

"Do psychologists get their revelations into the human psyche by staring holes into the back of people's heads?" he asked without turning around.

Lindsay came very close to blushing. "I was trying to work up the energy to be polite," she retorted dryly. "Seeing as I was wasting my time, breakfast is on the table. Eat it now or pick it out of the trash later."

"Would there be any difference?"

"It won't be warm later."

Lindsay was trying to work up interest in her eggs when Mitchell limped in. She didn't bother to look up, but her profession had taught her a lot about peripheral vision. Mitchell moved slowly, as if navigating under water. His shoulders still carried that weight, but she thought she detected the first signs of life in those tired eyes. Maybe that foray into hormonal overload had been profitable, after all.

Pulling out his chair, Mitchell slid into it. "A regular little homesteader, aren't you? Cleaning, cooking, caring for the wounded. I bet you can take a mean bead on the rustlers, too."

Lindsay didn't bother to meet his gaze. "I've handled myself in some pretty tough cow towns."

She actually got a laugh out of him, a short, sharp bark full of sarcasm. "Is that why the sheriff sent you to bring me in?"

"Nobody sent me."

"You're just doing this out of the kindness of your heart?"

Carefully masking her apprehension behind her coffee cup, Lindsay shrugged. "It's because I think so highly of your detecting abilities, Mitchell."

"And you know how I feel about your theories in police work, McDonough."

"Just one big, happy, mutual adoration society."

She watched his eyes, anger chasing quickly across them and then dying. "Then why did you come?" His voice was harsh. His hands were clenched on either side of his plate.

"To restock your beer. How's your leg?" *Come after the answer, Mitchell. Work up the energy to wonder.*

He still hadn't picked up his cutlery. "Crippled, thanks to you."

She shrugged. "Well, if it gets worse, I brought a hacksaw along, too."

"A rusty one, no doubt."

"And dull."

"Why?"

She stopped just short of betraying her relief. He'd risen to her bait. "Because I used it on the last three agents I counseled."

"Why are you here?"

Carefully raising noncommittal eyes to him, Lindsay saw what she'd wanted, the first hints of antagonism, of challenge.

Of life.

"To help you," she answered evenly.

He smiled, a cruel expression on his face. "Because you know how I feel, I suppose."

"In point of fact," she said, her voice softer than she realized, "I do."

He was on his feet even before she closed her mouth. There was no mistaking the anger in his eyes now.

"You can only knock your plate onto the floor four more times," she advised, her mouth dry. "After that, we'll be out of china."

He ignored her. "Like I told Bob and Al," he said, in a voice so cold that it sent shivers down Lindsay's spine, "none of you can know how I feel. Not them. Certainly not you. You haven't even been in the damn field. How the hell can you know?"

"I'm not talking about field work," she countered as evenly as she could, fighting to hold his hot green gaze. "I'm talking about guilt."

He straightened, considered the food on his plate as if really weighing the idea of pitching it. Then he lifted his head, his eyes cold as death. "In that case, you just stopped talking." And he walked out.

Chapter 3

Where is he now?"

Lindsay shifted the phone to the other ear and leaned over to peer out the window. "He's back by the river."

Bob's voice sounded tinny and anxious over the line. "So he doesn't know you're calling?"

Lindsay had to laugh. "Are you kidding? My life's in enough danger as it is."

"Have you made any progress?"

"I've cooked him two meals. He threw the first onto the floor and just walked out on the second. At least the housecleaning's getting easier."

"Lindsay..."

Lindsay sighed. "I don't know. I think so." She didn't think she'd share the experience in the bedroom. Even her old professors wouldn't have considered that a therapeutic session. "He's beginning to talk a little, and he's not just sitting in one place anymore."

She could hear the soft chuckle on the other end. "Who'd ever have figured you and Mitchell in the same house for more than twenty-four hours without one of you committing homicide?''

"That's why I knew it would work. Kind of like an itching plaster."

"Do you need anything?"

Lindsay considered a moment, her eyes still on Mitchell's shadowy figure by the edge of the stream. "A football helmet?"

"You have my home phone number."

"Yeah. If he gets his hands around my throat, I'll call."

There was a pause, punctuated by static. "I'm still not sure I like this, Lindsay."

"Which is why I didn't wait around for your blessing. You're so... regulation."

"Now you sound like Mitchell."

"Perish the thought. What else is going on back in the real world?"

How could anyone stand in one place for so long without moving? Had she done that, folding down into herself so completely that the rest of the world ceased to exist, so that movement was a task and thought an agony? Mitchell had been standing on the same spot for three hours now, hands either in his pockets or rubbing at his leg, his head down just a little, the wind tugging at his hair. Lindsay wondered how much longer his empty stomach would wait.

"Everything's running right along here," Bob assured her, dragging her back from her thoughts. "We're just about to call in warrants on the Caldwell case, and the attorney general wants us in on the latest round of military arms heists."

Lindsay turned away from the window. "Who are you giving that to?"

"Smith and Tyler are already in Virginia."

"Are you going to put somebody inside the base?"

"That was the plan."

She nodded, her mind split between the soft comfort of the kitchen and the spare utilitarianism of the office. "Might try Billy McCoy on it. After all those years in

Special Forces, he has that wonderfully sly lifer quality about him.''

Lindsay heard a chuckle. "Tattoos and all. Yeah, thanks. That's even better. I'll take care of it.''

"You'll find my notes from the last bunch of arms thefts filed under whichever base it was. Bragg, I think. And—''

"Enough," Bob objected. "We'll take care of it. You have your hands full enough already.''

"Some jobs are just harder to leave at the office than others.''

"You haven't left anything at the office, old girl. You've moved in with it. By the way, your vacation's denied. You're on the payroll.''

Lindsay couldn't help but laugh. "Bob, will you marry me?''

"And do what with Moira and the kids?''

"Like I said, Bob. Hung up on regulations." Instinct turned Lindsay back to the window. Mitchell wasn't by the stream anymore. Stepping closer to the window, she scanned the empty meadow. "Any progress on Esperanza?" she asked, her expression drawn in bemusement.

"Nothing. Don't you dare leave that cabin without notifying me first. If anybody from that group got a bead on Mitchell, he wouldn't be safe in the contiguous forty-eight states.''

Lindsay grimaced. "Thanks, Bob. I needed the peace of mind." Speak of the devil. She'd just caught a glimpse of denim at the edge of the cabin, heading for the kitchen door. "Uh-oh. Coffee break's over.''

"Call tomorrow.''

"Right in between lunch and laundry.''

"And remember. Don't move without sending up flares.''

By the time the screen door slammed, Lindsay was seated at the kitchen table, immersed in a book.

"No dinner?''

She didn't bother to look up. "Not till I know you're going to eat it. Those last two rejects came out of my pocket.''

When Mitchell didn't answer, Lindsay looked up. He was leaning against the doorway, hands in pockets, the weight off his injured leg, the late-afternoon shadows settling in slashes across his face. At first Lindsay was going to say something, but his stillness was too complete, too purposeless. His eyes, darkened to a moss green, rested on her.

"I have an extra nose?" she asked, making it a point not to set down her book. She didn't want to betray the fact that just the way his gaze settled on her raised the most disconcerting goose bumps.

For a moment Mitchell didn't move. Then, as if lost in a dream, he slowly shook his head. "No...no."

He couldn't have told her why he was staring. It was something about her he was just noticing. Something he hadn't seen before, and he couldn't pin it down.

She certainly didn't look anything like she had in the office. There she was all efficiency and professional demeanor, casting meaningful glares over the tops of her hornrims, her hair never more than a strand out of place and her shoes polished to a military shine.

Here she was a different person. Looser, softer, her hair in seemingly permanent disarray, her clothing well-worn and faded. Comfortable. Most unlike her. Most...what? What was it that worried at him when he saw her now, her head tilted a little to the side, loose hair brushing at her shoulder, full lips slightly parted, her fingers stroking the cover of her book, as if reading it had been a sensual experience?

More than her actions. It was something about her appearance. It was too much for Mitchell, though. There hadn't been any constructive thinking going on in his head in too long for him to be able to pull an enigma like that out of the air and name it.

Shaking his head one more time, he turned away.

"Well, are you?" Lindsay demanded, finally giving up on the book and laying it down.

Mitchell stopped, his gaze centered on the cool, dark confines of the cabin. "Am I what?"

"Going to eat."

He furrowed his brow. His hand escaped his pocket to rub once again at a still-unshaven chin. Decisions, now. Expectations. Civility. He wished he could work up the energy to pitch her out.

"You threw all the old papers away," he finally said, still rubbing.

Lindsay frowned, not following him. "I cleaned up the mess," she amended. "Any articles you already cut out I saved. Otherwise I figured that the bad news would wait until you wanted to read it. Mailbox was empty, or I would have filed the bills for you, too."

Mitchell lifted his head a little, taking in a long gulp of oxygen. He was so tired. But night was coming. Maggie lived there, waiting to accuse him again.

"You just move right in," he suddenly accused. "Don't you?"

"I think we've been over this before, Mitchell," Lindsay retorted, getting to her feet. "Now, do you want to eat or not?"

He didn't turn. "Yes."

Lindsay wasn't sure whether she'd meant to go over to him, but he never gave her the chance. He disappeared into the darkness.

Dinner was eaten in silence—as were breakfast, lunch and dinner the next day. Lindsay didn't try to make him talk, deciding that nourishment would better see him through what she was planning. She cooked and cleaned and caught up on some reading, letting him settle into an absent-minded lull. Shocks were more effective with the unsuspecting, after all, and she still fully intended to shock him.

When she walked in on him after dinner, though, Lindsay almost lost her nerve. He sat in one of the armchairs in the darkened living room, staring silently into space, the shadows beneath his eyes no fainter, the taut lines of grief uneased.

She ached for him. Lindsay knew the weight that had settled on those shoulders, and watching him, it hurt her all over again.

Jason Mitchell was just too damn vital to waste away to a shell. He was too self-possessed to kill himself with blame. Even as she fought to keep a gentling hand at her side, Lindsay knew that this was the reason she was going to harass him back to life. Because someone like Jason Mitchell, who couldn't tolerate weakness in himself, wouldn't abide sympathy, either.

"What are you doing?"

Lindsay lifted her head from where she was crouched before the hearth. "Oh, good. You can still talk. I was wondering."

His eyes met hers. They were flat, unemotional, almost colorless beneath his frown. "What are you doing?"

Lindsay returned her attention to the task at hand, those eyes haunting her. "Well, unless memory and Girl Scout training fail me, I'm about to build a fire. I figured all those unread newspapers could be recycled into fuel."

"Leave it alone."

Picking up another of the papers she'd stacked alongside the fireplace, she tore it into strips and slipped it under the grate. The logs on top had been there when she'd first cleaned, the beginnings of a fire from some time ago. There was a healthy pile of ashes at the back, too, as if fires had been a common comfort in this house.

"I haven't laid a fire in years," she announced, her head still in past the screen, her words echoing around the soot-blackened chimney. "I figured it was about time."

"I said leave it alone. Don't you ever listen?"

Everything was ready. Reaching into her jeans pocket, she produced a packet of matches. "No. It's what makes me so lovable."

Lindsay eased back out to hear a decidedly ungentlemanly opinion being delivered behind her, but it didn't keep her from striking a match against the flagstone and tipping it into the crumpled paper. The funnies caught first, sending up a sharp flame that crackled like gunfire.

Smiling with satisfaction, she closed the screen and spent a moment enjoying the show.

"Nothing like a fire to make a place cozy."

She didn't get a corresponding opinion. That was when she pulled herself to her feet and faced Mitchell.

"Well, it's been over two weeks now," she said, settling herself onto the glass coffee table in front of him with an ease she didn't feel. "Have you decided?"

Mitchell turned wary eyes in Lindsay's direction, the flames sparking light and shadow along his features. The rest of him remained almost impossibly still. "Have I decided what?"

"Whether you deserve to live or not?"

For a moment he didn't move. His gaze held hers without emotion. His features caught the light in wicked patterns, making him look harsh and desolate at the same time. Tendons showed suddenly on hands that had tightened around the arms of his chair. Lindsay held her breath.

"I have to hand it to you, McDonough," he finally said, his voice so quiet she instinctively leaned forward. "You have guts."

"Not really," she disagreed with a little shake of her head that sent the light shuddering through the gold in her hair. "I'm impatient. I think that if you're going to throw yourself off a bridge over this, then do it and get it over with. Don't mess around so long that the task force suffers."

He stiffened, and Lindsay could see a muscle jump at the edge of his jaw. That little movement unnerved her more than the violent rages he'd once visited on her. "What kind of game are you playing?"

She shrugged. "I was about to ask you the same question."

"You think I'm playing a game? You think I give a good damn what you think at all?"

"I think you're wallowing, Mitchell. It feels kind of good after awhile, doesn't it? Almost friendly, like at least it's better than feeling nothing, which is what you felt at first. You can feel sorry for yourself now, eat at yourself over the horrible thing you did, and build your little chapel of guilt to Maggie right here in the mountains where nobody can interfere. That way she never really dies, does she?''

"You . . . bitch," he breathed, the fire finally lighting his eyes. A yellow blaze licked at the rims of his pupils, weaving in among the green, flashing with rage. "Who the hell do you think you are?"

It took everything Lindsay had to remain where she was. "Maggie's friend," she retorted. "I mean, you killed her, didn't you? You were the one who should have been there for her, and you weren't. Should I blame you, too, or are you doing a good enough job all by yourself?"

He was on his feet now, trembling with restraint, a hair-breadth away from striking out. Lindsay almost wished he could, that he might find that kind of physical release. The cruel challenge of her words flowed back from him in waves of agony. Self-recrimination, self-hate. He couldn't bear what he'd done. What he hadn't done. He couldn't live with it. Or so he thought.

Lindsay had once thought the same thing about herself. And the one thing she knew about Mitchell that he didn't yet know was that he was too fierce a fighter to give in to that temptation. So had she been, and it had taken another person to show her. Now it was her job to show Mitchell.

"So, what are you going to do, Mitchell?" she asked, getting to her own feet, still woefully short of his menacing height. "Sit here and rot? If you are, let me know so I can file you under permanent disability. All of us—including you—have better things to do with our time."

Lindsay was all set to walk past when Mitchell grabbed her. She gasped, the iron grip of his hands hurting her. Turning to him, she tried to face his challenge.

Something, though, changed in that moment. She met his gaze, the furious, hot challenge of him. His emotions were clearly boiling too far out of control for him to give voice to. The torment in him struck her like a physical force, like a great wind that battered her, cold and hot at once. And even then she was stunned by the thrill that shot through her.

She began to tremble.

Mitchell couldn't pull his whirling thoughts into focus. Lindsay had dared him, had goaded him to fight. She'd thrown down accusations like gauntlets and then turned to leave, unconcerned about his reaction. He couldn't let her go, couldn't let her torture him like this without giving answer.

But when he took hold of her, reaching out instinctively, something far more desperate took hold of him. She was so soft, her eyes large and dark in the firelight. Her skin was translucent. Her hair glowed like the sunrise. Suddenly he found himself wanting to lose himself in the sweet smell and soft comfort of her. She was a woman braver than any man who had fled the dark echoes of despair in this cabin, a woman he couldn't abide—a woman he suddenly needed more than life.

He tightened his grip. His breath rasped in his throat. Mitchell felt caught in a vortex, the firelight sweeping over him, yellow and red, full of rage and passion. Desire. Grief. God, how could he separate his feelings while she was looking at him like a doe caught in the headlights of a car?

"You think you pretty well know it all, don't you?" he grated, gripping her with bruising strength, trying to keep his footing. "Think you understand just how I feel?"

Lost in the maelstrom he'd unleashed, Lindsay could hardly find her voice. "I do." It was as if his fingers were brands, searing throughout her arms, her chest, to the very core of her. His eyes had caught fire, the very emotions she'd courted sweeping over their edges and setting him alight. Lindsay shuddered before him, at once terrified and mesmerized, the cool objectivity of her profession lost.

"Then tell me," he taunted, edging closer, his breath hot on her cheek. "Tell me how I feel right now."

You're wondering how the hell you could be so drawn to someone you can't tolerate, she wanted to say. You want to know why your knees are weak and your heart is hammer-

ing in your chest. Are you afraid or excited? Do you want
to run or stay? Can you do either on your own?

Lindsay couldn't form the words. She could do no more
than face him, just that act taking every ounce of courage
she possessed.

He was fire and smoke in the darkness. Fierce eyes and
granite features—stone-cold and hard above her, compel-
ling and terrifying her at once.

"Tell me, damn you," he whispered, moving even closer.
He shook her, his fingers digging into her skin, his chest
heaving with the pain of her earlier taunt.

"I . . . let me go. . . ."

Lindsay saw his mouth curl at her words. It gave him a
cruel, unforgiving look. The pain in her chest tightened,
stole her breath, her strength. Lindsay saw him close the
space between them and couldn't move to stop him.

Mitchell didn't know whether he meant to hurt her. He
didn't understand at all why he acted. Temptress and healer,
he saw both. Sought both. With brutal strength, he dragged
her to him, catching her head in his hand. She was limp in
his arms, but she was soft. She cried out in surprise, yet she
lifted her mouth to his.

And he took it. Her lips were silk, but Mitchell didn't
comprehend. She trembled beneath his onslaught, but he
didn't stop. He ran his hands blindly over her, his hold on
her fierce, his foray of her soft, sweet mouth desperate. Her
breasts were crushed against his chest, her neck arched un-
comfortably in his hold, but Mitchell didn't realize that. The
feel of her within his grasp, the taste of her maddened him
even more, stirring the raging furies that tormented him.

He should have felt the trembling start in her, should have
heard her sharp little cries as she struggled between flight
and surrender. Lindsay had brought her hands up to his
chest, but she couldn't seem to gather the strength to push.
She couldn't fight the storm she'd unleashed in him.

She couldn't fight the storm he'd unleashed in her.

Mitchell wasn't sure how he heard it over the roaring in
his ears. He wasn't sure what sanity dragged him back from

the brink of madness. It was only a small sound—the tearing of cloth—the final barrier of control.

He heard it and stopped. He realized that his hand was against her throat, that her blouse had split beneath his fingers. The firelight was molten along her skin, flowing along the swell of her breast. He'd torn her blouse to get at it, and suddenly the sight of the tear swept the madness from him like a harsh wind.

For a long moment Mitchell couldn't lift his eyes from the evidence of his crime. Lindsay had drawn down her hand, pulling up the material back over the exposed lace and skin. Stunned, speechless, whirling with recrimination, Mitchell withdrew his own hand. Then he drew himself away and almost stumbled with the shock of separation.

He looked up to find no less confusion in Lindsay's eyes.

"The blouse will come out of your paycheck," she informed him the surprised little sobs steeling her reserve. She was shaking, her hands up to her chest as if to protect herself. Tears swelled the liquid amber of her eyes. "Do that again and you'll be paying for a funeral. Yours."

Mitchell wanted to apologize. He wanted to explain. He knew, though, that he couldn't explain what he didn't understand. The anger and self-recrimination had become too mixed-up in something he still couldn't name. Instead of reaching out to her—what he wanted to do—he straightened, and his eyes were fierce.

"In that case," he answered, his voice even more harsh than his hands had been, "I suggest you decide if you really do know what I feel before taking me on again. There are no games here, lady. No games at all."

Lindsay stood where she was for a long while after Mitchell shut himself in the bedroom. She faced the fire, the rippling, ravenous flames mirroring so identically what Mitchell had incited in her, her tears falling as much from loss as fear.

When she finally turned from the dying fire to go to her own room, she still hadn't decided whether or not she would be there in the morning.

Chapter 4

Vulnerable.

That was the word Mitchell had been looking for. In her jeans and cotton shirt and tennis shoes, Lindsay looked vulnerable. It was a word he never would have used about her before these days in the cabin. At work, she had been the perfect automaton, brisk and pleasant and unyielding, wielding all her little psychological tricks to get what she wanted out of the team, then retreating behind her tortoise-shell glasses and cool composure when anyone had gotten too close.

But here she'd been a different person. Softer. Unsure sometimes, with a hint of compassion crumbling the edge of her reserve. Here she had been human.

Groaning, Mitchell slumped back onto his bed. He crossed an arm over tired eyes and bent his good leg. Usually this was the time that he feared the most, when the minutes of darkness collected into images of Maggie and that great, metal monster that had lured her to her death. Usually he waited, willing himself to survive until the dawn.

Tonight he didn't have to wait to be tormented. He'd been tormented from the moment he'd taken hold of Lindsay.

He could still feel her, the steel in her fury, the delicious comfort of her arms. The image of her breasts haunted him, so sleek and soft and pale in the flickering firelight, trapped beneath lace, her trembling hands crossed to keep him away. He couldn't believe what he'd done, couldn't comprehend the furious emotions she'd unleashed with her sharp words and bold cat's eyes.

He'd hated her. He'd wanted her. And he lay in bed, his fist clenched against his face, the hard ache in his belly refusing to die, wondering why a flash of vulnerability should ignite such a fire storm in him.

She should get the hell out. Nothing was worth what Mitchell had almost tried. What she'd incited. Lindsay got to her feet and began to pace the tiny den. Her feet slapped listlessly against the cool hardwood. Her eyes sought out something comforting in the titles on the shelves that filled one wall. Maybe there was something to read to ease her to sleep. A little mystery. Some harmless mayhem. Trauma inflicted on someone else.

There were classics, well-thumbed copies in hard covers and paperback. There were histories and biographies collected in untidy rows and held up by framed pictures of smiling couples. The lightest reading Lindsay could find was a book of anecdotes about baseball. She turned her attention back to the photos.

Three couples. Gathered on a lawn, separated into formal sittings, scattered over various holidays. Younger than Mitchell, some with vague resemblances, some not. Family? Friends? Did Jason Mitchell have friends? He never talked about them. Nothing hinted at a fraternal band that might have collected for football scrimmages and beer on someone's lawn.

He'd served his time both at school and in the military, having graduated from West Point and done a couple of tours in Vietnam. There was nothing in this room that be-

trayed that—no citations, diplomas, memorabilia. For all
this room showed, Jason Mitchell had been born last week
and knew six people. You couldn't tell that he had won two
Purple Hearts, a Bronze Star and several law enforcement
citations. No mention of his Eagle Scout years, either.

Mother, father, twin sisters, Lindsay remembered from
his dossier, all living somewhere back east. He had an older
brother who was now deceased. Maybe she was seeing the
sisters on his shelves. If so, they were beautiful women. But
if they were sisters, where were the parents, smiling shyly
when their son snapped them at a Christmas dinner? Why
weren't they represented, and what did that say about
Mitchell's relationship with them?

Lindsay turned away, not really wanting to know. It
would mean investing too much. The longer she stayed in
this house, the higher the cost of her actions climbed.

The room was too small. The house was too small, holding as it did all of Mitchell's specters and the fetid wind of
despair. Suddenly Lindsay couldn't imagine what she had
hoped to accomplish in this place, what miracle she'd assumed could be wrought.

How had Alex done it? How had he survived her acrimony, her silent wall of resistance? Had love been the key
when even a Ph.D seemed to pale before this task? It was
too bad, then, that she didn't love Mitchell. All of a sudden
it looked as if just respect and concern wouldn't be enough.

Yanking open the door, Lindsay stalked down the hall.
What she wanted was fresh air. What she needed was the
sight of the night sky, so constant and quiet as it arched into
infinity over the mountains. The world would go on, it told
her, if she failed here. She would do her best, and if her best
wasn't good enough, then she, too, would have to go on.

Another lesson Alex had taught her. Too bad he didn't
guest-lecture in psychology.

She realized her mistake the minute she threw open the
kitchen door. The meadow spread before her in slumbering
silver. The moon had just crested the mountains, gilding the
trees and shutting out the stars. The view was mystical, only

waiting for a ring of fairies to dance across the flowers. It was also being shared.

Mitchell whipped around at the sound of the screen door. Lindsay came to an uncertain halt, abruptly aware that she hadn't added anything to the oversize nightshirt she usually wore to bed. Her legs were bare and felt suddenly cold in the chill night. Instinctively she brought a hand to her throat.

Mitchell wore nothing but jeans, slung low on his hips. The moonlight slid over his torso like liquid and scattered through his hair. Lindsay couldn't see his eyes, shadowed by his fierce frown, but she knew they would glow on a night like this. Pale, ghosted, with a heat like a flame. Seeing him without her contacts, just a little blurred, she could almost imagine him a specter, as if captured between worlds on this moonlit night. He turned and tensed.

"Coming back for more?"

It was all she could do to keep from flinching. Even here, with the night wind sneaking under the loose cotton of her shirt, an uncomfortable warmth seeped through her. The darkness hid the furious blush that crept up her throat.

"Getting away, actually. That house was starting to feel too..."

He nodded, a small, jerky movement. "Small."

Lindsay felt his eyes resting on her and straightened, surprised. "Yes."

Now his gaze traveled, and Lindsay could feel it, hot and questing, along the swell of her breasts and hips, sliding over the long lines of her legs and back up again. His eyes were like swift fingers, dispensing shivers, so that even the cold Colorado night was too close, even the sky too small.

"Why don't you wear your glasses?" he demanded.

Lindsay started. "What?"

"Your glasses. Don't you really need them? Do you use them as a sign of authority or something?"

"Of course I need them. What kind of a question is that?"

He never let his eyes stray. Never moved a muscle, as he rigidly stood as a statue. "A question that suddenly occurred to me as I was holding you. I was wondering why you seemed so different here.''

Lindsay had no answer. His question made no sense, his observation even less. In the morning when the light returned, she would probably realize that just the fact that he'd made an observation at all was a step in the right direction. But there was no light now, no real illumination except the magic incandescence of the moon spilling silver over Mitchell.

"Aren't you going to tell me?" Mitchell demanded, suddenly needing to know. Why had she come out here, damn it? He had just begun to regain his silence, settle back into the lassitude that had protected him so well from the pain. Now she was here, her hair tumbled and dancing in the breeze, her lithe figure so deliciously hinted at beneath that piece of material she called clothing. Her legs, so long, so sleek, so inviting. He could almost feel the strength of them as they met his, as they wrapped around him to welcome him home....

He whirled away with an oath.

"Where are you going?" Lindsay demanded.

"Away from you."

She thought to follow him. The night was black and he was barefoot, striding blindly away from her. But Lindsay knew better. Even if she had the courage to wander into the mountains after a madman, she wouldn't have the temerity to court his magnetism once again. If he challenged her, she might just succumb.

Across the narrow valley, a screen door hissed shut and a shadowy figure slipped out of the house. Shrugging into a jacket, Artie checked to see that his gun was in place and then resettled his night glasses. He was in no mood for this. The guy walked too far in the middle of the night, he might just shoot him and take all the fun away from Mick, after all.

Damn him.

The sun had risen somewhere beyond the mountains,

sapping the deep midnight blue from the sky. Birds skipped across the meadows, and the first butterflies of the day were tasting the flowers. Lindsay sat on the back steps of the cabin in her nightshirt and jeans, glasses resting on the bridge of her nose in deference to lack of sleep and grainy eyes. Her fifth cup of coffee was in hand, her eyes were on the barely distinguishable trail that wound up from the creek.

Damn him and damn him again. Where the hell was he?

Mitchell had been gone over five hours. Five long hours of darkness and animal gruntings that Lindsay interpreted as the grumblings of a full stomach. He could be anywhere up on that mountain, hurt, crippled, maybe dead. Why had he run off like that, without so much as a thought of what it was doing to her peace of mind?

The thought brought Lindsay abruptly upright. Oh, good. That would certainly endear her to him when he finally came trudging back off the mountain. "Just where have you been, mister? Do you know I've been waiting here all night? Don't you have any more consideration than that?"

Yeah, Lindsay, she thought with a rueful grin and another long sip of coffee, one word of that kind of diatribe and he'd head straight back for the hills. And for good reason. If anybody said something like that to her, she'd head for the hills, too.

Still, it had been an awfully long time. Maybe she should begin thinking about calling someone.

When Mitchell did stumble into the clearing, Lindsay froze. She hadn't *really* believed he would have hurt himself. It had all been a game of Worst Case Scenario. But there he was, limping, disheveled and bleeding.

"Good God," she finally gasped, her mug hitting the stone step with a clang as she sprang to her feet. "Mitchell, what the hell did you do?"

Slowly, as if it required a very great effort, Mitchell lifted his head to take in the sight of Lindsay hurtling toward him.

"You weren't waiting for me, were you?"

Lindsay came to a halt before him, forcing him to stop, too. "In the frame of mind you were in last night?" She scowled up at him. "Why on earth should I wait to make sure you'd decide to come back?"

He didn't give an inch, even though weariness threatened to overcome him. "Then why didn't you follow along?"

Lindsay could do no more than smile. "I'm not *that* much of an idiot. I figured I'd wait behind and sweep up the pieces."

He nodded, as if this were something to consider. "Well," he announced, arms out for inspection. "The pieces have arrived."

Lindsay made a quick survey. His chest was covered with abrasions and his feet looked as though he had explored the entire mountain range. The blood was from his thigh, where the wound had evidently broken open again.

"What did the bear look like?" she finally asked, her head tilted to the side.

"No bear," he countered. "A cliff. It wasn't there a couple of weeks ago. I'd swear to it."

Lindsay hooked an arm around his back and turned to guide him toward the house. "Well, you'll sure know where it is now. Do you know any of the doctors in town?"

Mitchell shook his head again. He was dragging his right leg, as if there weren't any feeling in it. "No, thanks. I don't get along with doctors."

"Well, I don't do stitches," Lindsay countered, surprised at the fact that he was actually letting her take some of his weight. She wanted to shove her glasses back up her nose, but knew that one less hand would make all the difference in getting anywhere. "It's the doctor or another round with the alcohol."

Mitchell's scowl would have been much more impressive if he hadn't just lost a fight with a cliff. Lindsay took a long look at the cabin as they approached and knew that once inside she wouldn't get him back out. Without putting the matter up for a vote, she steered him straight for her car.

"Are you feeling better?" she asked dryly.

Mitchell winced as he lifted his leg. "Define better."

"Able to communicate without snarling."

He shook his head and tiny bits of leaves fell from his hair. "No. You're wearing glasses again. And you're in your nightgown."

Pulling open the passenger door, Lindsay navigated Mitchell in the general direction of the front seat. "At least I have a shirt on."

"Thank God."

Lindsay's eyes widened at his words, but Mitchell didn't seem to notice. All his attention appeared to be on folding himself into the little import Lindsay drove.

"Let's take my Jeep," he suggested after bumping his head on the door. "I'll drive."

"Thanks, but no. I'd rather arrive alive." Making sure all his limbs were safely inside, Lindsay shut the door on him. "Wait here. I'll get the keys."

Mitchell scowled. "Where the hell do you think I'm going to go?"

The car keys were in her purse on the kitchen table. Right beneath the phone. Lindsay dashed to her room to get some clothes, then, at the last minute, thought to call the office.

Bob wasn't in. Al was.

"Al, listen, get a hold of Bob for me, will you?" Lindsay asked, bending over to tie her tennis shoes. "Tell him that I need to get Mitchell in to get his leg looked at. He's not bad, but we're going to have to head over to Estes Park to see the doctor."

"Lindsay? Don't leave that cabin until we can get you some backup."

"Mitchell's not going to wait. Tell Bob. Bye."

Pulling her purse over her shoulder and stuffing the tail of her nightshirt into her jeans, Lindsay headed out the door.

Standing in the office he shared with Brent Sellers, Al stared at the dead receiver. Then he cursed. Looking around, he saw that there wasn't anybody else within help-

ing distance. He was going to have to risk it and take care of
it himself. With his gaze still looking out for some help, he
began to quickly dial.

Artie hadn't gotten back. Mick had waited for him, even
missing some of a TV program to watch the cabin. He'd
seen Mitchell stumble in from the creek, and the lady steer
him for the car, but he hadn't seen Artie.

Could Artie and him have had a fight? Maybe Artie was
lying up there someplace, in worse shape than the cop.

Mick lowered the binoculars and turned toward the
phone. If he called, there wouldn't be anybody to follow the
cop. If he waited for Artie, they might get away. And if he
just accidentally nudged the cop off the road, nobody could
say it was his fault. Mick took a quick look at his watch. He
could get it done and be back before the first spin of the
wheel.

With a sudden, huge grin, Mick traded his binoculars for
a gun and lumbered out the door.

"Are you okay?" Lindsay asked. They were heading up
over the pass to the north of the cabin, weaving in and out
on a road that hugged the mountain all the way up to the
sky. Beside her, Mitchell leaned rigidly against the seat, eyes
closed, hands clenched on his legs.

"You've read the file. You know damn well I'm not."

Lindsay turned her eyes back to the road. "But you drive
this way all the time."

"It's different when I'm riding."

She downshifted into a turn and took a precautionary
peek into her rearview mirror. There was a great big boat of
a car following her much too closely. Nothing tested Lindsay's patience more than a tailgater. Her first instinct was to
slam on the brakes. Then she remembered that she wasn't
exactly on the freeway.

"Have you had acrophobia all your life?" she asked, her
concentration focused on her driving.

Mitchell was in no mood to play. "Are you going to charge me for this session?"

With a scowl, Lindsay took a look at him. His lips were whiter than his knuckles. It made her feel repentant. "Just gas money," she answered a bit more gently and turned back to her tailgater.

Maybe if she just slowed and let him pass her. There was a truck lane coming up. She'd pull over.

"So," Mitchell said through gritted teeth. "Tell me about the glasses."

Lindsay kept her attention on the road. "What about them?"

"Why do you wear them at work? Why not here? Isn't that backward?"

"What does that have to do with anything?" she demanded, suddenly anxious. The car was too close behind her. Lindsay decided that was why she felt so impatient.

"It has to do with keeping my attention off the road we're on," Mitchell snapped. "Tell me."

"Glasses make me look older, all right?" Lindsay answered, gauging the distance between her car and the truck lane, hoping her shadow had more patience than she. "It's hard enough getting you guys to listen to suggestions, without having them come out of a twelve-year-old face."

"Wrong."

"What?"

"They don't make you look older, at all. They make you look harder. More distant. Do you wear them on dates?"

Lindsay hit her blinker, giving the guy in back of her plenty of notice. "That's none of your business, Mitchell."

"You're a beautiful woman, McDonough," he retorted. "But I didn't figure that out until you showed up in jeans and a work shirt."

The car behind slowed with her as she shifted to the slow lane. "Well, Mitchell," she countered testily, "don't expect me to wear jeans at work."

"Just take your glasses off so people can see you."

She turned, wondering at his interest. Something else took her attention, though. Something far more important. "Mitchell, you don't have your seat belt on."

He opened one eye just far enough to glare. "You're going to be my mother, too?"

"Everybody wears a seat belt in my car."

He turned away and let his eyes close. "Everybody except me."

She'd reached the truck lane. Swinging the little car far to the right, she gave the boat behind her plenty of room to pass. He didn't. Rather than take the free lane, he seemed to prefer a game of cat and mouse. Lindsay cursed under her breath.

"What?" Mitchell asked, his hands still clenched, his eyes still closed.

"You either put your seat belt on," she warned him, without bothering to look away from the road, "or I stop at the edge of this cliff until you do."

They were nearing the top of the pass. It wouldn't be too much longer before they ran out of passing lane. Then Lindsay would be forced to entertain this guy's bumper all the way back down the mountain. Maybe if she slowed a little more, just to give that guy back there a stronger hint. Then again, if she slowed much more she was going to start going backward.

"If you remember correctly," Mitchell retorted, eyes still closed, oblivious to the little ballet going on around him, "I didn't want to go on this field trip in the first place. Stop the car and I'll just walk home."

"Damn it, Mitchell, I'm not in the mood to deal with a six-year-old. Put the damn thing on!"

She had only taken her gaze off the road for a second. Only long enough to emphasize her point with a little strategic eye contact. It was at that moment that the car was hit.

Lindsay screamed. Mitchell whipped back against the seat and then shot forward into the windshield. His head struck it with a dull crack. The glass starred. He cursed. The car bumped over the uneven shoulder, perilously close to the edge of the mountainside. The next stop was a good five hundred feet down. Lindsay fought the wheel, her hands suddenly sweating, her mind reeling between reality and memory.

"How long has he been back there?" Mitchell demanded, a hand to his head as he turned to see what had happened.

"Who?" Lindsay asked, finally swinging the car onto pavement. She was all set to slow to a stop, her trembling making mincemeat out of any kind of reflexes she might have had. She had to get out of that car. Get some air. It was Mitchell's fault. If only he'd put on his seat belt. If only Patrick had listened to her.

She put a foot on the brake.

"Don't do that!" Mitchell snapped. "Hit the gas. Give yourself some room."

Lindsay looked over to argue the point, but lost her train of thought. She blanched. He was bleeding. Blood coursed all down the side of his face where he'd struck it. No. No, God, not that. Not again.

Patrick, I didn't mean it.

"Come on, damn it," Mitchell snarled, taking hold of her arm. "He's going to push us off the road. Drive!"

"I ... I can't ..." It had taken her six years to get over it. Dreams the size of Mitchell's and days that were a walk through hell. She'd fought so hard. Suddenly she was right back in that little Volkswagen on a rainy June night.

The car shuddered again, careened forward. Lindsay made another grab for the wheel, trying her best to pull herself together. "What's going on?"

"You're getting your first taste of fieldwork," Mitchell informed her, an eye on the other car following theirs. "That's what's going on. Now give this thing some gas. And don't put your foot near that brake until I tell you. You lose control if you ride the brakes."

Lindsay heard the roar of a powerful motor and looked up to see the big car edge up alongside them. There wasn't room on the road. The passing lane was ending. There was nothing but two lanes, no visibility and a lot of air.

"What do I do?" she asked, both hands tight against a slick steering wheel. Mitchell still hadn't let go of her arm.

He watched their pursuer, then turned to her. "Downshift. Give yourself more power."

Lindsay downshifted. The little car jerked forward, the engine screaming. The edge of the mountain seemed to face them, and the big car was closing in again.

"Hold on," Mitchell barked. "He's making another—"

The compact car lurched. Metal screeched as the two cars met. Lindsay knew that her car wouldn't stand a chance against the heavier machine that challenged her. It was only a matter of time before he pushed her over the edge.

"Faster," Mitchell commanded.

Lindsay shifted up and gained inches. She veered toward the center line so she could handle the curves and prayed that no one came shooting around one of the blind corners. Downshift. Gas. Upshift. Turn. Faster. Her heart was hammering. There was a knot of acid in her throat. She couldn't do it. They weren't going to make it, and she'd run out to find Mitchell lying dead in the road. Just like Patrick. Just like before.

"Come on," Mitchell urged. "Make him chase you. Make him put that car through its paces."

"This isn't a road race," Lindsay snapped shrilly, the sweat already beginning to trickle into her eyes.

"The only way you're gonna live is to win, sweetie," he retorted. "All right, now, downshift again. Pull some speed out of this thing. No, no, go straight. Don't turn."

"But the road—"

"I know. We're going to outsmart him. Now, keep your foot planted on that gas pedal until I tell you. When I do, I want both feet on the brakes. *Both* feet, got it?"

Shaking like a leaf, Lindsay nodded. She could feel rather than see the big car edging close enough again for another try. The road turned; it seemed to veer off at an angle only yards from where they were careening along. Feet. Inches.

They were going to fly off the road like brightly colored birds.

She hadn't even paid her car off yet.

"Now!"

Lindsay slammed both feet against the brake pedal. The tires shrieked. Lindsay had all she could do to hold on to the wheel as the car skidded in a wild curve toward the edge of the mountain.

"Oh, my God!" She couldn't even close her eyes and pretend she wasn't going to die.

Mitchell grabbed the wheel with her. They battled the car to a stop. Alongside, the big car shot past them like a loosed arrow and sailed straight off the edge of the cliff.

"Oh . . ."

Lindsay sat transfixed by the sight. The car seemed to soar, arcing out over the mountainside in lumbering flight until it finally lost to gravity and nosed down. The sound of its crash was distant, like a cymbal from a faraway band. Bright tongues of flame consumed it and a thick cloud of oily smoke snaked into the summer sky. The world was too silent for what had just happened.

"You can let go of the wheel now."

Lindsay's heart hammered in her chest. She couldn't breathe. Couldn't function. So close. They'd come so close, and she hadn't even been watching the road.

Again.

The adrenaline that had brought her to the top of the mountain raced unheeded through her. The terror choked her. The self-recriminations she'd left behind so long ago tasted like acid on her tongue.

"Lindsay, I said you could take your hands off the steering wheel. You can even get out and stretch a little until the police come."

She'd only taken her eyes from the road for a moment, a second, just to challenge Patrick's accusation. He'd been so vindictive toward the end. Especially the times when she'd insisted on driving home.

She'd thought it would be safer that way. She'd been sober, and her husband hadn't.

But she'd killed him, anyway.

Lindsay didn't even feel Mitchell pry her fingers from the steering wheel.

Chapter 5

Mitchell gave in to his first impulse. Turning his head only slightly, he delivered a sardonic smile. "Well, I have to ask you. Is fieldwork as much fun as you thought?"

He hadn't even gathered the control to keep the acid from his voice. Lindsay was ashen and shaking, staring blindly out front, tears filling her stark eyes. Frozen. Just what he would have expected from a desk jock.

Except that this desk jock had gotten the job done.

In a couple of minutes, he was going to have to start unraveling this little surprise. Right now, though, he had to take care of the matter at hand.

"Come on, McDonough," he prodded none too gently, easing her fingers from their death grip on the wheel. "If you want to play with the big kids, you have to learn how to get bumped around."

Her hands were like ice, clammy and limp. At his touch, she started.

"Patrick . . ."

Mitchell stopped short, Lindsay's hands still in his, his gaze fixed now on eyes that carried their own ghosts. He'd never heard such anguish in a voice in his life. Who the hell was Patrick? And why was she calling to him, when she'd just stopped inches short of high diving into a pile of rocks?

"Lindsay?" Mitchell was surprised at the tone of his own voice. It was gentler than it had been in ten years. Something in that suddenly lost face pulled at a too-familiar chord in him. "It's over. You did a good job."

She seemed to respond to the tone, turning to face him. When she caught a fresh sight of the blood on his face, her eyes grew impossibly large. She licked at dry lips.

"You didn't . . . you didn't put on your seat belt," she accused him, more hotly than Mitchell was prepared for.

"I won't make that mistake again," he promised, not even realizing that he still had hold of her hands. "Especially if I'm driving with you."

That was evidently the wrong thing to say. Lindsay grew still paler, if that was possible, and drew in a ragged breath. "It wasn't my fault. He came on us so suddenly. I couldn't swerve. . . ." Faltering, she shook her head. "No, damn it. You know what I mean."

"Lindsay, are you okay?" Mitchell asked, suddenly really wondering if she was coming unraveled.

It took Lindsay a moment with eyes closed before she could answer. When she did, it was with a certain amount of accusation. "You want to explain that crack about playing with the big kids?"

Mitchell had to grin. She sure didn't lose any time going on the offensive. "So, you were paying attention after all."

"I have a suggestion for you, Mitchell," she retorted, eyes open again and hands back in her lap. "But I think it's anatomically impossible. What do we do now?"

Her eyes strayed to the plume of smoke that stained the perfect summer sky. Occasionally cars passed behind them on their way around the mountain, but none stopped. It must have looked as if they had stopped to admire the view.

Lindsay felt her stomach drop away again. God, she was going to be sick. It was like a time warp tearing through the fabric of daylight, suddenly letting in rain and darkness where there had been none before. Giving brief life back to Patrick, only to take it away again.

For a moment she really hadn't been able to differentiate. You can only win one round with a load of guilt like that. Round two must surely go to guilt. Lindsay took a moment to thank whatever kind gods were listening that they had kept her from the edge, that the car hadn't been hit hard enough for Mitchell to be thrown out onto the road.

"Lindsay?"

She could hardly drag her eyes away from the evidence of their close call. "What?"

"Are you feeling better?"

Her response was automatic. "Define better."

That was all it took. Lindsay turned to find Mitchell giving her a dry smile; she broke out laughing. He joined in, the giddiness fueled by adrenaline and flavored with a feeling of reprieve. But they weren't being frivolous. They were venting the terror.

By the time he'd faced the police and an emergency room doctor with the touch of a lowland gorilla, Mitchell wondered what the hell there had been to laugh about. His head hurt, he was sporting a brand-new set of eight stitches in his head and another six to patch the incision on his leg. And that didn't even take into account his run-in with a nurse, who'd treated the scrapes on his chest with a bottle of hydrogen peroxide.

All in all, the day kept going straight downhill. And by three, he still hadn't had any sleep. Jason Mitchell was not in a good mood.

"Do you want to hear about the merits of a seat belt now, or do you think you're sufficiently chastised?" Lindsay greeted him when he finally wandered back out to the waiting room. She didn't appear to be in any better mood than he.

"We're getting out of here," was all he said.

Lindsay nodded without noticeable reaction and followed him out of the door. "You're welcome, Mitchell. I think I did a good job keeping us from the bottom of that gorge, too. But think nothing of it.''

He never turned around. "I don't."

Mitchell stalked out to the now-battered little car without further comment. He wasn't in the least pleased by his initial reaction to seeing Lindsay waiting out on that uncomfortable little plastic chair. She'd looked so tired, so deflated, as if all the spirit had been sucked right out of her.

Mitchell realized then that something far worse had happened to her in that car than had happened to him. He also realized that he felt an empathy for her—and wanted no part of it. How the hell was he going to ignore her when he found himself wanting to pull her into his arms, tell her it was okay and that she'd done a damn good job out on that mountain pass?

But if he told her that, somehow he'd cast lines of commitments he didn't want, either. He didn't want to feel protective of Lindsay McDonough, but damn it, he did.

"Do you want me to drive?" he asked flatly, stopping by the front grille.

Pulling out her keys, Lindsay shook her head. Then she thought of his white knuckles on the trip over. "Yeah," she conceded, her shoulders slumping just a little with the weariness that seemed to consume her. "I do. That way, if somebody tries to run us off the road going back, I can repay your gratitude."

Flipping the keys in Mitchell's general direction, she headed for the passenger side. It wasn't until Mitchell was safely seated behind the steering wheel that Lindsay fastened her seat belt. Mitchell frowned, but reached around and buckled his own belt.

"Have you talked to Bob yet?" Lindsay asked. She kept her eyes on her hands, where they rested on her lap. She was still feeling sick, jittery and numb. It seemed that the effects of flashback lasted longer than a close brush with death.

"I'll call when we get back. Who's Patrick?"

She stiffened, trying to remember. Had she called to Patrick, just as she had in those last moments? Had she somehow given herself away? She'd meant all along to tell Mitchell about her past, but she couldn't do it this way—not offering her vulnerable spot like the soft underbelly of a dragon to the knight's spear. Mitchell would never listen, the way she wanted him to right now. He'd pounce on her.

"My husband. Why do you think that man tried to run us off the road?"

His startled gaze straying only briefly from the road, Mitchell shrugged. "Any number of reasons. I don't live in an isolated mountain cabin just because I like the trees." Husband, he thought with some confusion. McDonough didn't have a husband. He'd never asked, but every other single man in the office had. What was the story?

Lindsay kept to the previous line of conversation. "Meaning the line to get at you is long."

He nodded. "Meaning that very thing."

Lindsay gathered the courage to look over at Mitchell. His face was still so drawn, the new stress just leeching more color from his skin and sharpening the taut lines. She would really have to watch him for a while. Once the adrenaline high wore off and he didn't have to rely on instinct to fuel him, he was going to crash hard. His nightmares waited for him in the rooms of that cabin just as much as his solace did, and he would realize that the minute he set foot inside.

She was going to have to watch herself, too. Her objective sense noted the tightening in her own chest at the sight of him, the instinct to protect and comfort. It was beginning to hurt her more and more to see the sleepless nights take their toll on Mitchell.

With a start, she realized that she had somehow lost her clinical eye with Mitchell. When she looked at him, she didn't see symptoms. She saw a man. A handsome, enigmatic man who fought hard for his principles and gave no quarter. A man who, obstinate and uncompromising as he could be, was fair and honest and strong. It would kill her to see him shatter over something he couldn't control. And that bothered her a lot more than she ever would have imagined.

"Did you see him at all?" she finally asked, turning back to the road they had traveled that morning.

"The guy in the car? Yeah. He was familiar-looking."

"He was smiling." Lindsay found herself more amazed than outraged. "Like he was on a carnival ride."

Mitchell shrugged. "Takes all kinds to make a world."

Lindsay had to laugh. "Now that's something I'll have to file away in my psychology textbooks."

"You can do that the minute you get back to the job tomorrow morning," Mitchell informed her.

Lindsay did her best to keep him from seeing her tense. Decision time. She should probably take him up on it and get the hell out while she had the chance. This psychologist was getting a little too close to the subject. But she knew that he wasn't going to let anyone else close again. This was going to be her only chance to help him.

"Fine," she answered evenly. "I'll report in right after you do."

"In person," he countered.

"You're going to Denver?"

Mitchell scowled. "*You* are going in person."

She gave back a small smile. "No, thank you."

He never looked over at her. "It wasn't an invitation."

"I think you'd better talk to Bob before making rash statements."

"Fine." His nod was terse and final. "He'll just agree with everything I said."

"She stays."

Pacing to the length of the telephone cord, Mitchell dragged a hand through his hair. "You've got to be kidding me. The last thing I need on my hands right now is an amateur!"

Bob's voice sounded weary. "Sounds to me that what isn't needed right now is a pain in the butt, and you're the only one who qualifies for that. Lindsay stays on the case.

If you want to come in, she follows. If you want to stay there, she does, too." The pause was small but telling. "Am I understood?"

Mitchell dispatched a furious look in Lindsay's direction before starting on the next leg of his walk. From where she sat at the kitchen table, Lindsay could see the storm clouds gathering. Good. More emotion. Another flash point. At least Bob wasn't letting Mitchell settle back into his stupor. She was glad she'd anticipated all this and taken the time to call Bob from the hospital waiting room.

What she wasn't so sure about was whether she was going to have the energy to utilize all this emotion. Now that the adrenaline had died in her, there didn't seem to be anything at all fueling her. Her shakes had finally disappeared, but so had all of her strength. She was only sitting upright at the table to keep from falling face forward into her half-drained cup of tea. Lindsay wanted to go to bed, and she wanted to do it now.

"You will not!"

Lindsay stared at the sharp command in Mitchell's voice. He was heading her way again, his stride choppy and his hand worrying at the edges of his new stitches. His hair was still tangled, his feet were bare and his jeans bloodstained and ripped. For all he'd been through, she couldn't imagine how he could still be on his feet, much less participating in a long-distance shouting match.

"I've told you before. This cabin is strictly off limits for the task force. I don't bring it here, and I don't want anybody else doing it. No baby-sitters!"

He shot her an acid glance. He hadn't allowed the task force to broach his sanctuary, he was clearly telling her, until *she* had shown up.

Good thing she and Bob had already decided not to let Mitchell in on Lindsay's call to the office. The police Bob had dispatched had kept a surreptitious watch all the way back to the cabin, and the agent he'd called up had settled in to work the accident with the local guys. The less Mitchell knew about the measures taken to protect him, the better for all concerned. Especially, Lindsay thought, for her.

In a flash of stellar logic, she decided that the best way to deal with the whole situation was to ignore it. If she shut her eyes, Mitchell would go away. She did precisely that.

"Somebody just tried to run you two off the road," Bob was saying on the other end of Mitchell's line. "I'd say that means that somebody found the cabin, after all."

Mitchell dragged his eyes away from the sight of the late-afternoon light warming Lindsay's skin. She looked so small and childlike sitting there with her eyes shut and her chin in her hand.

"I can take care of myself," he snapped into the phone.

"What about my psychologist?"

Mitchell couldn't help a dry laugh. "*You* sent her in here. *You* figure out what to do with her."

"Mitchell—"

"What's Al come up with on Esperanza?" Mitchell asked, interrupting the warning.

"He thinks that Esperanza's lawyer, Perez, tried to get in touch with Maggie. That maybe he had the proof we needed to connect the Wilsons to Esperanza. Problem is, Perez was found in a Dumpster yesterday afternoon, in no condition to ever enlighten us again."

Mitchell rubbed at his eyes, surprised at the sudden stinging he felt at the mention of Maggie. "Couldn't have happened to a nicer guy. Just wished I could have talked to him first."

He was so tired. Too damned tired for any of this. All he wanted was to sit in his chair on the porch and watch the shadows gather.

"How does Al connect Perez to Maggie?"

"A note in his calendar about Maria Suarez, her cover. Nothing else interesting found in his place, which, by the way, had already been tossed by the time we got to it."

"Meaning that somebody wants something they think Perez had."

"Kind of supports Al's theory, doesn't it?"

"Yeah." Mitchell tried to kickstart some action into his brain, come up with a question or a suggestion. He knew there should be a logical path to take, yet he couldn't find it. Finally he went for what he knew.

"I think this guy today was tied in with this," he offered, leaning against the kitchen door. "I recognized him from somewhere, and I'm sure it's fresh."

Until recently, another of Mitchell's talents had been a full and photographic memory. His trial on the thirty-ninth floor had short-circuited that, as if someone had cut the wiring. From the moment he'd lost Maggie's last words, he'd lost bits and pieces of everything else. The idea that he wouldn't ever get it all back crawled in his gut like cold worms.

"Are you coming in or not?" Bob asked.

"Right now I'm getting some sleep," Mitchell told him. "I'm sore and tired and in a bad mood...."

"No kidding."

Mitchell chose to ignore him. "Have Al check on a guy... Rick, Mike... no, Mick. Mick something. Prize-fighter's face, and not one that won often. See what the connection is."

"Any last name?"

Mitchell closed his eyes to better conjure an answer. His head still hurt, and his back needed stretching. And no matter which way he held his memory up to the light, no last name connected itself with the smiling Mick.

"Nah. Enjoys his job, though. He had a big grin plastered on his face when he ran into us."

"Lovely."

He also wasn't the kind of person who could have set this whole thing up himself, Mitchell realized, though how he could be certain of that he didn't know. Later. He'd figure it out later. He was getting too damn punch-drunk himself to think coherently. All he wanted to ask was what had happened to Lindsay's husband, and that damn well wasn't making any sense.

"Nobody will get close tonight," he finally said. "I'll call tomorrow from a secure line. See what Al can have for me."

"Mitchell?"

"Yeah."

"Are you absolutely positive this is all coming from Esperanza, and not somebody else just evening up an old score?"

"I'm positive."

"Then why did they wait two weeks to try and kill you?"

Mitchell straightened at that. He turned to see that Lindsay still kept her precarious balance on her hand as she dozed. There was only one thing, he realized, that had changed in the last two weeks.

"Maybe your psychologist had him in her chair, too. He probably hates her guts."

"If you think Lindsay had anything to do with this, I'm consigning you to retirement, Mitchell."

Mitchell rubbed at his face. "Yeah, yeah. Okay. This was the first time I've been out of the cabin. Is that what you want to hear?"

Bob didn't answer right away. Mitchell could almost see him rolling a pencil back and forth across his desk as he thought out his decision.

"Then maybe you'd better not come in, after all."

"I'll call you tomorrow."

"Sooner, if I'm wrong."

"You'll be the first to know."

Mitchell hung up, still pondering Bob's point, and turned to find Lindsay in the same position.

"C'mon, McDonough," he said. "I don't know about you, but I'm gonna get in some sack time before I tackle anything else."

She didn't react. Her chest rose and fell evenly and her eyelids lay without moving against her cheeks. She was asleep. Absolutely, soundly asleep.

Mitchell walked a little closer. How could she manage that? Her chin was still propped on one hand, her forearm straight and unwavering. Giving in to an absurd impulse,

Mitchell snapped his fingers within millimeters of her closed eyes. She didn't even twitch. If somebody had done that to him, he would have been facedown on the table. If he hadn't been already, that is.

It occurred to him then that this was the first time he'd seen her with her hair down. It floated around her face like a cloud, rippling from fawn to wheat with the breeze that winnowed it. There were freckles on her nose, just a few...just enough. They made her look kissable.

"McDonough!" he snapped, stepping back as if he had been bitten. "Come on. Get up."

Lindsay smiled dreamily and eased her head from the palm of her hand to the table itself, never once opening her eyes. And there she lay.

"Aw, hell!"

He should leave her where she was. Should just stalk off and throw himself onto that crumpled, unmade bed and be done with her. Instead, Mitchell found himself scooping Lindsay into his arms and carrying her out of the kitchen.

Even worse, she curled right up against him as if it were the most natural position for her to be in. A hand rested against his chest and her cheek nestled his shoulder. Her hair hung just below his nose, just close enough for him to smell the wildflowers in it. It should have made him madder. But all he could think of was how light she was in his arms. How comfortable.

With his arms full, Mitchell had to kick Lindsay's door open. When he did, he was surprised. His den was a mess.

Well, not really. It was just that her belongings overflowed the place. Clothing was tossed over the chair and makeup was strewn across his usually carefully ordered desk. The fold-out couch was unmade. A bra hung from it, brushing against a pair of sneakers that sat alongside on the floor.

He came to a stop before it all, actually amused at the picture. After all the cleaning she'd inflicted on his house, she didn't even keep her own room tidy. Mitchell wondered just what her place looked like. Probably a lot cleaner, now that she hadn't been in it for a few days. So, the psychologist kept an untidy life. If he'd seen this just coming from the office, he would never have believed it.

A picture. There was a photo in a frame on his end table, one he certainly hadn't placed there. The enigmatic Patrick, perhaps? Another mysterious gentleman in the psychologist's life? Come to think of it, nobody in the office knew what McDonough did in her off hours. For all he knew, she could live in a brothel and date Arab sheiks.

Mitchell stepped closer for a better look. The guy looked like Cary Grant. No, the guy *was* Cary Grant. What the hell was she doing with a framed photo of Cary Grant next to her bed? Was she crazy? Or was she just playing another one of her games?

Lindsay shifted her weight a little, curling into a more comfortable position. Mitchell looked down at her, wondering how she could get away with the image she projected at the office. Her glasses had slipped to the side of her nose and her hair lay in a tawny banner across her cheek. Her lashes were like soot and her mouth curled in a soft child's pout. She looked as if she was fifteen. How the hell did she manage to appear so godawful prim at work?

It was then that it struck Mitchell that Lindsay McDonough had something to hide. Some soft spot she protected with her glasses and designer suits and sleek hair. And, oddly enough, that was what made him angry.

The woman who demanded everyone else's secrets kept her own safe behind a glossy facade. And she played games with other people.

He went so far as to ease Lindsay onto the bed and cover her up. But when he stalked out of the room, Mitchell slammed the door behind him.

Artie knew he was being pulled off the job. He sat in the front room of the cabin, rewinding the wiretap reel and painting his scratches with Merchurochrome. That damn cop had slid through those mountains like a ghost, leaving Artie huffing and puffing on his trail like an amateur. By the time he'd finally trudged back out of the woods, minus field glasses and a lot of skin from slipping and sliding along in the dark, Artie had lost not only Mitchell but his patience. Then he'd walked back into the cabin to realize he'd also lost Mick.

The call he'd had to make afterward had not been a pleasant one. Nobody liked screwups. Especially screwups that left behind dead bodies. The boss was going to send in another team, and Artie was being relegated to the rear lines. But somehow he was going to be in at the kill. He owed that to Mick. After all, hadn't that been the last thing Mick had wanted? Just to get that cop.

It was the breaks that Mick had bought the big one. Breaks and bad luck. All the same, Artie wasn't gonna be able to watch *Wheel of Fortune* without thinking of Mick laughing and scrunching up his face to try and figure out that damn puzzle.

Yeah. He'd do the cop for Mick.

The storm invaded Lindsay's sleep first. We've sure had a lot of those this summer, she thought, snuggling more deeply into the pillow and pulling the covers over her ears.

Storms didn't particularly bother her. She liked the sound of spattering rain and the distant rumble of thunder like the bass drum from a marching band. She didn't like the lightning, though. It lanced through her sleep and refused to be ignored. Tonight, the lightning slashed and sizzled against her eyelids until she couldn't even hide from it beneath the covers.

She'd been thinking of getting up and watching the pyrotechnics from the porch. There wasn't going to be any way to sleep through this nonsense. But when she started to move, certain inconsistencies nudged her subconscious.

When had she gone to bed? And why was she still in her shoes? Lindsay eased one eye open to realize that she was still in all her clothes. Beyond the den window, the sky was certainly dark, the lightning and thunder shattering it and rattling through the little cabin. How had she ended up in bed? The last thing she remembered was sitting at the kitchen table, listening to Mitchell yell at Bob. Or more particularly, sitting at the table with her eyes closed, trying to ignore Mitchell. She must have done a good job. She'd managed not only to make him disappear, but the entire afternoon, as well.

Lindsay sat up and swung her feet to the floor. Mitchell must have put her to bed, which explained the shoes. He wouldn't have thought to be that considerate. Lindsay was surprised, in fact, that he hadn't just left her in the kitchen.

She looked around, seeing that nothing had been disturbed. He really must have dropped her and run. No big surprise there. She wondered if he'd seen Cary. It would have been so interesting to see his reaction, if he'd had any.

Taking a look at her alarm clock, Lindsay saw it was eleven. P.M., she assumed. She felt as if she had gotten a full night's sleep, and the storm still raged unabated around her. Nothing to do but get up and watch. With a shrug, she got up to change the rumpled, stale clothes she'd worn to bed before proceeding to the porch. She was slipping a T-shirt over her head when a hoarse cry split the air.

Lindsay jumped. The shirt suddenly seemed difficult to manage. What was happening out there? Was that Mitchell?

"Maggie!"

When she heard that, Lindsay started for the door. She was still stuffing her shirt into her jeans as she ran out into the hallway. The house was dark, and lightning slashed through the halls, giving erratic life to the shadows. Mitchell's door was open. Lindsay didn't hesitate to go in.

He was sitting up, and he was shaking. Not trembling, not shivering, but shaking so hard the springs creaked. The storm lighted his face like a death mask. His eyes were gaunt and hollow, the creases that bracketed his mouth suddenly harsh. When he turned to her, Lindsay wondered whom he saw.

"Mitchell?" She greeted him gently, seeing the sweat glistening on his chest. "It's me, Lindsay."

Don't waste time. Get him oriented as fast as possible. Get him past this and use the experience at the same time. She had to break this cycle, and now looked as good a time as any to do it. But she had to get by the pain that seared her at the sight of him.

"Get . . . out," he gasped, turning away.

She neither raised her voice nor came closer. "No."

"I have to . . ." He was facing the window, daring the storm that had taunted his memory. Lindsay waited for him to finish his thought, waited for him to move. He did neither.

She walked up to the bed. "Come on, Mitchell. Let's go watch from the porch. At least there's a breeze out there."

She didn't want to say how rancid this room smelled. Awash in terror and fury and failure. She wanted to get him away so he could face the truth, whatever it was.

Her words seemed to galvanize him. Mitchell turned on her, an eerie light flickering across his eyes, giving him an air of menace. "Leave me alone, psychologist. Let me rot in peace."

Again his energy buffeted her, surrounded her. Lindsay almost staggered before it, but she held her ground. "We've already buried Maggie, Mitchell. Isn't it about time you did, too?"

Mitchell heard none of the gentle concern in her voice. All he heard was the challenge. It was enough to bring him to his feet. "I don't want you here, McDonough. I don't want you in my house or my life or my dreams. I sure as hell don't want you picking apart my memories like some damn vulture, until you leave me in pieces. Go play your party games with some other sucker. I don't like your sense of humor."

"Ah." Lindsay smiled suddenly, still toe-to-toe with him. "You've seen Cary. I wondered."

Her words brought him to an uncertain stop. "What the hell difference does it make?"

"You're curious, that's what. I've been waiting for some signs of life."

Mitchell felt as if he were shadowboxing. And losing. His mind was still reeling from the images the storm had resurrected. The smell of the rain, the chill of the wind. Suddenly he was talking about curiosity and Cary Grant.

"What?"

Lindsay shrugged, squinting a little at him in the shadows that were blacker now that the lightning was easing. "Come sit out on the porch and I'll explain."

He actually went. Still chilly with sweat and flushed with shock. Barefoot and bare-chested, he followed the bobbing head of Lindsay McDonough like a pup on a leash. Jason Mitchell walked away from his nightmare and out into the cooling night air, and couldn't explain why he felt better for it.

Chapter 6

"From the beginning."

"What?"

Her eyes carefully on Mitchell's face, Lindsay curled a little more easily into her wicker chair. "Everything that matters. Your dream. That night."

He didn't move. "No."

"Are you afraid?"

Mitchell faced her, the expression in his eyes lethal, as cold as the bottom of a well. "Don't ever say that to me again."

"You're acrophobic, Mitchell. I thought you'd be familiar with the word." It was an effort, but Lindsay kept her voice quiet, passive. "It makes you angry to be afraid?"

She could barely see him squint as he wondered what it was she was doing. He stood at the edge of the porch, the muscles in his shoulders as tight as new rope, his right hand jammed into his pocket, positioned to do battle.

"Everybody's afraid," he finally said, turning back to face the wind that swept in from the mountains. The rain had died, but the thunder refused to concede, ambling through the mountains in an almost endless rumble.

Lindsay could see Mitchell's left hand working. Opening. Closing. Opening. He didn't even seem to notice. Lindsay countered his defensive posture with one of non-threatening acceptance.

"Then what was wrong with being afraid that night?" she asked softly.

Mitchell didn't answer. The wind tugged at his hair and cooled the sweat on his chest. The thunder was like a familiar companion now, the lightning tracing filigree patterns across the sky and outlined the mountains. Storms were beautiful things. He used to come out here all the time and watch them, soaking in their energy and wondering at their awesome display. Now he cowered in a corner remembering.

"Maggie should have alerted you somehow that she'd already arrived," Lindsay said.

"She didn't have a chance."

"Then how could you have been prepared to defend her?"

"I should have been prepared for anything."

His hand was moving faster, clenching tighter. A muscle was working in his jaw. Lindsay pressed right on. "Even though Maggie knew you couldn't tolerate heights?"

"Yes."

"Even though the two of you worked out a system where you never had to go up into places like that?"

"Yes." Stronger. Angrier. "Yes!"

"And you don't think it was good enough that you won out in a firefight with three other men who had automatic weapons?"

Mitchell turned on her. "I didn't save Maggie, did I?"

Lindsay flinched at the agony in Mitchell's voice, the raw grief that lanced her chest. It was all she could do to sit still before it.

Mitchell quivered under the weight of his words. He dragged in a desperate breath, his eyes glinting unnaturally in the half-light. Pulling his other hand out of his pocket, he raked both through his hair. The nightmare pounded through him, echoing in his head and swirling in his gut like acid. Maggie's face, her voice. Accusing him. Begging him. Dying without him.

He looked down at Lindsay, who delivered her own accusations as quietly as if she were trading recipes, and he wanted to shake her, to show her exactly how the pain felt. He couldn't bear it alone anymore, but didn't know how to ask her to share it.

He wanted to feel her arms around him, but knew that if she moved to hold him, he would lash out.

"Do you want to deal with it, Mitchell?" she asked in that damn psychologist's voice. Impersonal. Passive. Professional.

"Deal with it?" he demanded, bending over so that his hands rested on either side of her. "Deal with it? How the hell am I supposed to do that?"

He was too close. He ached too badly. Whipping away, Mitchell pulled an ashtray from the table and sent it sailing. It crashed into the wall. "I can't even remember it!"

A lamp followed, then a vase, a wicker and glass table that smashed against the wall and splintered. Lindsay sat through it, waiting out the storm and struggling to stay away.

Once started, Mitchell destroyed his porch blindly, ferociously, his breath escaping in harsh curses and his eyes glittering. All the poison that had festered within him these last two weeks broke free. The sound of it echoed and crashed through the little room, its most vile sound the sobs of a strong man.

Through it all, Lindsay sat in her corner and watched. Waited. Prayed. She had brought this infection to a head, and now she was going to have to treat it. If only she could rely on the traditional tactics—word games, small nods and the comfort of a cozy office. She didn't have the luxury, though. She'd invented these rules as she'd gone along, and

she couldn't back down now. She couldn't leave Mitchell
with nothing but questions and frustration and guilt.

When there was nothing left to throw, Mitchell sank into
a chair, shoulders heaving with the exertion, hands over his
face. Beyond them the storm had died, leaving behind a cool
breeze and the smell of rain. The porch suddenly felt cold—
cold and lonely. Lindsay saw the storm pass in Mitchell as
well, and timed her next words to stir it once again.

"I'm not cleaning that up."

For a moment he didn't seem to hear. Lindsay waited
without moving. Mitchell's head finally came up and his
ravaged eyes swiveled slowly to where Lindsay sat only a few
feet away. His answer was as scathingly succinct as the look
he delivered.

Lindsay smiled. "Now, there's the Mitchell I know and
love."

Getting to her feet, she walked over to him. He didn't
move away or protest. He didn't seem to have any energy
left. When she received no objections, Lindsay knelt down
before him. She took one of his hands and held it, just
waiting while he sorted out what he wanted to say next.

Lindsay wondered if he could feel the clamminess of anticipation in her hand. She had relived her own trauma that
afternoon, and had just seen its end once again. Poor Alex.
He had had to dodge crockery for an hour before she would
let him come close.

She wasn't going to give Mitchell that chance. Not just to
save him the pain, but to save herself, too. It had begun to
hurt too much to see him battle his ghosts, had begun to be
much more than just a matter of consideration for a fellow
worker she respected. She couldn't bear to watch Mitchell
go through any more.

For a moment Mitchell looked down at the hand that held
his—small, slim, capable. She didn't wear polish, he realized. Nothing fancy at all about her when you got down to
it. Should he be mad at her for forcing him to face himself?
Should he charge her with his own failures?

Slowly Mitchell turned to take in the extent of the destruction. He felt as if his own dreams, his own self-respect, lay shattered in that pathetic pile of debris. He had somehow lost the fragile facade of courage—that delusion that had seen him through war and then had disappeared in a flash of lightning—the fantasy all men hold that they won't fail.

They fail. They sell out. And then they have to face the nightmares.

"I thought it was getting better," he finally said, his admission barely a whisper, his gaze once again on a hand—his own hand, now, one he had never considered or questioned before. Strong enough, quick and efficient. But curiously slow to act when heights were a factor. "I thought after today..."

He had felt it. The energy had filtered back into him, trickling through leaden limbs and easing the tight weight in his chest. Up on that mountain he'd performed, and after. He'd done some thinking and found it almost comfortable. Maybe it won't be so bad now, he'd thought. Maybe I can get a few hours' uninterrupted sleep.

Before giving himself a chance to look in Lindsay's eyes, Mitchell launched himself back onto his feet. Once more Lindsay waited, her attention still on him, her hand now clenched against her thigh.

"It doesn't get better all at once," she answered quietly, wondering at the overwhelming urge to stand up and put her arms around him. "It can't. You still wake up and think Maggie's alive. You'll probably see somebody who looks or sounds like her. You'll be in a high place, and suddenly—"

Mitchell whirled on her. "Stop!"

Lindsay shook her head. "You have to know, Mitchell. If you're going to deal with it."

Mitchell captured the bronze of her gaze and shuddered. It was there, just as he'd feared. The compassion. The tenderness. Lindsay's eyes were liquid with it, and Mitchell thought he detected a tear on her cheek. Damn. He didn't want her sympathy. Sympathy only made it worse, under-mining his strength and demanding his participation.

All the same, he couldn't quite pull his own eyes away. The only light now spilled out from the kitchen and settled across Lindsay's cheeks. Mitchell could just make out the color of her eyes, a warm nourishing honey. He could still see the crease between her brows, the purse of her lips. The hand clenched on her leg.

Why did she give such a damn, when until now even he hadn't? And why did that thought cut through him as sharp as pain?

Shoving his hands back into his pockets, Mitchell delib-erately turned away. "Is that what you taught your stu-dents at the college, McDonough? That this kind of thing takes a while?"

"Grief counseling isn't usually a requirement for crimi-nology."

"Is that right?" He threw his taunt over his shoulder, not strong enough to tempt himself again with her softness. "Well, where did you learn this particular lesson? I mean, you never had a practice, isn't that right? You went from the schoolroom to the conference room. Where does this wealth of experience come from?"

"Common sense," was her answer.

"No," he retorted, spinning around on her now. "I really want to know." His voice had a hard edge of defense to it. Distance. Walking back to his chair, he stood over Lindsay. "You told me you understood what I'm going through. You *understand* guilt. Tell, me, Doctor, when did you become so proficient?"

When Lindsay looked up at Mitchell, the weight of her past shadowed her eyes. "When I killed my husband."

Mitchell lost his accusation. Inadvertently pulling away, he stiffened. "You what?"

"Isn't that how you think of it?" Lindsay asked, locking gazes. "That you killed Maggie? You didn't push her off the edge, but that doesn't make any difference. You feel re-sponsible. Complicity by failure to move. My guilt was a lapse in attention. I was driving the car the night my husband was killed. I looked away from the road to argue with him, and the next thing I knew, a car was spinning toward us. I lived; Patrick didn't. My fault.''

''But that's—''

''Ridiculous? I know. That's what the staff in the emergency room told me, and the police and my family. But they hadn't been the ones holding their husbands on the road that night.'' Lindsay saw Mitchell actually flinch at her words and she offered him a bittersweet smile. ''Sounds familiar, doesn't it?''

Mitchell could only meet her eyes briefly. His own ambivalence was reflected there, his nightmare echoed. It was hard enough to face when he had thought he was alone. To think she really recognized the decay that ate at him was like being stripped of all his defenses. The possibility that she was right . . .

''The only way to live through it is to work through it,'' she was saying, not moving from where she knelt before him, her head tilted back to watch him. ''Do you *want* to remember?''

Mitchell turned back to the solace of the night. The crickets had taken up again, chirping lazily in the darkness. A few birds braved the late hour. Somewhere a coyote addressed the moon. The things around him had once been enough to make him happy. He had once been content with his delusions.

''And I suppose you can do that, too.''

''I can try.''

Mitchell sighed, rubbing a hand across tired eyes. ''McDonough, is there anything you can't do?''

Finally Lindsay got to her feet. ''Not that I know of.''

He laughed, a short bark of derision. ''Humility won't help you worm your way into my confidence.''

''You haven't answered me, Mitchell,'' she accused him, close enough to see the taut stretch of the muscles across his shoulders, the unrelenting resistance. It made her want to reach out, to ease the strain with just her fingers. To breach his defenses. "Do you want to remember?"

Lindsay was surprised when he turned to her. She was shocked by the torment in his eyes. Mitchell looked like a man who clung to the edge. Wanting relief. Wanting answers. Terrified of the consequences, but too worn by the pain to care anymore.

"Yes," he nodded, his voice ragged, his face gaunt. "I want to remember."

Lindsay didn't even think about it. The minute she saw the anguish on his face, she drew him into her arms. Mitchell hadn't had any tears. Maybe he'd used them up for his friend. Lindsay didn't know. She had tears. She felt them, hot and angry and sad as Mitchell lowered his head to hers and clung to her.

Mitchell held on to Lindsay and couldn't believe it. Opening up to her had been the hardest thing he'd ever done. Like being flayed, nerve endings screaming and raw, the pain running over him like fresh blood.

He'd never allowed a thing like that to happen before. Not in Nam, not in the force, not since he'd joined Peterson. When Jason Mitchell had a wound to heal, he crawled back into his den to do it alone, shoving the images back into his past where they couldn't hurt him. It was just the way he'd always been. The way he'd been taught.

Maybe that was why the sudden feel of Lindsay's arms around him had come as such as shock. Maybe that was why he'd folded down into her like that. She'd wrapped herself around him like a barrier against the pain, turned to him instead of away, offered tears instead of counseling.

He couldn't understand it, when she'd spent so much time battering at him. He couldn't believe it, knowing she was the woman who had stalked the halls of the task force with such firm purpose. Lindsay's hair tumbled over his arms and tickled his nose with its scent. Her hands measured his back with gentle support. Her tears fell hotly against his skin.

Mitchell, who had always carried his pain in isolation, wasn't prepared for what those sensations did to a man still shaking with the weight of revelation. He held her. He buried his face in the cool balm of her hair. He lifted her tear-streaked face and kissed her.

Mitchell never heard his own surprised gasp. Just the taste of Lindsay's lips sent him reeling. He clutched her tighter, afraid of falling, of already having fallen and not knowing it. Her skin was so soft, her mouth warm and sweet as the honey in her eyes. The feel of her in his arms was at once balm and incendiary. Life surged in him where there had only been ashes. Emotion sprang from a dry well.

Mitchell forced Lindsay's head back with his kiss. Her neck arched within the span of his hand. Her hair showered over him, tangling in his fingers and torturing him with its silkiness. Her heart hammered against him. Her hands clamored at his back. Mitchell twisted a hand into her hair and pulled her even closer.

He edged her lips open, seeking the sustenance within. Lindsay yielded, and he took her. Sipping, suckling, sating himself on the flavor of her. Salt and secrecy, she tasted of both, and drew him deeper. Her tongue met his, parried and danced in a dark courting of desperation. Mitchell's head spun. His chest ached as if he couldn't get enough air. Was it empathy he drew from her or strength? Was it support he sought or comfort?

He lost his questions within the space of a breath. Lindsay sighed and Mitchell spiraled down into the sensations she compelled. He lost himself in the substance of her—the velvet of her cheek, the quick chill of a tear on her throat. Mitchell took Lindsay's face in both hands and followed the trail of her tears with his lips, drinking them like wine, savoring the sweetness of her skin and bathing in the scent of wildflowers that drifted to him from her hair. Need became want and exploded into desire, and Mitchell found himself running to catch up.

Lindsay couldn't feel the night around her anymore. The wind only lived where it touched her kissed skin. She'd acted on instinct, gathering Mitchell to her to protect them both from the pain. She hadn't realized what furies she would unleash. Not just in Mitchell. The musky taste of his mouth had set Lindsay herself on fire. The steel of his fingers in her hair had taken her strength. She'd lost her reason in his arms and been overwhelmed by the blind beauty of desire.

Mitchell's hand framed her throat and dipped into the hollow at her collarbone. Lindsay's body shrieked for him to hurry—to touch all of her, to take all of her. His lips swept her ear and she shuddered, shivers cascading through her like rain. Desperate, she mused disjointedly as she lifted her face to seek out his. I'm desperate for the taste of this man, and I haven't realized it till now. But Mitchell . . . His fingers found her breast and she forgot her objections.

Mitchell couldn't even think clearly enough to wonder. He had captured Lindsay with his mouth, and now mastered her with his hands. He met denim and cotton where he knew the softest of skin was hidden, and raged with impatience. He wanted to mold those high breasts in his hands, wanted to take them into his mouth. He wanted to lose himself in her, deep where her darkest flavors hid, where a man would find his most desired welcome.

Without asking or demanding, Mitchell swung Lindsay into his arms and carried her into his bedroom, never taking his mouth from hers long enough to allow her to protest. But Lindsay wouldn't have thought of it. She was drowning in the tide Mitchell had unleashed, her arms tight around his neck, her hands in his hair.

It had been so long. So long. She inhaled the rich scent of him and drank in his musky taste, clutched at the hard edges, the crisp hair that curled at his throat. He was so overwhelmingly male, his contours chiseled instead of molded, his skin harsh against her seeking fingers. His passion devoured her. His strength incited her. Lindsay felt herself being lowered to his bed and could think of nothing more than the sweet release of union.

His hands trembling with the cost of control, Mitchell rid Lindsay of her clothes. After dispatching his own, he returned to her.

There was no time for finesse, just for hunger. Just the coming together of two disparate people united by the loss they'd faced and surprised by the passion they had discovered in each other.

Mitchell captured Lindsay in his hands, burnishing the life in her to a fine glow, igniting the fire in her skin and fanning the ache that had blossomed in her. Lindsay writhed with the agony of anticipation, the sudden emptiness of waiting. She melted at his ravenous touch, arching against him and opening herself to entice him home. A hot spiral of desire coiled in her belly, crawled along her legs. Clutching at the soft skin of his back, Lindsay slid her hands down to cup his bottom and urge him to her. She was panting, her breath harsh in her own ears, the thunder of her pulse maddening. Reason fled and left only need behind.

Mitchell couldn't move quickly enough, couldn't consume enough to quench his thirst. His hands feasted on Lindsay, blindly searching out her secrets and opening them up for his tasting. He filled his hands with her breasts and bent to torment them with his mouth. Her moans only fueled his madness. When she arched once more against the touch of his tongue, he nipped at her tender nipples. The satin of her skin incited him, beckoning him to explore, to seek out the very core of her, the sweetest, darkest flower that wept for want of his touch. He found it, waiting, swollen, and savored its slickness with callused fingers.

His mind didn't identify the hard ache in his gut as need, couldn't separate the pain of his loneliness from the fury of his arousal. All he knew was that Lindsay waited, open and moist to accept him. He knew that her eyes were glistening and that she was crying out his name, begging him to join her. With a sound that was almost a groan of relief, Mitchell did so.

Lindsay couldn't have known. Even having seen him, having imagined . . . Mitchell met her, thrust deep—and she cried out with wonder. The night exploded. She threw her head back, suffocating, drowning, flying before a great wind. The darkness disappeared. Singing, shuddering, her body eased into ancient rhythms and drove Mitchell to madness. Together they broke through into the light, spiraled into oblivion and fell into exhaustion.

Sanity only returned with the darkness. A chill little breeze licked Lindsay's bare ankle. A sliver of moonlight nudged at her closed eyelids. Peace receded like a warm wave, and she suddenly found herself pinned within a tangle of arms and legs—Mitchell's arms and legs. He was snoring softly no more than millimeters from her ear. Lindsay could still smell stale after-shave. She felt the rasp of hair on her arm and the slow cadence of a heartbeat against her hand. Mitchell was asleep and she wasn't.

How had she gotten here? What on earth had possessed her to make love to a man whom, under normal circumstances, she could barely abide? She tried to think back, to reconstruct the series of events that might explain it, but nothing seemed to move in any logical order. One minute she had been goading Mitchell away from a nightmare, and the next she'd been in his arms.

Carefully turning her head, Lindsay looked over at him. For the first time since she'd walked through the cabin door, Mitchell looked relaxed. Quiet, as if the demons that had tormented him had fled with the sounds of their lovemaking. He appeared more human than she'd ever seen him, softer, the stern lines of disapproval all but gone from his forehead. A thick lock of hair tumbled over his eyes, and even the line of his mouth had gentled.

Lindsay couldn't help but think how that mouth had felt against her, searching, provoking, demanding, as if he could draw something from her. She thought of the power in the hands that now rested slack against her skin, of the fierce, tender way he'd taken her.

God, what was she going to do? Even now she was succumbing, wanting nothing more than to crawl deeper into the refuge of his arms. She wanted to stay and share the peace he'd gained such a tenuous hold of. But even as she started to draw a careful finger over the shadow that had collected across his chin, to test the delicious sandpaper of his beard and measure the steel in his jaw, Lindsay pulled herself away.

This couldn't be. She couldn't walk on both sides of the line and expect to do either of them any good. She couldn't possibly court the idea that this might happen again. It would be tantamount to suicide. If only her body still didn't sing so deliciously. If only she didn't care.

"Where are you going?" Mitchell asked without opening his eyes.

Lindsay didn't turn from the edge of the bed where she sat. "I'm going in search of my common sense."

She didn't hear any pause before his answer. "You mean this isn't part of the prescribed treatment, Doctor?"

"It's not part of civilized behavior of any kind that I know of." Why was she snapping at him, when only minutes before she'd pleaded with him? How do you regain a professional distance when you've whimpered in a man's arms?

"Well, hell," Mitchell drawled, his voice as dry as hers. "And here I thought I was involved in a new experiment in hypnosis."

Lindsay closed her eyes and drew her arms across her belly. So, was this the way it was going to be? "Does this mean we're going to just chalk this up to bad timing, or do you plan to keep sniping at me about it?" Why did she feel so suddenly desolate, when she'd never wanted to be in Mitchell's bed to begin with?

"I plan on getting some sleep. After that, if you're interested in going back to Denver, I'll be more than happy to pack your car."

"Good," Lindsay retorted, lifting her head just a little to escape the sting of tears. "Then I won't have to worry about any more of the furniture suffering damage."

"Or the psychologist."

That brought her around. Mitchell lay on his side, tousled and sleepy. His eyes were as cold as winter. "Why don't you just get the hell away from me?" she snapped.

Mitchell only smiled. "It's my bed, McDonough. You're the one who has to leave."

She didn't even bend to retrieve her clothes. Gaining her feet with an almost regal grace, Lindsay turned away from Mitchell and walked out the door.

No! Mitchell wanted to scream. He bolted up in the bed, longing to run after her. *Don't go. Don't let me feel this bed grow cold.* He saw Lindsay stalk out, her hair drifting across her sleek back, her naked stride proud and beautiful, and he wanted to drag her back to him.

How could he have done that? How could he have attacked her when she'd given him back his life? Mitchell thought of the bitter words he'd flung at Lindsay and bit off an oath.

She had accused him of being afraid. She hadn't known how right she'd been. He was afraid now. He was terrified. For two weeks he'd been numb, damn near dead. It had been Lindsay who had broken through the ice, but she'd done it by making him need her. And Jason Mitchell didn't want to need anyone. He couldn't afford to.

He had to use Lindsay to get his memory back, to put Maggie to rest and get on with his job. And then he had to put Lindsay back on her shelf where she couldn't hurt him, either. But he couldn't do that when his body still thrummed with the ferocity of his passion for her.

It was still two hours until dawn, that time when sleep healed, when dreams waned toward the sun. His eyes still on the empty doorway, Mitchell knew what his sleep would hold. He swung himself out of the bed instead and went to take a shower.

Chapter 7

Y ou're not packed."

Lindsay looked up to see Mitchell standing in the kitchen doorway. Barefoot and clean-shaven, he looked curiously young, like a callow boy standing out under a tree on a spring day. All the same, the sleeplessness dragged at his eyes.

"Why should I be?" Lindsay asked, deliberately returning her attention to the paper she was paging through. Terrorists, elections, street gangs. The usual goings-on. For once, she wished she could be back there with all the world crises. It seemed so much simpler. Her palms were still clammy and her heart was racing. She couldn't let Mitchell know that just the sight of him badly unsettled her.

His movements a shade uncertain, Mitchell padded into the kitchen and pulled his mug from the cabinet. "You're not going to slap my face and storm back to report to Peterson?"

"Report what?" she asked, sure he could hear the tremble in her voice and hating herself for it. "That a potentially explosive situation became just that? I...should have been more careful. I'm sorry. We still have to work on getting your memory back, if that's what you want.''

Lindsay hadn't lifted her gaze from the now-meaningless newsprint. Suddenly she felt Mitchell standing over her, his shadow stretching across her arms. Lindsay looked up.

"You're sorry?" he echoed in disbelief. "That's it?"

Lindsay didn't understand. "You want more of an apology than that, you're going to have to be careless with someone else."

He shook his head, the coffee in his hand forgotten. There was a real light in his eyes now, not just the spark Lindsay had worked so hard to ignite. She wasn't sure that it was a positive thing; it looked too cold for that yet. But it held life.

Mitchell searched her eyes for some kind of revelation. Finding none, he sank into the seat across from her. "I guess I was expecting you to run off screaming rape or something."

Lindsay couldn't help her first smile of the day. "It was hardly rape, Mitchell. It just can't happen again."

Taking a sip of coffee, he cocked an eyebrow at her. "Admirably objective, Doctor."

Lindsay gathered all her courage and faced him as calmly as she could. "We have work to do, Mitchell. Handwringing is only going to waste precious time."

Mitchell almost made a crack about ice queens. The flash of pain he caught in Lindsay's eyes stopped him, surprised him. The idea that the plastic shrink he'd known for four years could be vulnerable was still alien to him, even after what they'd shared. He almost expected her to put her glasses back on, just so she could peer over them at him. From somewhere came the thought that maybe that kind of behavior was McDonough's protection against the world, kind of like the cabin was his.

There's more to Lindsay than meets the eye, Maggie had always said with that complacent smile of hers. Maybe she'd been right. Mitchell sure wouldn't have expected the kind of passion he'd shared with Lindsay last night from the woman he'd faced across that desk all these years.

Taking a slow sip of coffee, Mitchell let his eyes stray to the tendrils of hair that clung to her neck. "So, we act like it never happened?"

Lindsay restrained herself from lifting a hand to the sudden heat at her throat. "Unless you can come up with a better suggestion that will still let us work together."

Mitchell let his gaze drift back to Lindsay's. The certainty in her voice didn't quite reach her eyes.

"Like I said before," he informed her, "you have guts." And eyes a man would sell his soul for. They'd been like hot amber last night, butterscotch melting sticky and sweet over him until he couldn't pull himself away.

The question was, could he do it now? Her eyes glowed in the daylight, too, warmer than he'd ever noticed. Her fingers wound around the handle of her mug, as if seeking purchase on a cliff face. Those fingers had tormented him the night before, and he didn't think he could forget it. That cool, professional voice had whispered and sung.

But like she'd said, *that* was last night. Today there was business to take care of.

"I have one question before I head off," he said. "What the hell does Cary Grant have to do with psychology?"

Mitchell could almost see her shoulders sag with relief. Her feeling was a palpable thing, shooting needles into his chest. Good or bad? Did he share her objectives? Or had his own objectives begun to change?

"Cary's my mile marker," Lindsay was saying, her smile less than apologetic. "When people have to deal with an emotional trauma, they retreat into themselves, marshal all their energies to deal with the problem. It's kind of like fighting an overwhelming infection. The body shuts down everything else and focuses all its efforts on that one task. Psychologically we do the same thing, retreat into ourselves to survive. One of the ways we have of telling that the emotional crisis is beginning to ease, is that a person becomes less self-centered. He's able to take an interest in his surroundings again. Cary is a dumb little inconsistency that would never have interested you three days ago."

Mitchell scowled. "Parlor games."

Shrugging, Lindsay kept his gaze. "It takes energy to ask questions."

"And is this one of the things you taught in school? Stupid picture tricks?"

She shook her head. "I got it from a colleague of mine. He uses Paul Newman. I admit to using some unorthodox methods, but you have to remember, most of my training is in theory rather than based on practice. I had to play catch-up when I got into the task force."

"Which just supports what I've said all along. If you can't do, you teach."

"I am doing, Mitchell. Maybe you haven't noticed, but I've been doing for about four years now. A lot of it's been textbook, and some has been spur-of-the-moment inspiration."

"So I suppose you want points for initiative."

"If not imagination. Face it, Mitchell, you're feeling better, and it wasn't Al Amato who got you there."

He scowled. "I'm feeling tired, McDonough, and if Al Amato had tried the kind of therapy you did last night, I would have punched him."

Lindsay stiffened instinctively. "I told you. . . ."

But before Lindsay could voice her protest, Mitchell was scraping back his chair and scooping up his coffee cup. "It's been fun, but I have to call the boss. When should I be back for lunch?"

"Whenever you decide to cook it," Lindsay snapped, getting to her feet, her patience lost after Mitchell's off-hand crack.

Mitchell turned around. "What do you mean?"

"I mean I'm not the maid, Mitchell. It's time you started pitching in. Oh, and don't forget the mess you left out on the porch."

Mitchell took a moment to assess the tight-lipped look on Lindsay's face. "I guess I can assume this is the next stage?"

Lindsay's nod was curt. "Participation. Do a good job and I'll recommend that Peterson lets you show up at the office again."

"Listen," he retorted, eyes narrowed and coffee cup aimed at her chest. "Nobody tells me when I go or don't go back to that office, lady. Especially you."

Lindsay just flashed him a smile. "Might be a good time to read the fine print on your contract, Mitchell. You can't set foot into work until I say so. Now I'll just get my purse."

"Over my dead body."

"Don't tempt me."

He held on tightly to his coffee cup to keep from heaving it at her as she started down the hall. "I'm going to town and you're staying," he ordered.

"Not unless you have a couple extra distributor caps. I have those, and the keys." Turning once more to emphasize her point, Lindsay smiled again. "I'll be ready in five minutes."

The ride to the local store started out in a rather tense silence. Since their destination was at the edge of the valley, there weren't any more passes to tackle, but Mitchell didn't seem to be taking Lindsay's maneuver with the distributor caps with any sense of humor. She sat alongside him without once looking away from the scenery, letting him fume and grimace in peace.

She should have felt better. Once Mitchell had started to climb back out of his depression, he'd done it at lightning speed. It made Lindsay wonder if there would be any merit in the study of the effect of life-threatening situations on a despondent patient. A good dose of adrenaline hadn't hurt at all. He hadn't come as far as being able to plan and coordinate. His thought processes were still too self-centered and scattered for that. But he had begun to move—a good sign in any circles.

Her theory had worked like a charm so far; the irritation she'd provided had been enough of a catalyst to force Mitchell in the right direction, Maybe too much of a catalyst. How did she explain her own actions the night before? When had she finally lost the last of her objectivity?

Lindsay sat in silence as the Jeep wound through meadows and stands of aspen and did her best to deny the pain that just the memory incited. Mitchell's eyes, so fierce in the darkness, the play of his hands on her. Lindsay fought to push the pictures away, and lost. She knew that no matter what happened to Mitchell, she would have to carry them with her for the rest of her life.

She'd gotten too close. She'd broken the cardinal rule. She should get the hell out. But she knew she wouldn't.

Mitchell stole a look at Lindsay when he checked the rearview mirror. He'd praised her objectivity only an hour or so ago. Objectivity, hell. If those weren't tears in her eyes, he needed glasses. Damn. He didn't want that now. Not when his brain was beginning to function again. Not when he had a case to solve.

It was like a power surge. Ideas, memories, plans were beginning to circulate in the sludge that had been his brain for the last few weeks. Tumbling and dancing, first one thought rising to the surface and then another, totally unrelated, each demanding attention. No coherence yet. Just garble.

And on top of that, he had his hormones throwing another hunk of debris into the whirlpool to bump up against him at odd times and agitate the whole mass into incoherence.

Objectivity. Yeah. He was going to be objective the minute he got McDonough out of his way and out of the line of fire. Then he could be objective—then he could be anything he wanted.

Mitchell checked the mirror again, scanning the dirt road that snaked off from the left. No traffic ahead, none behind. Was he safe? Had they staked out his cabin or just gotten lucky? And if they'd been watching the cabin, why hadn't they bothered him until he'd tried to cross that pass? Did Bob have something there? Did they want him just to sit home with his feet up for right now?

Why? He had nothing on them. Nothing more than what he'd given Al. Why would they be afraid of him? And if they were so afraid of him, why not just take him out at the cabin and be done with it?

Lindsay saw Mitchell rubbing impatiently at the stitches again and recognized his frustration. She knew his synapses still weren't working, his brain skills were rusty, as if he were trying to race a car without warming it up first. It was a tiring feeling, and she was certain it would wear on Mitchell quickly.

"If it'll help," she said, quietly, eyes still facing front, "try bouncing ideas off me. Sometimes it keeps them in order."

When Mitchell shot her a surprised look, Lindsay just smiled.

"I tried going back to work too soon after Patrick died. I found myself sitting in front of a class of thirty postgrad students, looking at the textbook and thinking that it was all mush. Alex had to pick me up and guide me back to my car like a three-year-old."

"Alex?"

"My brother. The brave soul who locked himself in with me when I wouldn't come out of the house."

Mitchell lifted an eyebrow. "Another psychologist?"

"A C.P.A."

Mitchell snorted, slowing the car and hitting the blinker. A weather-beaten little wooden sign at the crossroads proclaimed that Gabe's Grocery was somewhere down the left fork. Mitchell followed it. "C.P.A., huh? Now, there's an occupation that delves deeply into the human psyche."

"Watch those preconceptions, Mitchell," she warned, thinking about what her brother was capable of. "They could get you into trouble."

Mitchell offered a lopsided grin. "There's not much that can get me into more trouble than I am already."

Lindsay couldn't take her eyes from the appealing slant of his mouth. She couldn't even remember Mitchell joking at his own expense before, at least not with her.

"How long were you married?" he asked.

Lindsay almost flinched. *"That,"* she said, "is one of the things that can get you into more trouble."

"I was just wondering," he explained. "You talk like your husband's death damn near did you in. You must have loved him a lot."

Lindsay refused to look over. "I don't suppose you could go back to being curious about Cary Grant."

"Cary Grant isn't here picking my brain."

Still there was silence, punctuated by the wash of wind and the hum of passing traffic. Mitchell shot another look at Lindsay and saw her tense, her back stiff, her head held rigidly, as if she were defending herself from accusation. Why? he wondered. And why did it matter so much to him?

"I did," she finally said, her voice soft with hurt. "I loved him very much."

"But?"

Lindsay turned, wondering what he'd heard in her voice. "But nothing," she managed as evenly as possible, the arguments still ringing in her memory along with the frustration and guilt. "I loved him. We were married four years."

"I'm still not hearing the end of the story."

"He drank, Mitchell," she retorted, eyes ablaze. "Is that what you want to know? The reason I was driving the car the night he died was because he was drunk again. I tried to get him to stop. I begged, I threatened, I seduced. It didn't do any good. Seems it's an occupational hazard that women in care-giving roles sometimes end up with husbands who want care given. Anything else you'd like to know about it?"

Surprisingly, he had only understanding in his eyes. "Takes a while to get over the guilt, doesn't it?"

She couldn't even find an answer.

Flipping on the blinker, Mitchell slowed down to turn. To the left of the road sat a cluster of clapboard buildings with the sign Gabe's Grocery adorning one. Mitchell swung the car into the lot, gravel crunching under the tires, and switched off the engine. With one hand on the door and the other juggling keys, he turned back to her with a wry smile. "You'd have a lot to talk about with my mother. She spent twenty years having the same arguments with my father. She didn't have any luck, either. She buried him two years ago."

Before Lindsay could answer, he'd swung out of the car and headed into the store. She could do no more than slowly shake her head as she followed him in.

"Well, there you are," the proprietor was saying to Mitchell. A small, weather-beaten man with more teeth than hair, he couldn't have been much older than Mitchell. All the same, he looked like someone at the end of a cattle drive, brown and withered as an apple doll. "Wondered when you'd be getting back home."

"Gabe." Mitchell nodded back as he approached a counter piled high with potato chip holders, candy jars and shabby charity collection cans. "Mind if I use your phone? I've been having trouble with mine."

"Nah. Go ahead," the little man answered, slipping his plug of tobacco farther into his cheek as he eyed Lindsay. "Just leave the dollar on the counter. Nice to see you again, too, young lady. See you found him, all right."

"I'm afraid so." She grinned, keeping a bemused eye on Mitchell's retreating back.

Left to her own devices, Lindsay explored the little store as if it were a museum. Born and raised in one big city after another, she still considered a small-town store quaint. Every time she found herself in one, she browsed, as if she were in a small, disorganized library. She always enjoyed discovering the different shelving systems of each storekeeper—cereal piled atop dog food alongside aspirin, with toys and livery items crammed into any available cranny. She also noticed that in Gabe's store, the personal hygiene products were all wrapped in brown paper, like dirty magazines. It made her smile.

She gathered up a little stash, licorice and chocolate and a bottle of aspirin, while Mitchell disappeared into the back room. She didn't notice another car slow to a stop at the side of the store by the gas station. Nor did she see the driver waiting there, fingers tapping restlessly on the steering wheel, eyes on her as she passed in front of the window.

"What makes you think your own phone isn't secure?" Al was asking Mitchell.

"How fast we got followed. I shouldn't have used it last night, but I'm still...I was tired. Now, what have you come up with?"

"Mick Murphy. Sometime bagman, sometime mule for Wilson. You should have recognized him. You personally sent him up on a racketeering charge about five years ago. Because he was such an exemplary citizen on the inside, the powers that be let him go about a year ago."

Easing down onto the battered table that served as Gabe's desk, Mitchell picked up a Mount Rushmore paperweight and flipped it absently in his left hand. "Yeah, I remember now. Looks like something out of Damon Runyon. Lives for game shows. The warden would've loved him." Through the half-open door into the store he could see Gabe stalking Lindsay like a preteen at a dance. Good. It would keep him busy for a minute or two. "No concrete connection with Esperanza, huh?"

"Nada. And so far, we're still coming up with the big zero here. All of Perez's friends say he was a combination of Superman and the Pope. His record's so clean it squeaks. It seems we're the only ones who associate him with our friend Esperanza. And the Wilsons have gone into seclusion for the moment. I'm sorry, Mitchell. It just doesn't seem to be coming together."

"Well, I'll tell you what," Mitchell answered. "There's something else to think about, if Wilson's boys are after me. Something they're afraid of that I can't figure out. And they think I have it."

"What are you going to do?"

"I'm going to think about it. Where's Bob?"

"Waiting to talk to you," Al said. "Fill me in if you think of anything, Mitchell. We're hurting here."

"So, are you going to stay put, or do I have to send out the highway patrol to escort you in?" Bob asked within moments.

"I think I'm heading in, Bob. There are some inconsistencies I have to check out myself, and the only place to do that is the apartment. I also have a psychologist to deliver to you."

"No, you don't."

"She's no use in the field, Bob, and that's where I'm going to be. You don't have to worry anymore. I'm not going to jump off a bridge or anything. Now, take her back like a good boy and let me get on with finding out who killed Maggie."

"I'll make my decision when I talk to you in my office. When are you coming in?"

"When I get there. See ya."

He didn't wait for the predictable objections. Hanging up the phone, Mitchell went back out to quiz Gabe. If anybody knew whether there was anything unusual going on in the area, it would be Gabe.

True to Mitchell's prediction, Gabe *was* checking out the latest news in Morgan, Colorado. And that news was Lindsay. His wrinkled head only reaching her collarbone, Gabe was nodding furiously as Lindsay enthused about the area and the little store he ran. Shaking his head with some wonder, Mitchell strolled over to where the two stood by the side window.

"Been making yourself at home, I see," Mitchell greeted Lindsay.

It was Gabe who answered. "Your friend was just fillin' me in on your accident."

Mitchell turned to Lindsay with a silent warning. "She's no friend of mine."

"Acquaintance," Lindsay amended with a straight face. "Business associate. I was telling Gabe what I thought of the drivers out here."

The look on Gabe's face left no question as to his opinion of a man who would let such a good-looking woman remain just an "acquaintance." But it wasn't Gabe's way to butt in.

"Guy was a tourist, what I hear," he stated with a sage nod of the head, as if that explained it all. "Had a rental."

"Well, I think he saw a lot more of the Rockies than he wanted," Mitchell said offhandedly as he leaned against a shelf. "Listen, Gabe, a friend of mine was supposed to look me up. He stop in here? Big guy, looked like a fighter. Kinda simple. I was gonna show him the mountains."

If that car hadn't turned into a fireball, Gabe would have told Mitchell that the friend he wanted to find had been inside. As it was, the task of remembering seemed to require a certain amount of head-scratching on Gabe's part. He finally came up with a shake of the head. "Not him. Another guy was in, though. Rented the Backman place alongside of you. Said he was looking for someone to do some trout fishin' with."

"Oh, yeah? I haven't seen him. What did he look like?"

Lindsay could see the subtle change in Mitchell's eyes. It was almost a flattening, as he camouflaged his interest with casual curiosity.

Again, Gabe had to consult his cranium. "Thin guy. 'Bout your height. Couldn't really see him bein' patient enough to go for trout. He was always movin'. Pickin' things up and puttin' them down, you know. Drove a late model Chrysler. One o' them fancy cars."

Lindsay hadn't meant to look out the window. It was just that when she listened to Gabe speak, her mind drifted. This time her attention wandered right out to the lot by the gas station, where a late model Chrysler sat with its snout pointed her way. Inside, a set of hands was tapping in a syncopated rhythm against the steering wheel.

"Like that?" she asked without thinking.

Mitchell swung her way. She looked up and pointed.

Gabe leaned over to take his own look. "Yeah. That's him."

Lindsay caught a flash of movement as the driver noticed the activity in the store window and bent forward for a better look. Then the car engine was turning over. Whipping around, Mitchell ran out the door. Lindsay followed, her hands full of candy, not sure what she could do.

The point was already moot. By the time the two of them made it outside, the car was screeching off in the other direction.

"Are we going to chase him?" Lindsay asked.

Mitchell pulled to a stop at the bottom step. The Chrysler was just screeching around the corner and out of sight. One look at the Jeep was enough to leave him shaking his head.

"I don't think so. I know who he is."

Lindsay couldn't help but stare. "You do?"

Mitchell just nodded, his attention still on the empty road. "More low-level muscle. I'll get him later."

"What are you going to do now, call in?"

"No. I think I'm going to check out the Backman place."

Mitchell headed up the steps. Lindsay followed right on his heels. "You can't do that. Not alone. You don't know who else could be waiting over there. Policy calls for—"

Without warning, Mitchell came to a stop and turned on Lindsay. "Do me a favor. If you want me to deliver you back to Denver in one piece, stop quoting the manual to me. I know what policy is. I just don't follow it."

"But those men aren't following you around because they want fishing advice. They don't like you."

"And I don't like them."

Lindsay knew she should keep her mouth shut. She was out of her league here. Mitchell was the one in charge, and she would be the first to admit that no matter how unorthodox his methods, he got the job done. But suddenly, for no reason at all, she wanted him to take better care of himself than he usually did.

After all, she argued even as she silently followed him in to say goodbye to Gabe, she had a stake in him now. She hadn't put in all that time and effort on him, only to see it flushed down the toilet.

Her logic made perfect sense, but for some reason it didn't completely satisfy her as she handed Gabe the change to pay for her purchases and followed Mitchell out the door.

"Aspirin?" he asked, waiting by his open door with eyebrows raised.

"For when you get shot again," she retorted dryly, facing him over the roof of the Jeep. "I would have bought plasma and surgical equipment, too, but I have the feeling Gabe's fresh out."

Mitchell dispatched a heartfelt scowl. "That's what I love so much about having a partner. Unspoken support. Listen, like I've said before, when you've handled a piece, then come talk to me about it."

Mitchell was bending to slide into his seat when Lindsay answered. "Then show me."

He straightened, almost hitting his head on the roof. "What?"

"Show me how to defend myself," she said evenly, doing her best to ignore the sudden pounding at her temples. "After all, I have the feeling I'm going to need it."

Mitchell's expression held little encouragement. "Go back to your books, Doctor." He slid into his seat.

Lindsay got into hers and faced him again. "I mean it. You're the one who's always telling me that I should get out into the field to see what I'm talking about. Well, now's your chance."

"Not while my neck's on the line, thanks. I don't need surprises...like a bullet in the back from my partner." Revving the engine, he pulled onto the road and headed home. "You can pack while I check out Backman's. Then we're heading for the city."

Lindsay was already shaking her head. "I'm not letting you out of my sight."

His answering smile was grim. "Afraid I'll take off without you? It is a thought, isn't it? Don't worry, McDonough. If I don't deliver you back to Peterson, he'll never give me any rest. I'll come back for you."

"But what about that man? Won't he be waiting for you?"

"If he has any sense, he'll be a hundred miles from here by now. If he saw us talking to Gabe about him, he knows we'll have found out where he's staying. I'm looking for clues, not confrontations."

"And what about your memory? Are we just going to forfeit it?"

Mitchell took a quick look in her direction, his eyes stormy with surprise. "All in good time. Right now, I want to get some questions answered, and then put some distance between you and me while I find out the rest."

Lindsay was still trying to think of a way to change his mind when they pulled up before the cabin. She swung out of the car and stalked around to his window. Mitchell rolled it down.

"I'd be more than happy to break a window," Lindsay assured him. "But I assume you'd rather I use the door."

Without a word, Mitchell pulled out the keys and handed them over. Lindsay turned back for the cabin. She heard the car door open behind her, but didn't think anything of it. She heard Mitchell step out and pause. Tossing the keys in her hand, she decided that he was going to be surprised at how hard it would be to lose her.

She was halfway to the house when it happened. A freight train hit her in the side, sending her sprawling across the gravel drive. Lindsay gasped. The keys went flying. She heard them clink somewhere off to her left as the breath whooshed out of her lungs.

Gravel bit into her elbows. She heard her jeans rip. There wasn't enough air in her lungs to curse, but she was trying. Then she heard the soft command in her ear.

"Keep your head down."

Mitchell.

Mitchell was the one with his arms around her waist, his full weight on her back pushing her nose into the rocks. Lindsay valiantly fought for breath.

"If this is your idea of...distance," she finally gasped, "I think you're going to have to work a little harder on it."

"Shut up," he rasped in her ear. Somewhere someone coughed and Lindsay found her face back on the ground. "And keep your head down. Someone's shooting at us."

So much for her breath. Lindsay shoved her face into the ground all by herself and kept it there.

Chapter 8

He must be a hell of a shot," Lindsay finally gasped, wondering just what was responsible for those shivers racing through her. Certainly not the weight of Mitchell lying against her. It must be the adrenaline. The fear of dying. Funny. She'd didn't feel afraid. Just jittery.

"Why?" Mitchell muttered, his breath fanning her ear.

If he hadn't had Lindsay's arms pinned under her, she would have reached up to rub away the chills.

"Well," she said instead, trying to crane her head around. "A hundred miles is an awfully long way to aim."

There wasn't much to see. Just morning sunlight, the Jeep behind them with the driver's door hanging open, and a crumpled corner of her car. And half of Mitchell, where he was spread out flat across her, one hand on her to keep her still, the other holding a gun.

"Where did you get that?" Lindsay asked automatically.

"I said to shut up," he retorted, eyes swiveling to the tree line beyond the cabin. "We need to scoot back to the Jeep. Think you can do it?"

Lindsay followed his line of sight. She still didn't see anything. Just the aspen leaves trembling in the breeze, the tall grass sighing. There was a cluster of wood sorrel nearby, almost at eye level. Lindsay had never realized how delicate the flowers were—how perfectly crafted in miniature, like little blue stars scattered over the grass. It suddenly occurred to her how funny it was that she had to be shot at to appreciate wildflowers.

Giddiness now. Lindsay wondered whether Mitchell knew that his protective hand was covering her breast. The shivers centered a little more. She did her best to keep the quaver of laughter from her answer. "Right behind you, Kemosabe."

She heard the coughing sound twice more before they reached the open car door. It was a hollow noise that seemed to come from the trees off to their right. Each time Mitchell shoved her back down. Once a shower of gravel chips dusted her cheek. Lindsay was fascinated by how detached she felt from the whole thing. She just wished Mitchell wouldn't be so enthusiastic in trying to protect her. She was getting gravel tattoos on her cheek.

"Climb in."

Mitchell wrapped steely hands around Lindsay's waist and hoisted her onto the front seat. Lindsay flopped onto the upholstery like a limp fish and slid over, her head well below the window. Mitchell followed, moving a lot more nimbly than Lindsay thought a man should be able to do with all those stitches.

"Now, stay down," he commanded, hunching in his seat and reaching over a hand. "The keys."

Lindsay winced. She took a breath, steeling herself against his inevitable reaction. "They flew out of my hand when you hit me."

Another of those coughs and the windshield shattered. Lindsay shrieked and shrank back. Glass pattered over her like rain. Mitchell cursed steadily. After brushing off his own shower of glass, he made a decision.

"The shooter's on your side. We'll use the Jeep for protection." Lifting his head just a little, Mitchell quickly scanned the area. Another bullet pinged off the hood.

From her position on the floor, Lindsay watched with wide eyes. "Well, at least my car isn't the only one taking abuse."

Mitchell slipped the Jeep into neutral and slid back out the door. Lindsay couldn't think of anything to do but watch as he positioned himself against the side of the car and began to push.

Tendons popped out on his neck. The muscles on his shoulders and arms grew impossibly taut. Just when Lindsay was about to get out and help, the Jeep began to roll.

It rolled right up to where the keys rested on the ground, and Mitchell stooped to pick them up. Climbing back into the vehicle, he slid the keys into the ignition and passed the gun over to Lindsay.

"You wanted to shoot, now's your chance. Point it over the windowsill in the direction of the woods and fire. Keep firing until the clip runs out."

Lindsay eyed the weapon with some hesitation. "Are you sure?"

"You're firing cover so I can sit up far enough to see. You don't have to hit anything. Just make noise." Suddenly, briefly, his features relaxed. "This is the easy stuff, McDonough. You've already done the hard part."

Lindsay thirstily drank in the support in his expression. The giddiness was growing, the jitters infecting her hands. And when Mitchell looked at her like that, she could have sworn she could fly. Interesting stuff, this danger.

Taking a second to get the feel of the heavy weapon in her hand, Lindsay lifted it, rested it against the edge of the window and began squeezing the trigger. The gun made an impressive noise. Every time it went off, she jumped. She didn't even notice when she squeezed her eyes shut.

Evidently much more used to the noise than she was, Mitchell eased his head centimeters above the dashboard and steadily backed the Jeep up to the road.

"Stop," he snapped, jumping into the seat. "Hold on."

She did. Mitchell executed a flawless turn, spraying clouds of dust around him and screeched down the road. Easing her head above the window, Lindsay looked out just in time to see a man step out of the woods, gun in hand. The same man she'd seen in the store, she thought. Placing the gun on the seat alongside Mitchell, she slid up onto the seat and fastened her seat belt.

"I don't want to hear it," Mitchell said before she got the chance to remind him to do the same.

Lindsay turned to see that his concentration was directed to the road and the task ahead. The furrows alongside his mouth were taut, his brows drawn. His hair tumbled in the wind that whistled through the shattered windshield. He was frowning as he turned his attention to check at both the way they were heading and the way they'd been.

"So, what do we do now?" she asked, glancing backward, too.

All seemed peaceful on this Colorado afternoon. The empty landscape belied the pounding in Lindsay's chest, the shaking of her hands. People with guns crouched behind those box elders—people intent on killing Mitchell, and, since she was along for the ride, her, too. Lindsay wanted to soak in the scenery and let it calm her. Unfortunately, Mitchell's answer shattered even that peace.

"I told you. We're going to Backman's."

Lindsay swung around on him, sure he was goading her. The expression on his face hadn't changed any. Unfortunately, she recognized that look. It was what Al called Mitchell's "mongoose spots a cobra" look. Mitchell had caught a scent, and wasn't about to be talked out of following it.

Lindsay had to ask, anyway. "Are you sure that's smart? We're not exactly invisible anymore."

Reaching into his shirt pocket, Mitchell flipped her a fresh clip. "Do you know how to reload a Beretta?"

Lindsay glared at him. Reaching over to retrieve the gun, she dropped the spent clip and slid the new one home. The thought didn't escape her that she could very well point the thing at him. Unfortunately, she knew that it wouldn't change anything. They would end up at Backman's, one way or the other.

"What do you want me to do?"

Now Mitchell looked over, and Lindsay was amazed at the respect that colored his eyes. "Wait in the Jeep. Honk like hell if you see anyone coming. If I don't come out fast enough, get out."

Mitchell turned off into a narrow dirt road and nosed the Jeep into a stand of trees about a quarter of a mile down before cutting the engine. Then he turned to Lindsay.

"Remember. If you don't see me within four minutes of honking, get out and call for backup."

"I could do it now and save us all some time."

He just opened his door and stepped out.

"Wait," Lindsay said, sliding over toward him, the gun held out like an offering. "You forgot this."

Mitchell turned just as Lindsay reached the driver's seat. "No, you keep it."

Lindsay halted, astonished. "Get serious, Mitchell. The only thing I could do with a gun is start a race."

He actually smiled. "You already fired cover. Most times that's all it takes. I want to know that you have some protection."

"I have protection. I'm sitting in the middle of reinforced steel. What about you?"

He cocked an eyebrow. "Worried about me, McDonough?"

"Do you know what kind of paperwork I'd have to do if you died?" she demanded, trying her best to keep the real fear from her voice.

He grinned. "That's better. For a minute there I was afraid you cared."

Lindsay grimaced. "You've cured me, Mitchell. I'll never leave the office again."

"And just think," he retorted, leaning over to drop a kiss onto her lips. "It's probably only starting."

Unfortunately, Mitchell's little foray gave Lindsay plenty of time to think. She sat in the driver's seat surrounded by shards of glass, staring out a gaping hole in the windshield, her hand slick against the gun in her lap, wondering just what the heck she was doing here.

Her place was in the office, among the textbooks; her talent the calm, objective eye she brought to the sometimes horrendous situations the team handled. How was she ever going to be objective again after she'd fired a gun and escaped an attempt on her life? How was she ever going to be able to deal with Mitchell in that same calm, unflustered voice that so infuriated and focused him?

She had made love with him. She'd run with him and fought for him and been delighted by him. And here she sat in a Jeep at the edge of a valley, wondering whether Mitchell would outrun the bad guys or be trapped in that damn cabin while he searched for a reason for Maggie's death.

The worst part was that, as the minutes ticked away with nothing to break the stillness but lazy insects and distant birds, her anxiety for Mitchell blossomed in her chest like a hot cloud. Maybe if she contacted the University of Chicago now, they'd let her come back by the beginning of next term.

"Not a good idea to meditate right now, McDonough."

Lindsay jumped a foot, only to realize that not only was it Mitchell who had addressed her from the other side of the car door, but that she'd instinctively brought the gun up to shield herself from danger.

Fortunately, Mitchell was quicker than she.

"Whoa," he warned, immediately putting a hand up to push the barrel away. Easing the gun from Lindsay's grasp, he shoved it into the back of his jeans and opened the door.

"No problems, I assume."

Lindsay couldn't quite catch her breath.

"Glad to see me, too, I see." Casting a jaundiced eye at the mostly nonexistent windshield, he shook his head and pushed out a few remaining chunks of glass before starting the engine. "I guess this will have to do. I really don't think it'd be a good idea to go back for your car right now."

"Don't ever do that again," Lindsay finally blurted out.

Mitchell turned bright eyes on her. "I missed you, too, McDonough."

"This isn't funny, damn it," she snapped. "I'm not used to it."

The humor in Mitchell's expression died. "You wanted to know about me, now you do. This is me, Doc. This is all of me. Get used to it."

"But it's not me," she answered without thinking.

Pulling the car out, Mitchell turned toward Denver. Lindsay faced forward. The wind tugged at her with angry fingers. The sun was too brilliant. She was still shaking, and the cloud in her chest had turned to acid.

It hadn't been the fear that had shaken her as the minutes ticked away and Mitchell hadn't returned. That had been bad, stretching her tolerance until it felt like frayed rope.

But then Mitchell had appeared at the door of the car, and she'd felt that rope snap. It was the relief at seeing him alive that had melted the rest of her reserve.

How could she have known how desperately she'd waited, how sure she'd been that he wouldn't come back, that she would have to leave that valley alone? Lindsay leaned back in the seat, eyes closed, and let the wind flay her.

Damn you, Jason Mitchell. How did you do this to me? Her heart raced. Her eyes stung with surprised tears. Jason had come back safe, and Lindsay had realized how far she'd come from the moment she'd first walked into his house. Damn him.

"Are you okay?"

"Just shut up and drive."

She didn't see him frown or notice that he was watching her as much as the road. "Well, since you asked," he answered, "the place has been cleaned. Somebody knew we were coming."

"Of course they did. Don't you remember the welcoming committee?"

"He didn't have time to do a job like that." For a moment there was just the sound of the wind as it rushed past them. "Which makes me wonder what my apartment is going to look like."

"Mitchell?"

Surprised, Mitchell looked over. "Yeah?"

She looked as if she'd just seen her first death. White and shaky and small. Mitchell was surprised by the stab of compassion he felt for her. It was rough to be thrown into a situation like this, no matter who you were. He was going to have to drop her off fast. Especially since he didn't have any time to waste to pull over and just hold away the shakes like he wanted to do.

Damn. Where had that thought come from? He knew better. The last thing he needed at a moment like this was to be distracted by personal feelings. Not that he had any, of course. Not for McDonough. It was just that she'd been through so much, that she'd handled it so well. Then she opened her eyes, and he saw the surprise in that soft amber. There were a dozen emotions dancing there, more than he could sort out. And each one of them pulled at him in a different way.

Damn.

"Do you always feel so...alive when you're in a situation like that?" Lindsay asked in a voice that should have belonged to a small child.

"Alive?" he asked a bit hesitantly, remembering at the last moment that he couldn't afford to pull over right now. He checked the rearview mirror for company, then turned to see that she was sincere. "How do you mean?"

Now Lindsay allowed herself a rueful smile. "I felt like I could fly back there."

The only way Mitchell could answer was to keep his eyes on the road. "C'mon, Doc. Surely you've read about that in your textbooks."

Eyes on her hands, she nodded. "I know. The danger high. The same phenomenon occurs in battle. A life-threatening situation heightens sensory reception, slows time, gives one the feeling of euphoria. Adrenaline and endorphins. I guess I wanted to know if what I felt was the usual mix."

"Were you afraid?"

She thought about it a moment. "Sporadically." She didn't tell him that she had felt more afraid when he was in danger than when she was. Or the part about wondering whether the exhilaration was due to the danger or to his proximity. She could still feel his hand at her breast.

Mitchell scowled. "Careful," he warned. "That kind of high is as addictive as drugs."

Lindsay knew what he meant—that delicious clarity brought to the world with the sound of a gunshot.

"You should know?" she asked.

He didn't even favor her with an answer.

"I think that that's what got Maggie into trouble," Lindsay finally ventured.

Mitchell looked over then, not bothering to veil the surprise in his eyes. "Maggie was as solid as a rock, McDonough."

Lindsay just shook her head. "She was undercover with the Wilsons, undeniably the nastiest bunch we've run across. You've been there, Mitchell. You know the appeal of the tightrope. She called me one night to tell me she was having the time of her life. And that wasn't like Maggie. I was trying to talk Bob into getting her out when she went up for that sale."

Mitchell couldn't think of anything to say. Lindsay's admission was one he wouldn't have listened to a week ago.

"Do you think it was your fault that she didn't reach you in time to tell you she was going up for the buy?" Lindsay asked.

Mitchell shrugged. "I don't know."

"You've wondered."

"Of course I've wondered."

Lindsay nodded, tucking flying hair behind her ears as she turned to face him. "Do you think that maybe she got too caught up in it and decided to go in alone?"

He didn't agree readily. After all, it was Maggie they were dissecting, and she wasn't there to defend herself. "Maybe."

"You learned about the sale from the buyers, right?"

He nodded.

"Why not from Maggie? Why didn't she let you know she was going to be there? You tried to get hold of her. The message was on her machine. But she didn't try and get you."

Mitchell swung a look of accusation on Lindsay. "You'd better not be saying she was compromised."

Lindsay's reaction reminded Mitchell that she was the one who had hired Maggie, who had nurtured her during her first difficult days and shared her successes and failures. "What I'm saying is that I should have picked up a warning signal from her before she had a chance to do something stupid. Which means that her death was as much my fault as yours. I should have gotten her out sooner."

Before he realized it, Mitchell was defending her. "You couldn't have known what would have happened."

"Neither could you," she retorted evenly, "but that doesn't stop you from beating yourself over the head with it."

He wasn't having any of it. "That's different."

"You're right. You refuse to deal with it. I don't."

For a long moment there was only silence, punctuated by the whistling wind and the tap of Mitchell's fingers against the wheel. Lindsay held her breath.

"I'll call Peterson from a booth," Mitchell finally said, as if continuing a line of thought. "Let him know what happened. After I drop you off at the office and trade this the Jeep in for something that works, I'll check the apartment and the drops Maggie and I used. Maybe she did get something from Perez and left it for me."

"And that's it?"

"When I don't have somebody trying to shoot my lights out, I'll take the time to play mumbo jumbo with you."

"I don't think it's going to be that easy, Mitchell."

"It'll have to be, McDonough. Business isn't going to wait for me to feel all better."

Lindsay didn't know why she said it—an instinct she didn't credit, an emotion she decided not to confront. All the same, she faced him, her own eyes unyielding and strong. "You know where to find me when you need me, Mitchell. I have a feeling it'll be sooner than you think."

It took Lindsay a moment to decipher all the odd looks she was getting when she walked back into the office. Everyone was glad to see her, even more glad to see Mitchell, and there was a lot of backslapping and bad jokes going around. Bob emerged from his office to bestow smiles and greetings and an invitation to a private conference, then he caught sight of the look on Mitchell's face. But when Lindsay settled into a seat next to Mitchell, she saw the bemusement on Bob's face and remembered.

Her clothes. Her hair. She would never have been caught dead looking like this in the office before. Without thinking, she lifted a hand to the disheveled mess that had once been a braid and flinched. As a result of everything that had happened in the last few days, she'd completely forgotten her appearance. It made her feel even staler than that afternoon after the emergency room.

"I thought you were going to warn me when you left the cabin," Bob said without preamble, his eyes on Mitchell.

"I did," Mitchell retorted. "From the phone booth."

"The phone booth in Westminster, Mitchell. Ten miles away doesn't count. I'd also like to say that I'm not wild about you dragging the staff psychologist around on your cops and robbers chases."

"You're not the only one," Mitchell and Lindsay answered simultaneously, then traded frowns.

"I'd be happy to hole up in my cabin for the duration," Mitchell went on, knowing perfectly well that neither Bob nor Lindsay believed him. "But there's a friend of Mick Murphy's out there who doesn't feel the same."

"We have an A.P.B. out for him. What are you going to do now? You want a safe house?"

"I want you to sign the receipt for one psychologist, and then I'll head out and check our drops, see if anything turned up from Maggie. I think she must have gotten something and been in the process of sending it on to me, else nobody would be so interested in seeing me dead."

"But why leave you alone while you were in the cabin?"

Mitchell shrugged. "Because it's not there, I guess. Maggie knew better than to use it as a drop. That's why we set up our spare. To stay away from home turf. I'll throw her place if it's still clean, too."

"Al's going with you on this one." Before Mitchell could protest, Bob raised a hand. "You're not going by yourself. That's the end of it."

Mitchell acquiesced with a shrug. Hauling himself to his feet, he delivered a final glare in Bob's direction. "I'm leaving now. If he wants to come along, make sure he's a couple of steps behind."

Lindsay watched him turn to her, his expression melting for only a fraction of a second before it gained new steel. "Stay out of trouble, McDonough. If you behave, when I get back I'll actually teach you to do more than start races."

"You're welcome, Mitchell."

Lindsay was still looking after him when the door swung shut again. She'd almost forgotten her boss, seated on the other side of the desk.

"You've worked a miracle, Lindsay," he said with real wonder.

Lindsay shook her head. "He's running on adrenaline and caffeine. Have somebody with him when he crashes. Better yet, have me with him when he crashes."

"What do you mean?"

Lindsay turned on Bob, wanting to make him understand the situation without sacrificing Mitchell's privacy.

"He hasn't had a good night's sleep yet. I would bet he won't for another while."

Bob lifted an eyebrow. "You think he's still fragile?"

She smiled. "Don't ever use the word around him. Yes. I do. And I don't think it will help things to have him alone, or even to have one of the men with him when he tries to let down."

Bob was shaking his head, his attention on the pencil he was rolling over his desk top. "I don't like the idea of your being this close to a critical situation, Lindsay."

Leaning forward, Lindsay recaptured Bob's attention. "Mitchell's the key to this case, isn't he?"

Bob shrugged. "Looks like it."

"Then he needs to be protected, from himself as much as from Esperanza's people. I can do the one if you'll do the other."

"A safe house isn't as nice as a cabin in the woods."

"A safe house is just where she needs to be."

Lindsay and Bob both started, so caught up in their conversation that they hadn't heard Al open the door. He stood there now, his forehead creased, his eyes anxious.

"Are you all right, Lindsay?" he asked. "I heard about what happened."

"I'm fine," Lindsay assured him, seeing her unaccustomed appearance reflected in his attitude, too.

"What the hell was Mitchell thinking of?" he demanded, turning to Bob. "You told him not to leave that cabin. Now he's not safe anywhere. I hope you chewed out Turner for not staying with him."

"Turner just called in. Somebody neatly sabotaged his car so that he couldn't get back to the cabin before Mitchell. I accepted his profuse apologies. Now you can accept mine, Al."

Al began to look uncomfortable.

"I'm afraid it gets worse," Bob said. "Mitchell is now your charge. He thinks Maggie might have dropped something for him before she went up that night. He wants to check."

Al came to attention, outrage displacing the anxiety. "Is he kidding? He looks like he's dead on his feet. And the word's out that he's bolted. Let me do it alone, Bob. Or I can take Brent. Make him stay here. We can do it for him."

"Mitchell?" Bob retorted, eyes wide. "The only person who's made him do anything he hasn't wanted to is Lindsay."

"Then you do it," Al insisted, turning on her. "You know what Esperanza's like, Lindsay. Mitchell just isn't up to par yet. Esperanza will cut him up like salad."

Lindsay just shook her head. "Not this time, Al. Like I told Bob, I'm no miracle worker, and until Mitchell gets his answers, he's not going to stop. Keep him in sight. When you're finished, see if you can get him back to the safe house out on Elm."

Al turned to Bob for verification and got a nod. It didn't seem to appease him at all. He just shook his head, frustration pulling at his features. "I'm telling you, I have a bad feeling about this."

"You'll feel worse if Mitchell gets away from you," Bob assured him. "Now get going."

The sight of a newly invigorated Mitchell seemed to seal Lindsay's reputation with the rest of the staff. Suddenly she was the woman of the hour. She didn't want to burst everyone's bubble by admitting how tenuous Mitchell's hold on well-being was. Instead she nodded and smiled and escaped to her office, to repair her appearance and pack a briefcase full of work to take with her to the safe house.

Lindsay had to admit that she could use a little peace and quiet until Mitchell came back. She hadn't had much sleep herself, and the death of all that adrenaline running through her body had made her feel like day-old news. She wanted to get a fresh supply of clothes from home and then hole up in that nondescript little house in the suburbs for a nap.

Bob pulled the car up before the ghost-catcher Lindsay had turned into a painted lady. Three stories of gingerbread, the house had been built in the days when Denver was still courting silver. Now it was just another carefully tended echo of the past.

When Lindsay stepped out, she felt the draw of the place much as Mitchell must have responded to his cabin. Home. She'd deposited her memories here and collected warmth. Antiques from her grandmother, kindergarten sketches from nieces, dried flowers from the occasions of her life. She smiled as she mounted the steps. She hadn't realized how much she'd missed it.

The first thing she noticed was the screen door. It sagged a little out of line. Lindsay pulled on it and saw that her front door was ajar, as well. A cold thread of dread snaked up her back. She looked around her, expecting to see something else out of place on the quiet, tree-lined street. Mrs. Boulton was watering her lawn a couple of houses away, and down the street the Greeson kids were skateboarding.

Lindsay turned back to her front door and pushed it open. She must have cried out, because Bob was at her side before she thought to call to him. She was shaking, the revulsion of assault eating at her.

Someone had gotten into her house and thoroughly demolished it.

Chapter 9

The sun had set again by the time Mitchell finished. He shouldn't have made such a big deal about going to the drops himself. After an entire afternoon of putting up with Al's concern and rooting around in debris and empty mailboxes, he didn't think he could take another step without stumbling. The high Lindsay had tried so hard to break down had long since dissipated and died a horrible death. Hunger gnawed at his empty stomach, and his stitches ached and scratched.

Al pulled up before the nondescript one-story brick house and shut off the engine. Mitchell didn't even feel the car stop. He was running on empty.

"Pick me up in the morning," Mitchell instructed, his hand worrying at the stitches that crept along his hairline. His head was throbbing.

"Why don't you just stay put for a while?" Al demanded. "Get some sleep. Brent and I can do your running."

Mitchell turned on his friend, his expression hard. "I said pick me up. And bring Maggie's file with you. I want to go over it again."

"Mitchell—"

Mitchell opened his door. "Y'know, I have the most uncomfortable feeling you're about to tell me that I won't be safe unless I stay put." Turning to deliver his final message with his eyes, Mitchell smiled. "Don't."

Then he let himself out of the car.

No matter what he said to Al, Mitchell was glad to be getting out for a while. Things were beginning to move beyond him, the puzzle pieces falling without a pattern, and he couldn't seem to drag them together anymore. It would be good to get even a couple of hours sleep. It would be better to get more, but by this time, he knew not to expect it.

Mitchell thought of Lindsay, the way she'd waited for him in the cabin, walking in the shadows one minute and tormenting him the next. Funny how he wished she were waiting again.

He never would have told her, but he missed her already. It was just beginning to sink in that he wouldn't see her when he opened the door. She wouldn't have dinner ready, wouldn't stuff wildflowers into peanut butter glasses and put them on the table in this battered, abused little house. She wouldn't ever do those things for him again, and suddenly, inexplicably, that ached in him worst of all.

When he threw open the door, Mitchell came to an uncertain halt. He blinked, disoriented, sure he was only fantasizing.

No. She was really there. Lindsay sat curled up on the faded brown couch, her hair loose and shining in the soft light thrown off by the table lamp, her eyes on him. Waiting.

"What are you doing here?" Mitchell couldn't understand the impatient edge to his voice, when what he really wanted was to settle next to her and let her ease him to sleep.

His weariness had evaporated with just the sight of her. Waiting for her answer, he shut the door.

Lindsay lifted her head a little as if she, too, were having some trouble distinguishing reality. "Bob says I'm the punishment for your leaving the cabin. I have to stay here, too."

Dropping his athletic bag onto the rug, Mitchell approached. Even through his own conflicting reactions, he could see something heavy in her expression, a pain he'd never noticed in her eyes before. "What did you do to deserve that?"

"I...went home—" The words caught as Lindsay's voice quavered. Straightening her back, she retrieved control. "Somebody doesn't like the company I'm keeping."

Mitchell slowly lowered himself to the couch alongside her. Suddenly his chest hurt. He couldn't seem to ask what had happened. He couldn't see any signs of injury, but that didn't necessarily mean anything. Her eyes were haunted, her hands clasped in her lap. Without realizing it, he reached out and took her fingers into his hand.

"Are you all right?"

Lindsay nodded, the tears she'd been fighting so hard filling her eyes. "They were already gone. But my...it wasn't just that they searched the house. They ruined it. My pictures, my grandmother's desk, my needlework...."

Mitchell couldn't help a smile. "You do needlework?"

"I did," she answered, her control threatening to fail again. "It's all gone."

"I'm sorry," he said, a hand to her cheek. "It's not fair."

He knew what Esperanza's people were like. He'd seen the job they'd done on his apartment and Maggie's place. He could well imagine what kind of devastation they'd left behind at Lindsay's.

What had they found, he wondered? What kind of comfort did Lindsay McDonough surround herself with? Was her house spartan, plush, with modern art—or potpourri and lace? After working with her for four years, after making love to her, Mitchell couldn't imagine. After missing her for four hours he wanted to know.

"You're damn right it's not fair," she sniffled, her lips edging upward just a little in response to his touch. "I lose everything and then get punished by ending up with you again."

Mitchell still hadn't moved, his fingers slowly drifting back and forth across the velvet of her skin. "You really do needlework?"

Lindsay tilted her head, her expression growing dry. "It's so hard to accept?"

Mitchell shrugged. "I don't know. It seems too...homey for you."

"What should I be doing in my spare time?" she demanded. "Big game hunting?"

He shrugged. "Racquetball and aerobics, I guess. All that upwardly mobile stuff."

Lindsay grimaced. "Preconceptions again, Mitchell. Don't you think people would think *your* hobby strange?"

Mitchell wondered at the tone of their conversation, woven around their held hands and the feel of her cheek against his fingers. Sharp and soft, the essence, he guessed, of the lady in question.

"What about my hobby?" he demanded, only half serious.

Lindsay tilted her head and the light cascaded down her hair. "Woodworking, Mitchell? Is that the kind of pastime Sam Spade would indulge in?"

"I'm not a detective," he countered. "I'm an agent."

"I'll bet J. Edgar Hoover never ran a lathe."

"You make a chair, it lasts," he said. "You make an arrest, it doesn't. A man needs some sense of permanence in his life."

"Of completion," she suggested, eyes wide, mouth quirked. "Accomplishment."

Mitchell halted, unsure of the waters he was testing. "I guess."

"Of creation."

His eyes widened. She was taunting him, but she wasn't. Mitchell tried to imagine Lindsay with a sewing hoop in her hands, making delicate crosses across an expanse of linen, her glasses slipping over her nose, her hair in disarray. Maybe he could have at the cabin. But she was different here, and he couldn't say how. He didn't like it as much, either.

So he answered with a shake of his head. "You're beginning to sound like a guru, McDonough. The only thing I create is chairs and tables. The only things you create are pictures—and trouble."

"How do you know?" she demanded, eyes sly and enticing. "There's a lot you don't know about me, Mitchell."

When Mitchell answered, it was with a lot more truth than he realized. "I'm beginning to figure that out."

Mitchell found himself drawn closer by her words. They incited a wonder in him, a challenge he hadn't anticipated. He would know her, he thought, his eyes on the tremble of her lips. He'd slip in beneath those whiskey-tinted eyes, edge into her soul where the mysteries waited.

Lindsay wasn't sure she was breathing. She couldn't imagine that Mitchell wasn't able to hear the sudden pounding in her chest, couldn't feel the heat in her cheek. He leveled those green eyes on her and she stumbled, everything that had happened whirling and lost within their depths. There was unbearable life in his fingertips as they grazed the edges of her mouth.

You're tired, she told herself. You're trying to assimilate loss and disruption. Still, that wasn't reason enough to explain the awful turbulence in her. Lindsay knew that if she didn't pull away soon, she wouldn't at all. And that would seal her fate forever.

"Are you as tired as I am?" she finally asked, her voice too tremulous before the look of certainty in Mitchell's eyes.

"Probably."

Funny. His voice sounded as uncertain as hers. Could he be as unprepared for the chills as she, the sweet ache that had suddenly ignited like a hot summer sunrise, spreading fiery fingers across her as it grew?

Tired. I'm too tired for this, Mitchell thought, still unable to pull away from Lindsay. His body was listening. He felt the surge of desire at his temples, deep in his gut. Just the touch of her was bringing him back to life.

"What kind of furniture do you have?"

"What?"

"Style. What style?"

"Antiques, family things."

Another puzzle piece that fitted but didn't. A different facet of her.

Mitchell thought how he should be working on the case, retracing steps and reevaluating logic, and all he could think of was how much he wanted to taste the honey in her again. How luscious her mouth looked when it was parted like that, waiting.

He edged closer, his gaze drifting back to her lips. His hand brought her face to him. Mitchell could feel her breath on his cheek, warming him in short, erratic pulses. He could smell the soft drift of her perfume. It was like dipping his head into a bouquet of dark flowers.

Her lips. He met them and thought how tremulous they were. How surprised. He felt her hesitation begin to melt and drew her closer.

"No," Lindsay groaned, jerking away. "No, Mitchell. It's a mistake."

Mitchell knew she was right. Still he couldn't move. She was so warm, so soft. He wanted to find his way back to her arms. His chest ached with the struggle. Mitchell approached, even as Lindsay reached the last of her control.

Lindsay gained her feet. "No." She was pleading now, with herself as much as Mitchell. "It should have never happened before, and it can't happen now. I'm going to my room and I'm locking the door. I'd appreciate it if you'd do the same."

"What about my memory?" he goaded, surprised by the real pain of separation.

"Tomorrow . . . later. Like you said."

"I think you're right, Lindsay," he argued, not moving from his place on the couch, his hands clenched to keep away from her. "I don't think I'm going to have a chance for later."

"Then tomorrow. When we've both had some sleep."

His answering grimace was wry, taunting. She knew damn well what he could expect from sleep. He was pushing her unfairly, Mitchell knew that. But he couldn't stop. Suddenly it seemed as if only Lindsay could keep the ghosts from returning, only she could cushion him against the terror.

"God, Mitchell, please," she begged, shying away as he got to his feet and held out a hand. "Don't do this to me."

Her hesitation boiled in him, acid and emptiness. Mitchell stiffened, chilled by her rejection, and reclaimed his hand.

"You don't have to worry about me, McDonough," he finally told her, wishing he could pull himself from the turmoil in her eyes. "I know when the line's been drawn. I won't step over again. I'm heading back out at dawn tomorrow. If you want to get some feel for a weapon, be up before then. We'll work in the basement."

"I'm not . . ."

Unyielding now, he shook his head. "Maybe I should have left that in the command department. I'll wake you about five. When I go, I'm leaving a gun with you, so you might as well know how to use it. And get back into some real clothes." His eyebrows quirked as he took in the sleek lines of her skirt and sweater. "Don't you wear jeans in Denver?"

Lindsay turned startled eyes on her apparel, not understanding his question.

"I went back to the office before coming here. Why?"

Mitchell just shook his head. "You afraid to let those people see you without a dress on, McDonough?"

Lindsay glared. "Not everyone relishes the role of rebel, Mitchell. If I didn't enjoy wearing these clothes, I wouldn't."

"Did you bring anything more comfortable to wear?"

"I seem to have forgotten my jeans at the cabin," she retorted, defensive fire sparking in her eyes. "Bob thought it would be counterproductive for me to try and retrieve them. He also forgot to mention there being a safe house dress code. Satisfied?"

"No." He stared at her, once again caught by something—an anomaly, a disparity. What was it about Lindsay that once again seemed wrong?

Then he had it. "Armor." He nodded to himself, eyes a little wider with his discovery. "That's it. I'm going to bed."

Lindsay saw him turn; even then she couldn't believe it. "Mitchell? What the hell are you talking about?"

Mitchell didn't turn back, forcing Lindsay to follow him down the hall. "You, McDonough. You might as well have a chastity belt on. Which bedroom is yours, just so I don't stumble into it by accident?"

He didn't wait for a reply. Turning into the first one, Mitchell shut the door. Lindsay found herself standing out in the hallway, wanting more of an explanation than Mitchell had seen fit to give her.

"Mitchell!"

The door swung open by inches and an overnighter plopped onto the threadbare carpet by her feet.

"Remember. Dawn," came the muffled voice as the door shut again.

Maybe it's the stress, Lindsay thought, still planted before the solidly closed door. *I've lived through more than one lifetime worth of setbacks and surprises these last few days. They're catching up with me. Otherwise I would have been able to follow what he said. I would have at least belted him for it.* Slowly she retrieved her bag and headed into her room.

When she reached a mirror, she stood before it, still trying to understand. The same old Lindsay faced her, hair once again combed into order, outfit appropriate for her profession. Rose linen skirt and matching sweater, gold rope necklace, pumps. What was wrong with that? There was a

little more color in her cheeks, and her eyes looked brighter, almost glowing. She noticed that her hand kept straying
over her clothes, as if making sure they were still safely in
place.

Would she have succumbed? If Mitchell hadn't backed
off, would she once again have found herself in his bed in
the morning? There was no way to know, of course. She was
safely closed behind her own door, shielded from his demons and desires. Yet still her hand roamed, remembering,
wondering. And her mind, so exhausted that it did nothing
but spin, danced around his last accusations.

Nothing to do but get that sleep, she decided, slipping out
of her clothes and folding them into neat piles. That tight
discomfort in her chest was just the result of finding her
house ruined, her belongings torn apart like the prey of wild
animals. The constriction in her throat was the residue of
terror. She was just tired.

But she knew she wouldn't get any sleep.

Lindsay finally climbed into bed about eleven. At two she
was back on her feet again. By now she recognized the
sounds. She didn't even have to separate the thrashing from
the moans. Slipping into her robe, she walked out into the
hall.

His light wasn't on yet. Lindsay stood before his door,
torn. Wanting to go in and knowing instinctively that he
wouldn't let her this time. He wasn't in his cabin where he
made the rules. He was on somebody else's turf, exposed
even in an empty house. Lindsay waited for a few heart-
stopping moments, hand to chest, his pain echoing in her,
and then walked on into the kitchen.

Mitchell couldn't breathe. He didn't know where he was
at first, the unfamiliar room smothering him. How long had
he been asleep this time? Probably not long. His body still
felt wasted and stale. He needed a cigarette, and he hadn't
smoked in ten years.

Maggie had come so close tonight, her voice strident, her
eyes wild. Insistent, outraged. Dying in the air, knowing he
wouldn't reach her. Shouldn't it begin to ease? When would

his penance be over? Or would he spend the rest of his life trying to escape sleep?

Swinging out of bed, Mitchell padded to the door. These guys had damn well better have stocked beer in this dive. If they hadn't, they were going to hear from him, that was for damn sure. Yanking a hand through his hair in an attempt to keep the shakes at bay, Mitchell walked into the kitchen in just his shorts.

The first surprise was the beer on the table. Open and cold, waiting like a gift from a sympathetic genie. Then Mitchell realized that there was somebody else in the room, settled into a kitchen chair, her own beer in hand.

"Join me?"

He lifted his head, aching all the way down his back, feeling as though he had sandpaper under his eyes and a hot rock in his chest. When he saw Lindsay, Mitchell sighed.

Wrapped in a blue terry cloth robe, she sat in sweet disarray at the side of the table, beer in hand, her expression carefully passive. Mitchell didn't know how she did it. If she'd tried to approach him any other way, the acid that was eating at him would have spilled over into destruction. Somehow the remembered vulnerability she offered defused the dream. Rubbing at his eyes, Mitchell lowered himself into the chair across from her.

"You're losing sleep over this, McDonough. You have rings under your eyes."

"The wonders of makeup, Mitchell," she countered, taking a first pull from her bottle. "Nobody will ever know."

Facing his own beer, he shook his head. "Makeup can only count for so much. After awhile stress takes its toll."

Lindsay watched him. "I know."

She waited. Mitchell picked up his beer and drained it in a couple of long gulps, the condensation trickling over his fingers. The room was dim, only the stove light offering a small pool of white in the corner. The summer outside whispered. The house answered, creaking with age and indifference. Mitchell set the beer down and decided it wasn't enough.

"You ready for another?" he asked, lifting himself to his feet.

Across the table, Lindsay watched his movements without reaction. "Thanks, no," she demurred, lifting her bottle. "I'll work on this one awhile."

Mitchell nodded and went after his own. Lindsay wanted to tell him to put some clothes on. The frail light illuminated him far too clearly. He moved with too much power, even as tired and battered as he was. Lindsay found her eyes straying over the well-remembered lines of his body and took another long pull from her bottle. She'd been right before. She was too tired for this. Her own body was already beginning to sing.

"So," Mitchell said, turning back to her. "What's this magic you want to work on me?"

Dropping back in the chair, he began rolling the bottle across his forehead like an ice pack. Lindsay saw the squint in his eyes, the tight line of his jaw. She accepted her victory silently and worried over the pain she might inflict. He'd had enough already.

What was it they said in medicine? "We have to hurt you to make you feel better?" Tell that to a man with eyes as brittle as old glass.

Did all therapists come to this point, she wondered, when they couldn't distance themselves anymore? When the pain became their own? Or was it just this time, because she couldn't look at Mitchell without thinking of how gentle those clenched hands could be?

He was right. She'd sheltered herself in theory, and now she had to face reality head-on. Only now she had to do it with a man she couldn't decide if she hated or loved.

"Are you looking for clues," she asked, "or answers?"

Setting the bottle down, Mitchell lifted his gaze to Lindsay. She saw the determination there, the ravages of grief. She saw a man who didn't know how to quit, even as his subconscious battered at him without relief.

"Both," he answered. "I'm missing part of the picture, McDonough. I want to know why Maggie won't let me sleep, and why Esperanza won't leave me alone. I've looked everywhere else I can think of, and it hasn't done me any good. Maybe the answer's somewhere in me." He stopped, his decision his own, his request made without reserve. "Maybe you can help me find it."

"It might not be easy to find."

Mitchell snorted. "Looked at my file lately, McDonough? Nobody seems to think I know what easy means anymore."

Lindsay just nodded. "When?"

Mitchell shrugged. "How long does it take?"

"This isn't like an operation," she retorted. "There aren't any guarantees."

Mitchell finished off his second beer and took a moment to look at it, as if making a decision. Then he glanced at Lindsay and offered a crooked grin. "Well, I seem to be free right now. How 'bout you?"

"Do I really have to lie on this thing?"

"Close your eyes, Mitchell," Lindsay suggested with the barest hint of a smile on her lips. "You'll never know where you are."

Mitchell scowled at her from where he lay stretched out on his bed. "I feel like something out of a bad book."

"You're too tall for any of the furniture," she reminded him. "And if you're not completely comfortable, it's real hard to relax."

"You won't make me bark like a dog?"

"Only at staff meetings. I told you, Mitchell. It's not hypnosis. It's relaxation response. I'm not dangling any watches or spinning any wheels. Now just lie back and close your eyes."

He offered one last grimace before succumbing. "Last time somebody said that to me, I was in Tijuana."

Lindsay couldn't help but grin. "We're dealing in memories here, Mitchell. Not delusions."

Lindsay opened the window just a crack, then returned to the chair she'd placed a few feet from the bed.

"First thing I want you to do is tighten every muscle you have," she instructed.

"Every muscle?"

"Just cooperate. At least one of us would like to get back to bed sometime in the next week or so. Okay, clench everything."

At Lindsay's request, Mitchell had put on jeans and a T-shirt. She could see the muscles along his chest and arms bunch up beneath the fabric. He was grimacing, his hands in fists, his toes curled.

"Okay, now you're going to release one muscle group at a time, starting with your toes and working up to your head."

"At this rate," he grated through clenched teeth, "I should discover something about September."

Even so, his feet relaxed, then his legs.

Lindsay nodded, urging him on. "Feel the warmth spread up from your feet as you relax. Can you hear the wind outside? Focus on it, the rhythm of it, the soft sound. Listen only to that, and to my voice . . . good, now your shoulders, your arms . . . ."

Lindsay worked him through the routine until she saw the lines ease on his forehead. When she'd done this in the past, she had used a temperature sensor on the patient's finger. The more relaxed a patient became, the higher his temperature. The higher the temperature, the better chance he would reach the alpha level, the brain wave pattern her old professor had called the emotional melting pot. It was here memories were stored without censorship, here feelings ran free and inspiration bubbled. The incidents on that building would be more easily accessible here.

"Feel heavy, don't you, Mitchell? Still hear the wind? Listen to it, listen to its music. I want to talk about Maggie now. Is that okay?"

Only Mitchell's lips moved. "Yeah."

Good. He was balanced just this side of sleep, where speech was an effort, where sounds were magnified and suggestion impressive.

"Describe her to me, Mitchell."

A pause, then his chest lifted with the effort of remembering. "Solid. She was solid."

"You were friends."

"Yeah."

"You miss her."

A longer pause, his voice hushed. "Maggie was always there."

"Do you want to know what happened to her? To get the men who set her up?"

"Yes." Breath. "No."

"It's okay. Tell me what it is you want."

"I want," he said finally, "Esperanza."

"I think I can get him if you'll help me. Will you picture Maggie for me? Will you describe her to me when you saw her that night?"

Lindsay waited. She saw the emotion flicker across Mitchell's features, saw him draw Maggie up from his subconscious and shy away from her. Lindsay wanted to reach out to him, to gentle the memories with her hands. Her breath caught in her throat. She wrapped her fingers around the arms of her chair, willing him to succeed, aching for the torment she was producing.

"You've just reached the top, Mitchell," she murmured. "It's dark. A storm's coming in from the mountains. Can you see her?"

"Yes. She's...fighting. With Wilson's men. The guys she came up with."

"What can you hear?"

"The wind. Thunder. Miguel, the big one, screaming in Spanish... my gun. I have to get my gun up."

His breathing was growing ragged.

"Can she see you?"

"Maggie..."

"What is she doing, Mitchell?"

His voice was a whisper, cold as a night wind. "I don't...know. She's..."

Come on, Mitchell. Bring it up for me.

"She's what? Is she talking? Is she calling out?"

"Yes. To me. She's asking me to help...God, what have I done?"

"Mitchell?"

He was fighting it, his body bucking, his voice anguished. "No...no, I can't. The wind. It's all space and wind out there."

"Maggie. Look at Maggie, Mitchell. What is she doing?"

With a great shudder, he jerked straight up. "No!"

Lindsay came out of her chair. Mitchell was on his feet gulping for air like a drowning man, hands out to keep her away.

"No, no, no!"

Lindsay followed him, trying to keep a distance, wanting to put her arms around him. "Mitchell, it's okay. Settle down."

"Okay?" he demanded, whirling on her. "Don't you dare tell me it's okay! Nobody's scrambling *your* brains. You pick at me like a vulture and don't do any more than..." Words failed him. Shaking his head, he struggled to get past the revulsion she'd resurrected. The failure.

"What did you see?" Lindsay asked, forcing herself to face him.

"I saw Maggie sailing over the edge," he snapped. "I saw her die. Again. Just like the dream. And she still didn't tell me anything. So what do we do now, Doctor?"

Lindsay stood her ground before his venom. She knew he wouldn't want to hear it. She wasn't sure she did. But they'd run out of choices. "We do it again."

Chapter 10

Lindsay wrapped her hands around a mug of hot coffee and watched the steam spiral toward the ceiling. The sun was just struggling its way into the sky. Outside, the air was still cool, its humidity gathered into dewdrops on the untidy back lawn. The neighborhood was waking, and Lindsay could hear traffic from the nearby interstate. She could smell the pungent coffee in her hands and the bacon she'd fried for Mitchell. Later, if she felt up to it, she'd pull out her work or maybe the embroidery she'd been working on for her sister.

Just like family, she thought with a disparaging smile. Like Ozzie and Harriet, with the little woman getting up to see her man off to work. Only her man wasn't her man, and what he was off to was a manhunt. And, if you wanted to press a point, she hadn't really gotten up. She'd been up.

Lindsay still couldn't quite believe that Mitchell had dealt so well with the attempt to retrieve his memory. After she'd told him that they would have to repeat the procedure, he had stalked off, out of his room and into the kitchen where he could consult a bottle of beer. When Lindsay had shown up, he'd turned to her, nodded quickly, and tilted back the bottle to finish it.

But, he'd informed her in no uncertain terms, they wouldn't do it right away. *He* wouldn't do it. Two nightmares in one night were quite enough for him, thank you. He was going to retire to his bedroom—alone—and familiarize himself with the insides of his eyelids in the hope that he'd be coherent when Al showed up.

Lindsay had watched in silence, unable to even gather the strength to nod. When Mitchell had locked himself behind his door, she had sat down in the kitchen. And that's where he had found her two hours later.

"Sorry we can't take time to go over the joys of owning a gun before I leave," he apologized in a too-bright voice when he found Lindsay at the table before him. "But we took up so much time on games last night that I'm running a little late. We'll do it when I get home." He had his holster slung over his shoulder and a jacket in his hand. The jacket ended up over a chair. The holster didn't seem to bother him at all where it was.

Casting a jaundiced eye in his direction, Lindsay scowled. "Slow down, Mitchell, before you break something."

"What's the matter, McDonough?" he demanded with a feverish glint in his eyes. "Can't you handle life on three hours' sleep a night? It must be an acquired taste."

"Have some coffee," she suggested dryly. "Maybe you'll perk up a little."

His smile was sharp. "Can't say it's done much for you. I thought you'd like me better this way."

She smiled back, and her response was still dryer. "I don't like you *any* way. And if Al sees you like this, he's going to drive you straight to the nearest mental health facility. So give all of us a break and revert to form."

"Why didn't you go back to sleep?" he asked, pouring a cup of coffee for himself. "I'm the one with the nightmares."

As he set the pot back, he saw the warm bacon and eggs on the counter and turned to her. "These for me?"

"Yeah, I'm saving the porridge for Goldilocks."

Mitchell returned with the plate and cup and settled in across from Lindsay. The morning was still dim, but his eyes weren't. They sparkled with energy.

"Doing drugs, Mitchell?"

He seemed sincerely confused. "Drugs? What are you talking about?"

Setting down her cup, Lindsay shrugged. "I spend an hour panfrying your brain last night, and you look like you spent a week in a spa."

Not exactly. His skin was closer to gray than tan, and he had a set of circles under his eyes. The incident on the road had left technicolor patches over his left eye. Lindsay couldn't have imagined that anyone with that list of assets would look so deadly handsome, but Mitchell did. For some reason, it only served to shorten her temper.

For a long moment he looked at her, and Lindsay could see some calculating going on behind those bottle-green eyes. Then he set down his cutlery.

"Memory," he finally said, his expression honest. "I thought last night that what you did was a failure because I couldn't remember what Maggie said. There was something else I didn't consider, though. Something else was said that I *did* remember."

Lindsay actually recovered some of her enthusiasm. "What?"

"Miguel. Remember I told you he was yelling in Spanish?"

Thinking back, Lindsay nodded.

Mitchell leaned closer. "I didn't remember hearing him before. In the nightmare, I just see him. I only hear the wind. Last night I heard his words. All of them."

"And?"

"He was calling her a bitch, demanding to know what she did with it. He knew she had it, now where was it?"

Lindsay felt his excitement infect her. "What? What was it he thought she had?"

"The link. I'm convinced of it. She had the evidence that tied Wilson in with Esperanza, and they were desperate to get it back. They brought her up to that buy to make a point with their friends who had the money. Nobody double-crosses the Esperanza team."

"But where is it? What did she do with it?"

"That's it," he sighed, slumping a little as he went back to his food. "I don't know. I've been every place I can think of where she might have hidden something. Her place, mine, the drops. Somebody had been to the apartments before me, so they must still be looking."

"Well," Lindsay said, "they didn't find anything in mine. What next?"

"Next I head off with Al to check out some sources. Al's bringing Maggie's file with him, so I'm going to go over it again, see if anything sparks. For the most part, Maggie was a predictable person. I should be able to tell where she'd leave something for me. By the way, did I tell you that you're a good cook?"

Lindsay lifted an eyebrow. "I'm just grateful you're not throwing your food onto the floor."

Mitchell gave her that crooked grin again, the one that begged for patience and urged humor. Lindsay found herself grinning back and not knowing why.

"So, what's *your* agenda today?" Mitchell asked, returning his attention to his food once more.

"Sleep," Lindsay answered without hesitation.

His eyes were on her again. "Why didn't you go back to sleep when I did?"

Lindsay consulted the swirl of cream in her coffee. "Probably because you forgot to tell me what an unqualified success last night's session was. I was up, trying to think of a better way to do it."

"But I have the answer," he retorted, lifting cautious eyes, his food once again forgotten.

"You have one of your answers," Lindsay disagreed. "We still have to look for the rest."

He wasn't finished with his breakfast. Lindsay saw him consider it, the appetite dying in his eyes, the enthusiasm slipping away. He toyed with his fork, tapping it slowly against the rim of his plate. Lindsay wanted to take that hand. She wanted to take back everything she'd said, just to see the light in his eyes again. All of which was another problem that had kept her awake while he slept.

"Yeah," he finally said with a short nod as he pushed his plate away and got back to his feet, the fork falling with a dull clank. "I said I would. I will. We'll do it when I get back, okay?"

Lindsay followed to her feet. "I'll be here."

Mitchell stood before her for a moment, his eyes dark, his jaw tight. Traffic droned in the distance like the rush of an ocean, and a few birds sang in the trees.

Lindsay felt the stillness in the room like a weight, dragging them down, pulling them together. She saw Mitchell unsteadily lift his hand to her, as if he couldn't help what he was doing. His fingers brushed her cheek, infusing her with some of his warmth. Lindsay wanted to tell him to stop, to keep his distance. Her heart stumbled. Her knees wilted. She ached with the question she saw in his eyes and responded without wanting to.

It was a moment before either of them acknowledged the bell. Al leaned on it again, this time with enthusiasm, and Mitchell reclaimed his hand. Lindsay rocked on her feet, as if unable to break the contact.

"I don't suppose I get a lunch pail to take to work," Mitchell suggested with a sly smile, his voice husky and intimate.

"Catch me in another lifetime," Lindsay retorted more lightly than she felt. "Now don't keep the carpool waiting."

"Needlework something for me when I'm gone," he suggested and bent to brush her lips with the briefest of kisses before retrieving his jacket.

Lindsay did her best to match his mood. "I know just the saying to cross-stitch."

Al must have thought the two of them had been slaughtered. He was banging on the door by now. Mitchell just ignored him.

"What saying?"

Lindsay shook her head. "You'll see it when it's finished. Now, go let Al in before he starts using his head."

Lindsay followed Mitchell to the door, all the while thinking that there she was again, back in TV-land with the Nelson household. Maybe she should do some kind of study on it later. "Disorientation in Forced Use of Safe Houses." Or maybe she would just call it the "Pseudo-Nelson Syndrome." Find yourself cooped up in a small living space with an attractive male and you begin to envision The Ties That Bind.

"Where were you two?" Al demanded, almost having fallen in as the door was opened.

"Making mad, passionate love," Mitchell told him, slipping a companionable arm around Lindsay's shoulder and offering her a patronizing smile. "And may I say, my dear, you were wonderful?"

Lindsay answered with an elbow to the ribs. "You forget, Mitchell. Al knows us much too well to fall for that."

She wasn't so sure. Al's expression had gotten a little befuddled. It probably didn't help that she and Mitchell ended up exchanging significant looks.

"Get out," she insisted, a hand to each back. "Both of you. The sun's up, the birds are singing. There's crime out there waiting to be fought."

Mitchell headed out without protest. Al turned for a final look at Lindsay. "Is she all right?" he asked no one in particular.

Lindsay slammed the door in his face. She didn't see him look at Mitchell and rephrase his question. "Are *you* all right?"

Lindsay wondered how Mitchell had ever managed to sit in that cabin for two weeks without going stark, raving mad.

One day in this little cracker box, and she was ready to crawl the walls.

It wasn't that she was uncomfortable. The team had stocked the kitchen with all the staples and quite a few luxuries. The silence didn't bother her. She lived alone in a house without even a radio. Lindsay enjoyed silence. But then, she mostly enjoyed the silence in her own home.

She tried to sleep away the morning, only to wake about noon to find herself tangled up in the sheets, staring at a ceiling that bore scars made by the room's previous occupants. When she tried to evaluate the dossiers of four new candidates for the task force, more often than not she ended up standing at the front window, looking out at cracked sidewalks, identical brick houses and savagely mown lawns. It didn't even do any good to try to do her cross-stitching. She just couldn't keep her mind on it.

Lindsay finally resorted to pacing, measuring off each of the five rooms with careful steps, a cup of coffee in hand, her eyes on her progress. It didn't occupy her the way she wanted it to. She still found herself rehashing the same questions she'd wrestled with the night before.

Mitchell.

He was getting better. Anybody could see that. He had energy. He had purpose. He'd even begun to discover a sense of humor Lindsay had never witnessed before. Couldn't that be enough? Where was it written that she had to dissect him any further?

Lindsay had lifted her coffee to her lips before she realized that she didn't really want it anymore. She set it down on the end table by the door and continued her path through the dining room into the hall. The question wasn't whether he should eventually know and deal with everything that had happened. He should. But why should he have to do it now? Why couldn't he complete his case and give himself a little breather before tackling the big question? And then when he did, Lindsay could recommend somebody else to help him answer it.

It wasn't that she didn't want to help Mitchell. She'd proven her intent by walking into his cabin in the first place. She just didn't think she could be useful anymore. She'd lost her impartiality, her distance. How could she really expect to help him if she couldn't stand back far enough to clearly see what was going on?

How could she possibly come out of this unscathed?

Lindsay looked up, to find herself in Mitchell's room. He had almost invited inspection by leaving the door open. Lindsay saw the jeans he'd worn the night before thrown over a chair, his T-shirt crumpled alongside the bed. Clothes spilled from his bag, and he'd left a couple of extra clips for his gun on the dresser.

Even standing in the doorway, Lindsay could smell him. His tang and the musk of his after-shave mingled in the air and tantalized her memory. She could imagine him stretched on the bed, scrunching up his face in an attempt to lighten a session in hell.

That shouldn't make her cry. There wasn't any reason she should be standing in this doorway, wiping at her eyes and struggling against the emotion that squeezed her throat dry. Except maybe that she was drawn here.

It was the first day in what, six, that she hadn't spent with him. She hadn't realized how much he'd filled her days, colored the empty spaces she'd never known she had. For so many years now Lindsay had carefully compartmentalized her life, doling out her pleasures and attending to her work. But that was all gone—the small comforts and bits of life she'd gathered in her house, the links to her family and the past. The cozy environment she'd collected for her future had been shattered.

Now all she saw in her life was Mitchell. No house, no pictures, no seascape over the fireplace or oak coatrack in the front hall. She'd been thinking of all those things during the night and she'd been surprised to realize that they had begun to dim for her, even before she'd lost them. She had collected pastel comforts and then been confronted with a vivid challenge. And the challenge was what stayed with her.

Mitchell.

Lindsay gave her eyes a final swipe and turned away. What was she going to do? She had the most awful feeling she was falling in love, and it just so happened to be with the last person on earth she would have chosen.

He yelled at her. He didn't trust her. They'd never been able to pass one working day without trading at least half a dozen barbs.

He incited a life in her she'd never known before.

He was arrogant.

He had more courage than any man she'd known.

Lindsay paced faster, Patrick's harangues haunting her for the first time in almost two years, as certain as ever that she didn't ever want to go through that kind of turmoil again. She had her solitude. She had her comfort, her friends and family and career to fulfill her. She didn't need someone new to torment her.

The problem was, he was tormenting her already.

Mr. Esperanza was not happy. Only four more days until he was going to make his final move—and suddenly there were problems. A large man, with hooded eyes and petulant, fleshy features, Mr. Esperanza sat behind his desk like a great frog waiting for flies. The fly he waited for today was Artie.

"I've had it with all of this," he complained in a high, wheezy voice. "Nobody listens, nobody does his job. Am I the only one in this organization who knows how things should be done?"

"The cop made him, Mr. Esperanza," his assistant said diffidently. "Artie felt it was the only course open to him. He knows the cop could trace him back to you."

"In that case, we make sure nobody can question him to find out, don't we?"

The younger man nodded.

Esperanza scrawled a signature on a letter and sailed it across his desk. "Everything else is ready?"

Picking the paper out of thin air, his assistant nodded again.

"All right, then. We're ready to move on Saturday. The cop has someone baby-sitting him. We've been assured that the two of them can't sneeze without my knowing. Let the cop play his game. We'll let him do our looking for us. When he finds what we want, we let Paul finish him. If he doesn't find it by Saturday, it won't matter anyway, and we give the United States one agent's life. Generous, don't you think?"

"Artie's here, Mr. Esperanza."

Esperanza waved away the announcement. "Take care of it."

Mitchell made it a point not to invite Al inside. He could smell steak on the broiler, and he decided that he didn't want to share even that small pleasure with the baby-sitter Peterson had stuck him with. Of course, if he really thought about it, Lindsay was a baby-sitter, too. It was just that he found himself looking forward to the concern in her eyes. The way it looked on Al made his stomach curdle.

"I'm home, darling!" he called, throwing his jacket onto the chair. He unbuckled his shoulder holster and was slipping off his gun when he noticed the variety of coffee cups sitting on various articles of furniture. "Lindsay?" He'd gathered four by the time he found her at the stove.

"Was the coffee very bad or very good?" he asked, waving the cups in her direction before depositing them in the sink. "Or is this your way of trying to replant a coffee crop?"

Brushing her hair off her face with an arm, Lindsay turned to him, roasting fork in hand. "Now I know what the lions feel like in those little cages in the zoo," she snapped.

Mitchell grinned at the frustration in her eyes. "Oh, it's going to be a fun evening at the ranch tonight, isn't it?"

Lindsay was not amused. "How often do you end up in these places?"

He took a moment to look around at the circa 1950 aqua tile and barely functional appliances. "Oh, not often. Usually I bring eight or nine books and a bottle of bourbon."

"That's it," Lindsay decided, reaching over a glowing broiler to turn the steaks. "I forgot the bourbon."

Giving into an impulse he couldn't name, Mitchell kissed the back of her neck. "I'll bring it home tomorrow."

Lindsay straightened like a shot. "This is not home!" she retorted. "I don't appreciate being sneaked up on, and I have a feeling you're winding up to call me the little woman. Do, and you're going to find yourself with some new ventilation holes."

Mitchell made it a point to look around. "I only see innocent parties here, lady. Now, are you going to have gun class before or after dinner?"

He couldn't tell what was eating at Lindsay, only that something was tumbling around in her eyes and pulling at her mouth. She looked as if she'd been raking hands through her once-neat hair, and the slacks and blouse she wore were actually rumpled. That, coupled with the ceramic trail she'd left through the house, added up to cabin fever of the worst kind. And people usually didn't begin to exhibit that syndrome until they'd been indoors at least a few days.

"Can you make the salad?" Lindsay asked, turning back to her task.

"That's it, hard day at work and I have to come home and fix—"

Lindsay whirled on him again before he could finish. He punctuated his joke with a sly grin. It didn't seem to help.

Lindsay was quiet during dinner, picking at her food and going through almost as much beer as he did. Mitchell couldn't figure it. He'd never seen good old McDonough this distracted before. He found himself wondering how she'd react if he used some of her own medicine on her.

"All right," he announced suddenly when she stood to put the dishes away. "That's enough. Come with me."

And before she had a chance to protest, he had grabbed her hand.

"Mitchell . . ."

"Shut up and take it like a woman. I'm going to give you a back rub."

Lindsay balked, almost pulling away. "I don't need a back rub."

"Well, I don't have any tranquilizers with me, and that's the only other thing I can think of that would work right now." Slipping an arm around her shoulder, he guided her toward her room. "You are about as pleasant as a cat in a dog show. You wouldn't by any chance be—"

He almost lost a rib that time. "Don't even suggest it," she snarled.

Mitchell just propelled her on.

She balked as they stepped through the door. "Not in here."

Mitchell lifted an eyebrow. "You're too big for the furniture, too, Lindsay. And like an eminent doctor once told me, you can't relax unless you get comfortable."

"Why are you doing this?" she demanded, unable to meet his eyes.

His smile was a little wistful. "Because I don't want you working on my subconscious tonight in the mood you're in."

He hadn't meant to hurt her. Mitchell saw the sudden tears, the harsh stillness that took her, and knew that she felt ashamed. He sensed the emotions swirling in her and found himself wanting to protect her.

"Lindsay?" All of a sudden she was so fragile, so small in his hands. He thought that if he held on too tightly, she would just shatter. Mitchell was stunned by the hard ache that thought set up in him. The urge to hold her, to gentle her. McDonough was the most self-contained person he knew, yet he wanted to touch the susceptible places in her and heal them. He wanted to nurture her.

"Care to talk about it?"

Lindsay's head came up a little. She caught her breath. "Talk about what?"

Mitchell leaned closer, held on more tightly. "I want to help."

"Help?" she echoed. "You help me?"

His smile was wry. "A definite change of pace, I know. Why don't we sit?"

Lindsay shook her head. Mitchell lifted her chin with a finger until she faced him. "Come on, McDonough. It's your turn to be pampered. Give in gracefully."

"Damn it, Mitchell," she retorted without much energy. "I didn't like being cooped up. I don't like being left out, and you come back making stupid jokes. I'm entitled to be crabby."

"This," he said, "is not crabby. This is upset. Take it from one who knows."

Where he got the inspiration, he never knew. Mitchell wasn't usually long on empathy. Whatever it was that moved him that moment also prompted him to turn out the lights and pull Lindsay onto the bed. He felt her stiffen and smiled.

"Okay, my methods are just as unorthodox as yours," he said, sitting down with her. "Bear with me, anyway."

He arranged the two of them in a comfortable position, so that he was sitting with his back against the headboard and Lindsay was leaning against his chest. By the time he'd wrapped his arms around her and brought her head against him, she had relaxed a little.

"See?" He smiled into the soft cloud of her hair. "This isn't so bad."

"Why are you doing this?" she asked, her voice too small, too tight.

Mitchell had to grin. "Seems to me I said the same thing to you, and you never came up with an answer that satisfied me. I didn't believe it, when you said you just wanted to help."

"Help what?" she countered, still stiff in his grasp. "I'm just suffering the effects of losing one household and ending up in one I don't like. I'm feeling cornered."

"And you're tired."

"And I'm tired."

"From trying to figure a way of helping me."

She had no answer to that. Mitchell felt her tense and wondered if she knew how clearly she was sending him messages. He wondered just as much if he knew what he was doing. The scent of wildflowers she'd captured in her hair drifted up to him. He could feel the stiffness in the slim line of her arms and waist. He could hear her breathing—sharp and quick, as if she were fighting pain, and Mitchell found himself fighting the same pain.

"What's the matter with helping me?" he asked quietly, wanting so very much to touch the faint moonlight he'd found in her hair. "Don't you want to anymore?"

He heard a sob catch in her throat and looked down, as if he could divine some truth from her shadowy profile. As if he could assuage some of the ache in his chest.

"Lindsay?"

She shook her head. It took a moment for her to find her voice. "No." She dragged in a breath to complete her admission. "No, I don't."

Mitchell realized he had tightened his hold on her. "But why? We've made such a great team so far."

"Yeah." She laughed almost bitterly. "I've tormented you and you've fought back. Definitely one for the books."

Mitchell had never seen Lindsay like this. He couldn't imagine what to do about it. It was as if she were losing her sense of purpose, stumbling over convictions she'd never questioned before. As long as he'd known her, McDonough had never hesitated.

But then, how well had he known her all these years? He felt tears on his arm and was surprised.

"What is it that you don't like anymore?" he asked, carefully restraining himself from tightening his hold, from stroking a gentling hand through her hair. Lindsay wouldn't allow that. "Me? No, it can't be that. You never liked me to begin with. Did I insult you one time too many or expect you to do too much? If you don't want to fire a gun after all, tell me."

"You made love to me." Lindsay couldn't believe she'd said it. The words caught in her throat like acid. She felt Mitchell stiffen against her and knew that she wasn't going to stop crying anytime soon. "You made love to me, damn it, and suddenly everything's changed. I can't stay objective. I can't be dispassionate. How the hell am I supposed to do you any good when I can't keep things straight myself anymore?"

"But you've convinced me, McDonough," he retorted. "I believe you. I have to get this dream finished with and go on with my life. I have to bury Maggie. You've got to do that before you quit."

"But don't you see?" she cried, turning in his arms. "I can't hurt you anymore."

"What?"

Lindsay saw the confusion, the disbelief in his eyes. She saw him struggle with what she was trying to tell him.

She dropped her head a little, unable to keep eye contact. "You can't think that I don't know what I'm doing to you. I've been deliberately chipping away at you with an ice pick until I reached a live nerve. Well, you're all nerves right now, Mitchell. Every time I strike, I spark pain. I . . . just don't think I can face it anymore."

With the gentlest of fingers, Mitchell lifted Lindsay's chin. "Because we made love?"

She looked up at him and wondered if he saw the truth. "I don't know. I think that's part of it. There's just so much I can't untangle. All I know is that I'm chickening out. You win, Mitchell. You were right all along. I teach. I can't do."

She couldn't believe it. Mitchell was smiling. It was the last thing she had expected. And it wasn't a smile of triumph or glee, either, but one of support.

"There's only one problem, McDonough," he said, leaning very close. "I'm not letting anybody else within ten feet of my brain. You start the job, you finish it."

"But, Mitchell, I told you . . ."

He nodded. "I know. You can't be objective. You don't know if you'll do okay, or I'll end up a mass of vanilla pudding on the floor. Tough. You're the one who's gotten me this far, you're damn well going to stay on to the end of the line."

Lindsay did her best to blink away stubborn tears. "Did anyone ever tell you that you don't listen well?"

"It doesn't matter. I'm not changing my mind."

Mitchell couldn't say later why he did it. But then, he'd never questioned actions like that before. Lindsay was clearly fired up to give him a really good dressing-down and battle for her right of refusal. He could see the glint in those honeyed eyes, the full promise of her mouth. So when she opened it to protest, Mitchell simply silenced her with a kiss.

She really did spark fire. Mitchell caught it the minute his lips met hers, a primal heat that swept through him like a wind. He cupped her face in his hand, wrapping his other arm around her so that he could bring her closer. She bucked against him, brought her own hands up. They reached his chest and stopped. Mitchell heard the moan gather in her throat, felt the purr of it with his thumb. He eased her lips open and sought her tongue.

Lindsay stumbled into the whirlwind and couldn't find her way back. Mitchell surrounded her, his scent, the rasp of his breath, the touch of his hands. She twisted in his arms, intent on pushing him away. Instead she found his chest and rested there. His tongue plumbed the depths of her mouth, skimming, sweeping, sipping until it felt as if he had found the very essence of her. His fingers danced along her cheek and throat, dipping into its hollow and settling over the wing of her collarbone.

Lindsay couldn't understand her submission. She had tormented herself about this very thing all day, struggled to steel herself against the life Mitchell had resurrected in her.

It wasn't right. She couldn't allow him to continue. She felt him unfasten her top button and couldn't recover her resolve.

She was dissolving, her bones melting like wax, her skin shimmering. His fingers sparked pain, an ache that sought the center of her and grew. His lips awakened her, his tongue pleasured her. Lindsay felt him slip his hand toward her bra and arched to meet it.

Lace and velvet. Heat, warming his fingers, drawing them closer to the core. Mitchell wrapped himself around Lindsay, brought her home. He eased his way in between the silk of her bra and the soft comfort of her breast. He heard her gasp and felt her nipple contract. Button hard and ready, waiting for him to taste, begging for his touch. Mitchell couldn't breathe, couldn't pull himself away from the sustenance of Lindsay's mouth. He cupped her breast in his hand and felt the throb of her heart. He wanted to tease the nipple with his teeth, to fill his mouth with her and torment that tight little bud with his tongue. Mitchell wanted to taste all of her. He wanted the ripples of her pleasure beneath his fingers. He wanted her comfort and her life, where nightmares disappeared and the world waited outside.

A shaft of lightning shot through Lindsay—a sweet quicksilver bolt that shook her, woke her. She was lying in Mitchell's arms, twisted around so that his fingers could find her breast and his mouth could savage hers. She was panting, aching, arched in his hold so that he could better savor her, so that she could better receive him. She felt his hand at her breast—a rough warmth that had incited the lightning—a gentle communion, a sweet torture.

Before she could give in to the pleas of her body, she pulled back. Her brain told her it was good, but she sobbed with the loss of his touch.

"Damn you!" she cried, stumbling away. "What are you doing?"

Mitchell tried to recapture her. "What am *I* doing?"

"What am *I* doing!" she retorted shrilly, pushing her hair back. "What are *we* doing? I just finished telling you that one of the reasons I'm having so much trouble is because we made love, and suddenly I find myself right back in the clinch.''

"You weren't unconscious," he countered as hotly as she. "I didn't sneak up on you, Lindsay."

"You did!" she insisted, crawling away from his reach. "Do you know how long I...? How much...? God, Mitchell, I'm not used to this."

He was on his feet, too, driven by a longing for the solace he'd lost with her retreat, by the guilt at having taken advantage of her. "You're not used to what?" he demanded. "Attention? Making love? Tenderness? If that's the case, McDonough, maybe you'd better fit it into your schedule a little more. It might do you some good."

"What the hell do you know about tenderness, Mitchell?" she shouted, her open blouse forgotten, her chest heaving with the frustrated tears she sought to control. "If you did, you probably wouldn't be living alone."

"A condition you know nothing about," he said sarcastically.

"Widowhood is not a choice."

"But isolation is, McDonough. And you've managed to isolate yourself from everyone at the office. Hiding behind your glasses and dress-for-success clothes and ice queen attitude. Hell, every one of the people in that task force almost dropped dead when they saw you in jeans. What are you afraid of, Doctor? What are *you* hiding from?"

The phone rang out in the hall, a sharp little sound that splintered their control.

"I'm not—"

"You bet you are," Mitchell assured her, a finger to her chest, his eyes glinting with fury. "You're two completely different people. Better let the casual side loose a little more, McDonough, or you're going to break like an old clock spring." Heading out to the ringing phone, he turned for one last barb. "And trust me. Nobody will give a damn."

Lindsay couldn't move from where she stood, alone in the darkened room, shaking, a hand to her mouth to stifle the sobs. Mitchell flicked on the hall light to answer the phone and the light poured in across the floor, turning the carpet the color of pea soup. Lindsay kept her eyes down as she fought to regain her composure.

Damn him. How could he, after all she'd been through? How dare he accuse her of cutting herself off? Hadn't she just spent the last twelve hours flaying herself with the pain she'd had to inflict on a brave man? Hadn't she waded through her own confusion and done her best to find the right way for Mitchell?

She had been right the first day she'd decided to take him on. Staying in close proximity with a recovering Mitchell was going to prove untenable, after all. She wasn't going to do either of them any good by sticking around just to fight. She'd pack up and get out, and recommend him to someone who could see him through a more traditional therapy. And then she might just call Chicago.

But she couldn't think that far ahead. Suddenly it seemed too much of a task to even move from the room. Tears spilled over her fingers, splashing along her throat and sliding down along the hollow of her breast, which was cold and empty after the fire of his hand.

She couldn't give that up, and she didn't know how to ask for it again. Looking down, Lindsay saw that her silk blouse was in disarray. Her slacks were rumpled and limp, and she was in her bare feet. Her first reaction was that she had to straighten up. Her second was that she never would have thought that if she'd been in her jeans—if she'd been out in the cabin, alone with Mitchell.

Lindsay lifted her face to the light, listening to the mutter of Mitchell's voice out in the hall. Was he right? Was she another person when she was away from work? Away from people? Had she always been like that, or had it only been since Patrick had died? Since Patrick had started drinking?

Lindsay didn't know. She couldn't pull an answer out of the turmoil in her mind. All she knew was that she suddenly felt lost. She'd lost her boundaries and forfeited her detachment. The things she'd collected to define her were being loaded into a trash hauler, and here she stood alone in the dark, wanting no more than to return to the haven of Mitchell's arms.

"Get your things together."

Lindsay started, dropped her hand. Mitchell swung the door open a little so that he was silhouetted in the light. He looked big. Menacing. Lindsay wanted to flinch away.

"Lindsay, we don't have time," he said, his voice losing its harsh edge. "That was Al. One of his snitches just told him that Esperanza has found us. We have to get going."

Absently, Lindsay nodded. "Good. You can drop me off at the office and head out on your own. I'll give Bob the name of a friend of mine for you."

Suddenly Mitchell had her by the arms. "Lindsay, listen to me. You and I are heading off to another safe house. We're doing it now. Let's get going."

"But why?" she asked, looking up to see that she couldn't find his eyes in the darkness. She didn't know whether he was angry or not. "It's your perfect chance to get rid of me."

"I told you why before," he answered, his hands tight around her, his voice giving no quarter. "Because we have a job to finish."

Lindsay shook her head. "Not with me."

He gave her a little shake. "With you."

"But why?" she asked again, peering close and still not finding him. "After what you said, I thought—"

Mitchell never hesitated. "You make me mad, McDonough. You really do. Sometimes I wonder if there's a brain in your head. But then I remember that no more than four days ago I was trying to remember why I wanted to live. I want the rest of it, and I don't want it from anybody but you. Now move."

Lindsay couldn't quite go yet. His eyes. She'd just caught them, and realized that the anger there had died. Why did that change things? Why did she feel better—and worse—at the same time?

Taking his hands away from her arms, Mitchell smiled down at her. Lifting a qualifying finger, he reached across and very gently rebuttoned her blouse, never taking his eyes from her.

"My turn to offer apologies," he said simply. "You were right. It's just ... well, I hate to say this, McDonough, but I'm afraid you feel awfully good in my arms."

Lindsay couldn't help but nod. "I know. It stinks, doesn't it?"

Mitchell just laughed. "Yeah. It does. Now, let's go before the bad guys get here."

This time she moved.

Chapter 11

Sometimes the government could be very efficient, and it was that night. On the tail of Al's phone call, Brent arrived with a couple of reinforcements to move Mitchell and Lindsay to a new location. Lindsay still felt frayed, not having had the time to assimilate one crisis before having to deal with another. It helped that Mitchell kept a steadying hand on her back. It didn't help that Brent kept an eyebrow raised at Mitchell's solicitude. Word must have already gotten around. Lindsay was unspeakably thrilled.

"What garden spot are we being dropped into this time?" she asked, stifling a yawn and the impulse to curl up against Mitchell in the back seat of the unmarked car and go to sleep.

"Out in the 'burbs," Brent informed her over his shoulder. The other front seat was taken up—literally—by Oscar Washington, one of the new agents on the team. Oscar had done his time in the South Bronx before trading up to the federal government. It showed in his menacing air, the wary rotation of his head as he moved. Oscar didn't trust anybody but other cops, and sometimes not even them. Lindsay was still trying to find somebody patient enough to pair with him.

"So why did Bob tap you for baby-sitting duty, Oscar?" Lindsay asked him.

Oscar flashed her a smile that showcased his gold tooth. "Because it's my place. He figured Esperanza hasn't heard of me yet."

"Hope you stocked something in there besides gin," Mitchell groused.

Oscar didn't lose his smile. "Ice."

"Thanks."

The drive to Oscar's condo took an hour. By the time everybody was convinced that they were clear of problems, Lindsay was having real trouble keeping her eyes open. By the time she walked in the front door, she couldn't think of anything but bed.

To say that Oscar's taste differed from her own would have been a severe understatement. The condo complex was a carbon copy of any number of newer buildings—white cubes collected into rows with a pool out back and a sauna for the swingers. Oscar had evidently decided that all he needed in his apartment was electronics and a water bed.

"There's only one bedroom," Lindsay observed dryly, wondering if she would get seasick in the thing.

"All the better to protect you," Oscar said, and leered.

Mitchell quelled the agent's enthusiasm with one glance. Lindsay chose to just ignore it altogether.

"Thanks, everybody. Now, if you'll all head out, I'll get some sleep."

"No, you won't," Mitchell disagreed. "Oscar, does this thing have a basement?"

"Sure."

"Mind if we mess up your walls a little? I need to teach her how to use a gun."

"Shoot, no, man. Go ahead. I got some straw down there to work off tension. Know what I mean?"

Mitchell grinned at him. "Sure do." He had spent time in the South Bronx with cops just like Oscar. Every one of them had decorated their basements in bullet holes. There was a lot of tension in the South Bronx.

Lindsay swung her head back and forth between the two. "We're going to shoot up Oscar's house? Are you kidding?"

Mitchell just shrugged. "Better than shooting birds. The neighbors might complain."

Lindsay rolled her eyes. Oscar grinned and followed Brent toward the front door. At the last minute, Brent turned to Mitchell and motioned him to follow.

"There's one more thing, Mitchell."

Mitchell just shook his head. "Let me know here."

Brent flashed a significant look at Lindsay as he edged the door closed. Mitchell shook his head again.

"She might as well know."

Now both Brent and Lindsay were staring at Mitchell. This was the first time in the history of the task force that Mitchell had shared information with Lindsay without having his arm twisted behind his back. The "Need to Know" policy had followed him from the service. That, coupled with his natural distrust of those he called civilians, always added up to cooperation only under coercion.

"Don't look like you swallowed a goldfish, McDonough," he snapped. "Whether you realize it yet or not, you're every bit as much on the run as I am. Something happens to me, you're gonna need to know what you're up against. Now shut your mouth and listen, for a change."

She scowled. "Thanks, Dad. Your confidence is overwhelming."

Brent grinned. "Al must have been wrong."

Both Mitchell and Lindsay turned on him. "He was."

"And here I thought I was seeing the makings of a new team."

"Sellers," Mitchell warned. "Did you have something to tell me or not?"

"It's that guy we were watching out for. Artie Manion."

Mitchell's interest returned. "Yeah?"

"We found him. Or rather, what was left of him. He and Perez must have had the same friends."

"Wonderful."

"The worst part is we can definitely place him at the Esperanza camp. If we had caught him alive, we might all have been able to go home and get some sleep."

"Thanks, Brent."

Brent nodded and opened the door. "Okay, Mitch. Watch your back, okay?"

"Watch yours. You're the one with Quick-Draw McGraw out there."

"So," Lindsay asked as Mitchell shut the door. "Is that good news or bad?"

Pulling a hand through his hair, Mitchell sighed. "Both."

"Are you sure about this?" Lindsay asked as she and Mitchell reached the basement, to find it empty except for a couple of bales of hay and a mattress. The rough outline of a human was sketched in magic marker across the mattress. Two clusters of holes marked his vital areas. No wonder Oscar had a water bed, Lindsay thought dryly. That way he couldn't set it up for target practice.

Mitchell clicked the gun's silencer home and handed over the weapon. The Walther PPK fitted too neatly into Lindsay's hand. "Brent left me an extra weapon. You're going to have it on you at all times from right now. You might as well know what to do with it. Besides, you were the one who asked."

"I know," Lindsay nodded a bit dispiritedly, looking down at the gun in her hand. "I did, didn't I?"

Mitchell put his hands on her shoulders and turned her to her target.

"I still can't believe he keeps this down here," Lindsay said with an uncertain shake of her head. "It's kind of like having dead bodies in the basement."

"I'll take you to Oscar's home turf someday," Mitchell suggested, bringing both hands around to cup hers. "This will all make more sense."

Lindsay tried her best to keep focused on the target across the basement. Unfortunately, Mitchell had folded his body around hers to help her steady her aim. His arms bracketed hers and his breath was fanning her ear. And no matter what her brain told her about the inadvisability of being attracted to him, her body had already made up its mind.

"Do you have to stand quite so close?" she protested, doing her best to keep her respiratory rate under control. "I can't shoot with sweat running in my eyes."

"I'll back up as soon as I know you've got the idea," he promised, his voice too soft. His legs fitted so neatly against hers, his hips firm against the small of her back.

"Both hands," he instructed.

"You or me?" Lindsay asked.

Mitchell chuckled, and Lindsay could feel it through her back. "Both of us. You when I let go. The right hand's for firing, the left to steady your aim. Okay?"

Lindsay nodded, and her head hit his chin. She had her arms outstretched, the target across the room pinned by the silencer.

"Okay. Wrap your left hand around your right and pull back a little. That does the steadying. Now squeeze the trigger."

Lindsay pulled. The gun backed in her hand and she bumped back against Mitchell. There was a pinging sound and plaster sprayed off the wall.

"Sorry."

"It's okay." He resumed his position. "You're pulling. Squeeze. Steady pressure."

"Are you sure about this?" she repeated. "At the rate I'm going, Oscar's going to need a plasterer in here."

"He won't mind. Now squeeze."

She did. The bullet thunked into the mattress, just to the left of the outline.

"Better. Again."

She did it again. And again. The holes marched closer and closer to the top bunch Oscar had made, and Mitchell continued to murmur praise and support in Lindsay's ear. After awhile she forgot to ask him to back up. It seemed the most natural thing in the world to have him there to support her. Then her third clip ran out and Mitchell stepped away.

Lindsay turned to him. She stopped just short of asking him to come back. The basement seemed colder, the gun heavier. He was digging into his pocket for the last clip he'd brought down, his eyes on the progress she'd made.

"Okay, McDonough," he said, facing her with clip in hand. "Load up. This next round, I want it emptied."

Lindsay barely had the clip slid home when Mitchell jumped at her. She started.

"He's over there, McDonough!" he shouted in her face. "He's got a gun. Fire!"

Lindsay turned and fired. Fired the clip dry as Mitchell yelled into her ear. When the gun clicked empty, she lowered it. Then she looked for her latest path of holes.

"I'll be damned," Mitchell breathed, walking over to examine the evidence. He reached out a finger to the lower cluster and turned back to Lindsay with a surprised smile on his face. "Good student, McDonough. You killed him seven times."

Lindsay scowled, waiting for the adrenaline to dissipate, for her hands to stop shaking. "I'm thrilled, Mitchell. It's a goal every psychologist strives for."

"It should be if the psychologist has bad guys on her tail," he informed her.

Walking up, he took the gun from her hands and began to disassemble it. Lindsay could only watch, wondering at the economy of his movements—the familiarity of the task. He didn't even have his eyes on what he was doing.

"I'll clean it and make sure it's ready," he told her. "You make sure you fire it if you need to. Deal?"

Lindsay shrugged. "I guess."

Mitchell trapped her with his gaze. There was a purpose there Lindsay recognized. "No messing around, McDonough. I mean it."

Looking at him, Lindsay understood. They didn't have time for games. This wasn't hypothetical maneuvers at the office. This was the big time. If Lindsay didn't believe that, she would be dead. Lindsay believed it. She nodded and offered Mitchell a rueful grin.

"That split-second decision making must be part of the high," she offered.

Mitchell looked up from the gun and shrugged. "It only takes one mistake."

Mitchell smiled for her then, and she saw the doors of resistance open a little more. His expression reminded her of what they shared, how they would be able to depend on each other. It was the smile of a partner, and Lindsay accepted it gratefully.

"Time for refreshments," Mitchell decided, tossing the gun back to her and turning for the stairs.

Lindsay caught it and followed, wondering exactly what she did with the thing until she needed it. Her purse? A pocket, maybe? It would be a little conspicuous, and Lindsay didn't exactly want the shoulder-holster look this season.

"What refreshments?" she demanded. "All Oscar said he had was gin and ice."

"Sounds good to me."

She just scowled and prayed for coffee.

Twenty minutes later she would have settled for the gin. The icebox held a carton of sour milk and seven old oranges.

"Oscar did say he was a health nut." Mitchell grinned.

"There's some dry cereal up here," Lindsay offered from her place in front of the empty cabinets.

"Thank God we had dinner."

"But what do we do for breakfast?"

"We make Oscar take us out." Shutting the door, Mitchell lifted an arm to check his watch. "Okay, so refreshment period is over. It's just about midnight, and I'm getting tired."

"Getting?" Lindsay echoed with disbelief. "I'm exhausted, and I haven't been playing hide-and-seek with Esperanza's men all day."

Mitchell flashed her a grin. "I slept in the back of the car while Al drove. It was better than watching all the other people on the road screaming at him. Okay, McDonough, I guess the question is where we conduct the next session of remember and tell. Do water beds work for you?"

Lindsay was already shaking her head. "Mitchell, I still don't like this. I mean, I can't call out to check any of my theories with anybody. How do I know I won't make it worse?"

Mitchell shrugged. "You don't. But I'm the one who should worry about that, not you. And I'm not worried. I need to tap into that dream now, before things heat up again."

"Why?" she asked. "Do you think you'll learn something else?"

"I'll sure as hell find out if I won't, won't I? I'd like to know if there's anything else to expect out there—any hint of where Maggie left that stuff." Stepping up to her, Mitchell took Lindsay by the hand. "Come on, McDonough. Don't back out on me now. I don't know how much longer I'm gonna have the guts to go through with this."

He meant it. Lindsay saw the unwelcome hesitation in his eyes, the return of dread. She'd forced Mitchell into this. If she waited too long to do it, she might never get him back. He was right. It was now or never.

Shaking her head a little, she sighed, her gaze on the hand that was wrapped around hers. "Water bed, I guess. It's better than the floor."

Mitchell guided her toward the bedroom. "Depends on what you have in mind."

"I told you before," Lindsay protested, pulling away. "We're doing this on a hands-off policy, or you find another shrink. I'm having enough trouble dealing with it, as it is."

Mitchell lifted his hands in the air. "My thoughts exactly. Let's go."

At first Lindsay couldn't get used to the way Mitchell bobbed around on the bed. She sat alongside on the floor, thinking he looked like a tanker in a canal lock.

"I'm getting seasick," she complained.

"You should be up here with me."

"No, thanks. I guess Oscar doesn't believe in baffles."

"He says he likes the feeling that he's bobbing around on the ocean on a raft."

Lindsay leaned back against the wall and stretched out her legs before her. She was far enough away not to bother Mitchell, close enough to help.

"We're going to do this about the same way," she said. "Except that we're going to run the memory through your head like a movie. Like you're watching somebody else. Okay?"

Mitchell shrugged, the water already lulling him. "If you say so."

It didn't take as long this time. Within moments Mitchell was still and loose, the sensation of water surrounding him, buoying him. He was warm, his body too heavy to move. He could hear Lindsay's voice like a song, murmuring low, weaving in and out of the city sounds outside. His mind was clear as the sky after a summer storm.

"Picture the man—yourself—in your head," Lindsay was saying. "He's standing down at the bottom of the building, looking up. Do you see him?"

Mitchell looked at the figure in his mind. The wind whipped at his hair, and his hands were clenched. The man was afraid, but Mitchell didn't feel it.

"Yes."

"Take him up the elevator. Tell me about it. Tell me what happens in the movie."

He heard the creak of the cage, the rasp and clank as it slid home. He heard the thunder rumbling through the city and the mountains at its edge. The man hated the building.

For some reason, Mitchell saw that the building seemed to hate the man, as well. There was a menace in its size.

"The man is climbing onto the elevator," he said. "The elevator lifts. It's not smooth, and he doesn't like it. The car jerks like it's going to come loose from its moorings."

"It's gone up five floors," Lindsay said. "Fifteen...twenty. The top floor is just above the man. What does he see now?"

"The man turns. There are people there, underneath the light bulb. He can see them. They're fighting, two of them. The other two watch. No, they're yelling, too."

"Yelling what?"

"Maggie...it's Maggie they're yelling at."

"Yelling what?"

"Puta! Dónde está? Conoce su tienes. Dónde está?"

"What does she say?"

Mitchell couldn't understand it. The man didn't move. He saw Maggie there, knew she was in trouble. Mitchell was afraid for him, furious at him.

"Move, damn it! She doesn't have time!"

"What does Maggie say, Mitchell?"

"She says...she says...She's turning now." Lightning seared the edges of the building. He could see her eyes. They were stark, too bright, desperate. "No," he whispered, Maggie's eyes unaccountably frightening him.

"What, Mitchell? What do you see? What does she say to the man?"

"She's not looking at him. She's looking at me. She's talking to me."

"No. Mitchell, no, this is a movie, remember? You're sitting in the fifteenth row. You have popcorn in your hand and you're watching Maggie talk to the man. Look, Mitchell. Can you see it?"

"But she won't look at the man. She'll only look at me. And she's afraid, and the man isn't moving to help her." Mitchell struggled to breathe as the wind suddenly found him. "Maggie!"

"Miguel has her. God, he's going to throw her! Stop it!"

"The man is moving, Mitchell. See him? See?"

He tried to shake his head. The man won't be fast enough. He has his gun out, has it up. The other men turn to him, crouched. He doesn't see them. He sees Maggie. He's screaming at her.

"Maggie!"

"What is she saying? What is she trying to tell him?"

"Get out of here! Get back to your damn cabin, Mitchell. Get out!"

He's sobbing up there on that building with the man, screaming as the man begins to fire, stumbles to his knees with the sudden pain and fires again. The men fall around him like pins. The wind lifts the lid of the suitcase and lightning reveals the empty edge of the building. He and the man scream and scream, too late to help, too late to save Maggie.

"Mitchell! Mitchell!" Lindsay had him by the arms. Mitchell fought against her, flailing blindly, horror in his eyes, the residue of the dream ripping away his control. With it came the venom, the self-loathing, the failure that had been eating at him. It spewed out at Lindsay like hot lava, coursing down Mitchell's cheeks and welling up from his heart. Lindsay didn't feel the tears on her own cheeks, just as hot as Mitchell's, or the thudding in her chest.

"Mitchell, it's over," she soothed, pulling him close, finally beating back the images. "You've remembered. It's all over."

His arms came around her and he held on as if he would fall. Lindsay brought his head to her shoulder. She felt him shudder, his eyes shut against the pictures he'd resurrected, his breathing harsh with the cost of remembering.

"Shh, it's all right," she murmured, her own chest squeezed shut and bleeding. "You've done it. You've won."

His hold on her didn't ease. It was a grasp fueled by desperation. His lungs still struggled for air. Lindsay ached, longing to ease his pain. She held on to him, offering the silent support he could accept.

"Won what?" he finally gasped. "She was right. I should have gone back to my cabin for all the good I did her."

Lindsay backed away, wanting to face him. He turned from her.

"No," she argued. "You're wrong."

That brought him back around. "Am I?" Bitterness spilled into his expression. "What did you think she was going to say when she saw the one man arrive she knew wouldn't do her any good? When she knew, just by looking at me, that she was going to die?"

"She was your friend," Lindsay argued, holding on even as Mitchell stiffened to get away from her. "She went up there alone. She didn't even expect to see you. Why would she condemn you for trying to come to her aid?"

"Because she knew it wouldn't help."

"Mitchell, you're wrong."

He wasn't having any of it. Pulling away, he swung off the bed and got to his feet. Lindsay followed, afraid that all the good they had done would be undone. He had to understand. He had to believe, whether it was true or not, that Maggie hadn't gone to her death blaming him.

"What happened up there wasn't your fault," Lindsay insisted, following on his heels. "Maggie knew that."

"Maggie knew that I let her down," he retorted. For a moment he stood where he was, his head down. Then, dragging in a great breath, as if he couldn't bear the weight of his words, he slammed his hand against the wall. "Great way to die, don't you think, Doc?"

Lindsay saw the buckled wallboard and thought of the condition of Mitchell's porch. When she turned back to him, there was new purpose in her voice. "Think about it, Mitchell. Think about all the time you knew Maggie. All the cases you shared, the undercover work you did, stakeouts when it was just the two of you, and you had nothing better to do than talk. Did she ever say anything that would make you think she thought less of you for your acrophobia?"

He didn't answer.

"Well, did she?"

"That doesn't—"

"It does! She would never hurt you. Never! Not Mag. She didn't blame you, and neither does anybody else but you."

Suddenly Mitchell whipped around on her, his eyes fierce, his body so taut Lindsay thought he'd shatter. "Prove it!"

"How?" she demanded, fighting to stand her ground before the fury in his voice.

"You're the doctor. You think of something."

Lindsay straightened as much as she could and met his glare without flinching. "I wouldn't have been here all along if I blamed you. I wouldn't have put up with you for a minute."

She enunciated her words carefully, precisely, so that nothing could be misconstrued. Her heart hammered in her ears. She was buffeted by his torment, the indecision radiating from him like the heat from an arsonist's fire.

"If I thought you'd failed Maggie," she said, "I couldn't respect you. And if I didn't respect you, no matter what had happened, I wouldn't have made love with you."

Mitchell rocked on his heels, the conflicting emotions tearing at him. There was a rock in his chest, a heavy, intolerable burden that had Maggie's name on it. There was a sea at his fingertips, a calming, soothing sweetness that seemed too far away to reach. He wanted to believe her. Wanted to think that he hadn't blocked out Maggie's words because he'd known they were true—because she'd accused him.

"Lindsay..." He dragged in a breath, unable to think. Unsure how to ask. "I need ... I need you."

Tears filled Lindsay's eyes. As deliberately as she had argued, she lifted her arms to him.

Mitchell wrapped himself in her, buried his head in the veil of her hair. He drank her fragrance like water, tasted the tenderness of her skin like his first food. He filled his arms with her life and succumbed to her sweetness.

"Gently," she murmured at his ear. "Gently. I'm here."

Mitchell raised her face. He tasted the tears she'd spent for him and closed her eyes with his kiss. She brought her hand to his throat, claiming him, calming him. Mitchell tested the velvet of her cheek and then sought the dark pleasure of her mouth.

She opened to him, inviting him in, greeting him and slowing his impatient flight. Here, rest here, she was saying, and Mitchell sought to rest. He lifted her in his arms and carried her back to the bed, where the water rocked beneath them. She nestled beneath him, her hair a soft cloud on the sheet, her eyes soft and sure. Mitchell bent to reclaim her mouth, skimming its swollen edges and then dipping inside, testing, taunting, drawing her to him with his pleasure. He swept back her hair, delighting in its touch, and outlined the shell of her ear, her throat, the soft curve of her shoulder. He followed the flight of his fingers with his tongue, tasting the salt of her skin and the warm throb of her heart. He moved past the buttons he undid, past the silk of her blouse, as it fell away to reveal the mysteries of Lindsay McDonough.

Her bra was creamy lace and silk, a surprise beneath her tailored clothes. The material molded her breasts, lifting them to him, holding them from him. Mitchell traced the edges with his tongue, savoring the slick material as much as Lindsay's gasp of surprise. Her breasts answered his invitation, tautening beneath his touch. Mitchell stroked and squeezed, getting the feel of them in his palm, immersing himself in their softness.

God, he ached for her. His chest was on fire, his legs, his gut. He couldn't breathe, and she was running her hands along his arms, stoking the fire. Mitchell filled his eyes with her, her creamy skin, the delicious valley between her breasts, the soft swell at her belly, the line of her hips. She reached down and unzipped her skirt, sliding the material down and away, leaving behind garter belt and stockings. More lace. A scrap of silk across her hips. Mitchell moaned at the sight, surprised again, shaken by the sensuality that lay hidden beneath Lindsay's proper facade.

"You're so beautiful," he breathed in awe.

"You sound surprised." She chuckled, her voice husky and warm.

Mitchell had to smile, as he turned to feast on the light in her eyes. "I am."

She answered by reaching up to pull him back to her.

Lindsay's body sang beneath him, begged for him. Just the fire in his eyes fed the flames in her until they licked the edges of her, racing before his touch and inviting him on. The light in his eyes, fueled by need and desire, set her ablaze.

Mitchell bent to her, sealing his words with a kiss that took her breath. Then he turned his attention once again to the mysteries he sought to expose. He brushed her blouse away, down over her arms so that she greeted him in nothing but silk and lace. She did the same for him, stripping him until she discovered the evidence of his need, the power of his passion. Lindsay lay before Mitchell waiting, watching him as he lifted a hand to touch her.

Lightning. Sharp and sudden, flaring from his fingertips where they brushed her nipple. Lindsay moaned with it, lifted to it. Mitchell overwhelmed her. She lifted her hands to him and Mitchell turned his eyes once more to her and then, bending, returned to kiss her.

His tongue slipped over the silk at her breast. His teeth grazed the sensitive skin, sparking fresh aches in her like tiny shivers. Letting his other hand stroke her belly, he tormented her, his touch skittering over her, his tongue circling her nipple until she gasped with the urgency.

"Oh, Lindsay," he whispered against her. "I could lose myself in you."

Lindsay couldn't pull her whirling mind back to answer. She clung to him, his skin rippling beneath her fingers, his hair-roughened skin delicious to her touch. She wanted to beg him to rid her of her clothes, to take away the barrier. Before she could manage to say the words, he complied. Reaching up, he unclasped her bra. The cool air brushed her wet skin, igniting new fires. Mitchell returned to take her fully to him. He was so warm, so nourishing. She wound her hands in his hair and held him against her. She had never known such turmoil, such torment. But then Mitchell undid her stockings, rolling them away, unclasped her garter belt and swept a hand beneath her panties. Lindsay arched against him, wanting him there, waiting for him.

Mitchell slipped away the last of the silk. He couldn't bear to be apart from her any longer. He couldn't control a need that went beyond words or understanding. Easing his hand along her thigh, he sought her acceptance. Edged toward the darkest silk, the flower that opened for him. He heard her sharp little groan when he met her, slick and swollen beneath his fingers. He felt the thundering of her pulse as he stroked her, as he feasted on her breast. She cried out, her hips lifting in rhythm. Shudders built in her. Mitchell found her gaze again, drinking in the glazed pleasure in her tawny eyes, feeding off her joy, the delicious smile of her surprise on her kiss-swollen lips.

"Lindsay," he begged, trembling for control.

She merely held out her arms to him. Mitchell felt a sigh escape him, felt Lindsay's pleasure build in him and echo through his own bloodstream. He entered that dark garden, deeper, deeper as she wrapped herself around him and welcomed him home. He claimed her mouth again and when he felt Lindsay shudder around him, her nails clawing at his back, he followed her. He buried his head in the sweet comfort of her shoulder, drowning in the smell of her, the sight and sound and sensation of her. He spilled himself into her and fell exhausted into her arms.

The night settled upon them, frail starlight washing the walls and drawing shadows along their still forms. The breeze returned, and Lindsay could once more hear the traffic from the interstate. Her heart started easing back to normal and the sheen of perspiration on her forehead began to cool. Mitchell pulled her to him, fitting her against his shoulder and fingering her hair as he studied the pattern of the ceiling. Lindsay couldn't remember feeling such peace before. She just wished it weren't so transient.

"Why did you wear jeans up to the cabin?" Mitchell asked.

Lindsay turned to get a look at his face. "Why don't you smoke a cigarette like everyone else?"

He just grinned. "I can't figure you, McDonough. You wear a uniform like a nun, but your lingerie is straight off the Moulin Rouge. You act differently according to whatever you're wearing. You never give an inch in the office, but since you showed up at the cabin, you've redefined the meaning of patience and compassion."

"I've always been patient and compassionate."

"Have you always worn a garter belt underneath those androgynous suits of yours?"

Lindsay enjoyed a grin of her own. "That's for me to know and you to fantasize about."

"And every other member of the task force, once they find out."

That brought Lindsay up to her elbow. "I'm warning you, Mitchell. . . ."

Mitchell wouldn't face her. "I bet Al would lose the rest of his hair just thinking about it."

She gave him a good thump on the chest. "Hey! You stopped being funny."

Mitchell turned determined eyes on her. "Then tell me."

"Why?"

"Because it has to make some sense."

She just smiled again. "No, it doesn't. Why are you acrophobic, do you know?"

"No."

She shrugged. "There you are. I don't know why I wear the garter belt. I just like it. Maybe it's the rebel seeking to be free. Maybe it's just my little joke on the world. Who knows?"

He shook his head, his attention back on the ceiling. "I'm never going to be able to walk past you without checking under your skirt again."

"Mitchell."

He turned back to her, mischief replacing the seriousness in his face. "Yes."

"Are you feeling better?"

Now he smiled, and Lindsay saw that it was real. "Define better."

She nodded. "Good. Do you believe me?"

"About the garter belt? I'm not sure."

"About Maggie."

He lost some of his smile. "That's to be decided, I guess. I'll try. I'm glad you didn't send me to a different psychologist."

"The one I was thinking of would never let you get away with this."

"She a prude?"

"*He* believes in going by the book. And this, my dear Mitchell, is not in any book I'm aware of."

He drew her a little closer. "It should be." There was a new softness in her eyes, a completion Mitchell hadn't seen before. It made him wonder even more about her.

"What about Patrick?"

Lindsay might just as well have pulled away. "What about him?"

"Did he know about the garter belts?"

"If it were any of your business," she warned stonily, "I'd tell you."

Bingo, he thought, his gaze on the fist she'd just made against his chest. The gentleness had died in her, frozen so fast he almost wondered if he'd ever seen it. She lay against him like a mannequin, suddenly stiff and unyielding. *I should have recognized it before. Distance provides protection, and that's what Lindsay spent the last four years getting. Step too near the boundaries, and she peers at you over those glasses.*

"It must have gotten really rough," he mused, lifting a hand to stroke her hair.

Still she didn't relax. Nor did she answer.

He tried again, his hand brushing over her back and up again, seeking out the tension and trying to ease it. "You're right about the cabin, you know. When I was growing up, there were times when I just wished I lived all by myself, where nobody would yell at me, tell me what an idiot I was or throw things when they got mad, which was just about every evening. I thought if I were by myself, I could feel good about myself.''

He could see his words impact, her eyes close, her fist tighten. He knew her now; recognized the wounds, understood the barriers.

"Do you?" she asked in a very soft voice.

Mitchell thought about it for a moment. "I don't know. I think the cabin worked for a while. I got my peace, my distance. But it's not enough.''

He heard her catch her breath. It sounded almost like a sob, and it made him ache. "No," she answered. "It isn't, is it?"

"I'll tell you what, McDonough," he suggested with a soft kiss on her forehead. "Let's you and I get a little sleep and deal with the world again in the morning.''

"A sound idea," she agreed with a little more enthusiasm.

Mitchell pulled her closer, drawing on her warmth and easing himself to sleep with the murmur of her breathing. After this was all over, he thought, he would take the time to get to know her better. To see whether she would give him the chance to dip beneath her facade again. Was she a bloom that had been damaged by Patrick's frost, or had that bloom withered? Mitchell found himself wanting to know, and somehow as he fell asleep, finding out seemed to be part of the natural progress of things. He was pleased with his decision.

Mitchell slept the night away, nestled against the familiar warmth of Lindsay, a hand always over or around her, his leg thrown over hers.

Lindsay lay awake a long time after Mitchell fell asleep, just listening to him, counting the cadence of his breathing and praying it wouldn't be broken. Waiting in dread for the dream and then rejoicing when it didn't come. And then she, too, slept, the water lulling her, Mitchell's weight comforting her, the memory of what had happened as sweet as it was sad.

It couldn't happen again, and Lindsay knew it. Mitchell's invasion into her past had sealed that, resurrecting the acrimony she never wanted to face again. She would have to leave him and go on alone. She knew, though, that she would from now on measure all other men against Jason Mitchell. And that saddened her. Because however much they didn't get along, however clearly she knew they could never find anything together, she had never known a better man.

Chapter 12

The cabin!"

Lindsay's eyes shot open. She was lying in a lake, she thought, all blue and white, and the waves washed steadily around her. Her heart was tripping a mile a minute, and something heavy had just bumped against her. She turned her head to find out what it was.

Mitchell.

Suddenly she remembered and drew the covers a little higher. The sun poured through the window, lighting Mitchell as he jumped out of bed. Lindsay bobbed and swayed in the aftermath, trying to understand his excitement. He was grabbing his pants. She couldn't help but smile, perfectly happy to just watch the sleek grace of his body as he caromed around the room.

"Wake up, McDonough!" he insisted, grabbing her toes and wiggling them. "I have it!"

"You sure do," she said agreeably and yawned. Lindsay knew she shouldn't feel so content with herself in her present condition, but her body refused to cooperate. "And I am awake."

He pounced on her, hopping into a pant leg and pulling his shirt off the floor. "Then get up. We don't have much time to waste."

"For what?"

"I told you. The cabin. It's what Maggie was trying to tell me. Not that I shouldn't have left the cabin. That I should go back. She left her information there!"

He had succeeded in getting Lindsay's attention. She sat straight up in the bed, the sheet falling to her waist, her hair tumbling over her shoulders, her eyes alight. One leg away from being clothed, Mitchell caught sight of her and almost ended up on his nose.

"God, get something on," he commanded, turning away. "You're distracting as hell."

"I'm going to have to start with the garter belt," she teased, foolishly pleased by his remark.

"Pants, McDonough. Slacks and a shirt. We're not at the office today."

Lindsay slid out from under the sheet and headed for her suitcase. Since it was out in the living room, she had to pass Mitchell on the way. He suffered another setback.

"McDonough, I'm warning you."

Lindsay had to admit she derived a certain pleasure at seeing him at such a loss—Mitchell, the man who never made a wrong move. Even so, she scooted past him at a fair clip and didn't return until she was completely dressed.

"You're doing it again," Mitchell accused from where he stood by the front door, loading his gun.

Lindsay looked down at her attire in surprise. Slacks and shirt, just like he'd said. Just because the slacks were pleated khaki linen and the shirt pink silk shouldn't have made any difference. Even so, Mitchell was shaking his head as if she'd walked in wearing a bathing suit.

"We'll pick up your jeans at the cabin," he decided. "And your tennis shoes. You make me nervous when you're dressed like this."

"How can I make you nervous?" Lindsay demanded.

He ignored her. Giving the gun one last check, he slid it into his shoulder holster. "Do you have your weapon?"

Lindsay scowled. "I stuck it into my bra. Anything else?"

"I mean it, Lindsay. You're not leaving without that gun."

"Lighten up, Mitchell. I'm a big girl. When Al gets here, I'll be all ready to face the bad guys."

Mitchell took a look past the curtain at the living-room window. "We're not waiting for Al."

Lindsay swung on him. "We're what?"

He faced her, his words deliberate. "If I let Al know, he'll let Bob know, and Bob will refuse to let me up there. He'll send the locals, or maybe the National Guard. This one's mine, Lindsay. I'm not sacrificing it to the second string."

"Isn't that what they call grandstanding?" Lindsay demanded dryly, suddenly nervous. This Mitchell was almost whole, almost at full strength. He still had a score to settle, though, and it made him dangerous. She wasn't sure she shouldn't just get on the phone herself.

"And don't think of making that call yourself," Mitchell warned as if he'd just read her mind. "Help me out on this one, McDonough. I have to finish it."

"I know that, Mitchell." She wanted to reach out to him again. She kept her hands at her side. "But don't you think we can at least call in backup on this? Estes Park's a long way from here for Bob to help us if we need him all of a sudden."

"What do you want me to do, call him on the way up?"

"I want you to call him now."

Mitchell shook his head. "We're wasting time, McDonough. Make up your mind."

"Why me?" she asked.

Mitchell's grin was crooked. "I can't do *everything* alone."

Lindsay couldn't help an answering smile. "Wouldn't know that, to hear you talk."

"It'll be our little secret."

"Call him on the way up."

Mitchell made an X across his chest with a forefinger. "Cross my heart. Now let's get going."

"In what?" Lindsay asked.

Mitchell shot her a conspiratorial look. "Oscar keeps a Mustang in his garage. Hasn't driven it since New York."

Lindsay just shook her head. "The University of Chicago is going to look awfully good after all this."

It was a beautiful summer day. Clear, cloudless, with the sky arcing crisply over the mountains. If it hadn't been for the fact that she carried a handgun in her purse and was on her way to the scene where she had almost been shot, Lindsay might have enjoyed the outing.

Mitchell whistled as he drove, a low, atonal sound that grated on Lindsay's nerves. She tried her best to keep her attention on the fresh air that poured in through her open window. It didn't work. She felt worse with each mile, and it had nothing to do with what they were facing. It had to do with what she had realized the night before. She had enjoyed herself much too much this morning to feel good about what she had to tell him.

"Mitchell," she finally spoke up, her gaze on her hands and the unfamiliar weight on her lap that reminded her just how extraordinary her situation was right now. "Before we go any farther, I need to say something."

He shot her a quick look and returned his attention to the road. "What's that?"

"Last night. It can't happen again."

He didn't smile, but he didn't frown, either. "Seems to me I've heard that before, McDonough."

Lindsay stiffened. "Thanks for the consideration, Mitchell. I can tell you understand how difficult this is for me."

"Difficult or not, why bring it up now?"

"Because I should have last night. And this morning before we left. We've been through a lot together, and it blurred the edges of convention. And I . . . I let it. I'm not sorry about what happened. But I have to go back to my

own life when this is all over, and I can't unless I know the
boundaries will be redrawn."

"Between you and me."

She gave a stiff nod. "Exactly."

"Why?"

"That's a stupid question, coming from you," she retorted, still unable to face him. "You're the one who's been
trying to get me fired since the day I walked in. You've accused me of everything from frigidity to psychosis. I don't
enjoy an adversarial relationship, Mitchell. I especially don't
enjoy it if I have to worry about sneak attacks."

"All right," he acquiesced. "You have me. You're not
frigid."

"You're not listening."

He smiled a bit wistfully, his eyes still on the road. "I
don't want to."

"Why?"

"I told you. You feel too damn good in my arms."

Again Lindsay found herself shaking her head. "Not
good enough, Mitchell."

"You told me you feel the same."

"Cocaine might make me feel good for a while, too," she
countered impatiently. "It's not enough of a reason for me
to invest in it."

Taking a moment to ingest what she had said, Mitchell
turned to level an accusing glance at her. "Come tell me that
again when you're in that house of yours, and you're the
only one around to roll down those stockings."

Lindsay looked, really looked into his eyes, searching for
something more than irritation. She didn't find it. She
wasn't exactly sure why Mitchell had chosen to pick this
fight, but she was more certain that it wasn't for the reason
she'd half hoped for.

Knowing she wouldn't hear the only thing that would
have made her change her mind, Lindsay turned back to the
scenery. Tears stung her throat and her chest felt hollow, as
if something that had taken root there had just died.

She knew it was the best thing that could happen. It cleared her way to leave, once this was all finished. She certainly couldn't stick around, with Mitchell always there to remind her of what she'd wanted and what he hadn't been able to give. Even so, she felt as if she'd just faced death a second time in her life.

The glade behind the house sang in the afternoon. Sunlight tipped the grass and warmed the honeysuckle-laden air. The cabin sat silent in the shade, Lindsay's car still where they had left it. Mitchell killed the engine and Lindsay got out, stretching her legs and inhaling the mountain fragrances—pine and wood smoke and the close aroma of earth. And even as she absorbed a landscape that didn't include asphalt and streetlights, she kept a hand on her purse, inches from the gun Mitchell insisted she carry.

It didn't look as though they would be bothered. Lindsay didn't see anything more in the vicinity than a marmot. When he scuttled across the field, she found herself wanting to follow. Instead she trailed Mitchell into the cabin.

Mitchell used the front door. Stepping up onto the porch, he found the correct key and bent to the lock. Lindsay kept her eyes on the surrounding woods. She heard the door slide open and saw Mitchell step in. She heard him come to a sudden stop, his steps echoing on hardwood. Lindsay was set to follow when she heard his surprised oath.

Lindsay turned into the house. Mitchell was hugging the doorway in front of her, his gun drawn, his eyes darting back and forth, looking for trouble. He put out a hand to hold her back as he advanced into his own living room.

Mitchell didn't have to worry about Lindsay moving too fast. She had stopped dead at the door.

The living room. All that beautiful, handcrafted furniture. It had been reduced to waste, the splinters piled in a heap in the center of the floor, the few odds and ends demolished, and food and paint splattered across the walls.

"Oh, Mitchell, no!" she protested, unable to take her eyes from the debris.

Mitchell gave all the rooms a cursory check. Lindsay didn't follow into the kitchen. She knew what would be left of the bright gingham room. She'd seen her own.

When he came back out, Mitchell's face was set, his eyes hard. He headed next for his den. Lindsay followed.

The books that had filled the shelves had been reduced to so much shredded paper all over the floor, the desk shattered and the couch eviscerated. Lindsay felt sick at the sight. Mitchell crouched in the middle of the room and picked something out of the debris. When he straightened, Lindsay saw that it was one of the pictures, one of the couples she'd wondered about. Someone had taken a knife to it, so that it hung in tatters in his hand.

"I'm sorry," she said, reaching down to retrieve one of the other photos. It had fared no better. The sight of the mutilation unnerved Lindsay, as if not only their pictures, but the people there had been injured, as well. She wondered what Mitchell felt, looking down at his life like this.

Mitchell's eyes were flat, empty, as he considered the photograph in his hand. "How did they know?" he demanded softly. "How did they beat us here?"

"What do you mean?" Lindsay asked. "They could have done this anytime."

"There are eggs smashed all over that kitchen floor," he disagreed. "I don't smell them. It wouldn't take long in this weather for them to start stinking. They've just been here, McDonough."

"But they couldn't," she insisted. "We only called Bob an hour ago. Nobody else knows."

"Somebody knows," he retorted, throwing the picture back onto the pile on the floor. As he did, he was struck by something. Lindsay saw his head come up, his attention turn to the back of the house. He bolted, his shoes cracking over the paper.

Lindsay followed right behind, knowing he was headed to his workroom, knowing what he'd find. He must have known, too. He didn't make a sound when he flipped the light on.

The fluorescent shuddered to life in what had once been a meticulously kept room. All Lindsay saw now was devastation. The machinery had been destroyed, battered into pieces that littered the floor like dead bodies. The wood collected for new projects was no more than kindling. The sight hit Mitchell like a physical blow. Lindsay saw him flinch and stiffen.

"They were my grandfather's," he was saying, his hand still on the switch, his gun by his side. "He was the best cabinetmaker in Boston."

Lindsay reached out to him. At her touch, Mitchell whirled around. His eyes were unnaturally bright, hard with determination.

"Come on," he ordered, shouldering past her into the kitchen.

Lindsay looked after him, then turned back to see that he hadn't even turned off the light. She did it for him, taking one last look around at the devastation and knowing somehow that nothing she'd lost had been so important. When she closed the door behind her, the workroom was once again dark. "Come on, what?"

Mitchell was back in the den, rooting around.

"Mitchell?" she prodded, stepping gingerly over the debris at the door. "What do we do now?"

Mitchell gave her a quick look before returning to his search. "We look for whatever it is she left us."

Lindsay found herself glancing over her own shoulder. "But they might come back. They might be watching us."

When he looked up this time, Mitchell offered her a slow smile that didn't quite reach his eyes. "Good. Because if they do, I have a debt to pay them, and I'd be more than happy to do it."

He wasn't making Lindsay feel any better. "Let's wait somewhere for Bob to show up. He said he was going to meet us. Let's go to Gabe's."

Mitchell didn't even look up this time. "We stay here."

She heard the steel in his voice and knew it was useless to argue. For the first time since she'd taken hold of it, Lindsay wondered if it wouldn't be a good idea to get her gun out. There were too many unanswered questions, too many coincidences in this mess to make her happy. And Mitchell would be the last to back away from it, which left her squarely in the middle with him. Why had she ever offered to help in the first place?

She took a surreptitious look at him. He was bent over a wall safe somebody had missed, checking the contents, his eyes impatient, his jaw set like steel. His body quivered with fury. The line between the job and his private life had been crossed. He had been violated, the home he'd kept carefully safe away from work vandalized.

The fight between Mitchell and the underworld had always been an impersonal one, fought on a kind of neutral territory. They might have tried to kill him, but that was business. They had never blindly punished him. But all that had changed. They had made it personal, and Mitchell wasn't going to forgive them. He wasn't going to let them get away with it, either.

"Where is it?" he asked, slamming down some folders he was holding. "Where would she have hidden it?"

He was scanning the room, evaluating it and the entire house for hiding places Esperanza's people might have missed.

Lindsay took in the scope of the destruction. "They might have found it."

Mitchell looked up at Lindsay, his eyes a little startled, as if he'd forgotten she was there. Digesting her words, he shook his head. "They wouldn't have done this. It's still around somewhere, whatever it is."

"When was the last time Maggie was here?" Lindsay asked.

Mitchell went back to his scanning. "Uh, I don't know. A while ago, I guess."

"Did she come here much?" Lindsay asked. "I mean, would she have known about any of your hiding places, or said anything about her own?"

He was already shaking his head. "She was only here a couple of times. She knew how I felt about letting the task force up here."

As he spoke, he got back to his feet and headed into the living room. Lindsay followed, but only to find him standing in the center of the floor, slowly looking around him. He'd been right before. The room was starting to smell.

"When you cleaned up," he said, "do you remember seeing anything unusual?"

"Mitchell," Lindsay retorted, thinking of the other mess that had met her that day. "I didn't see anything *usual*."

"You know what I mean," he insisted, turning on her.

"No, I don't. What would you have considered important?"

"I don't know. Notes. A diary, computer printouts. Anything."

Lindsay looked around her, trying to remember, wondering what would have happened to the things she'd saved. "I cleaned up newspapers, magazines, a few articles you'd clipped on woodworking and ecology . . . your bank statement." Stepping over a pile of wood and cushion stuffing, she bent to pick up a scrap of blue—the envelope that had carried the statement. It was empty and torn, like everything in the room.

"Nothing else?"

She tried to come up with something fresh—anything that might mean something. After a few moments, she shook her head.

"It was really pretty clean, aside from the cockroaches in the kitchen and the beer cans in the bedroom."

"I'm not interested in the beer cans." He turned toward the kitchen. Lindsay followed, only to bump into him when he whirled on her. "Clean, you said."

Lindsay backed up. "Yeah, that was my reaction, too," she admitted. "For the time you'd been here, things were pretty tidy . . . except, as I said—"

"That's it!" he cried, eyes suddenly bright. "Lindsay, you're a genius!"

"That's what?" she demanded, suddenly finding herself following him out of the room again. This time he made for the front door. "Mitchell, I know I'm a genius, but just this once, will you tell me why?"

"Because you just gave me the answer, Lindsay, my love," he crowed, throwing open the door and heading into the yard without waiting to see if Lindsay would tag along. "God, I can't believe I didn't think of it sooner."

"Think of *what*?" she persisted, taking a moment to close the door before catching Mitchell at the car. By the time she'd fallen into her seat, he had already thrown the car into gear. They spun out of the driveway in a screech and headed up the road.

"Damn! We almost had it!" One hand to the earplug he sported, the man who had personally hammered the life out of Mitchell's belongings stepped to the edge of the woods to see the Mustang disappear over the hill.

Another man, wider, lower to the ground and younger followed him out. "Mr. Esperanza isn't going to be happy."

"Well, have Davidson follow, see where they're going. We can't waste a lead like this. He's getting too damn close."

The second man lifted a walkie-talkie to his lips and barked an order.

"Should we let this guy's buddy at the task force know that the tip didn't play out?"

"No. We'll get Mitchell this time. Besides, he's on his way up here, anyway. We'll get in touch then."

The man stood watching the empty road, the silent house. He'd enjoyed trashing that one. A real work of art. But he would just as soon trash its owner. It figured that the guy wouldn't say anything when they for once had the house wired. Now they were going to have to follow him, to see where he went to get that damn book. If they didn't, Mr. Esperanza would reward them the same way he'd rewarded Artie Manion. And Paul Colombo was one guy who didn't want to end up in no trash can.

Pulling the plug out of his ear, Colombo motioned for his partner to follow, and headed along to pull out the bugs before going after Mitchell.

Mitchell picked up the other car almost immediately. "Damn!"

Lindsay craned her head around to get a look at what had sparked Mitchell's ire. "Problems?"

"Yeah. The black Pontiac back there. I think he's interested in where we're going."

"He's going to have to get in line," Lindsay announced dryly, trying to hide her nervousness as she turned back to Mitchell. "*I'm* interested in where we're going, and you haven't told me yet."

"To the post office," he answered, his eyes still on the car behind.

Lindsay thought about that for a moment. "The post office." Suddenly her eyes widened in comprehension. "Your mail. There wasn't any when I got there. That's why everything was so neat."

Mitchell nodded with a dry grin. "I had Ernie, at the post office, hold my mail for me while I was in Denver. I never asked him to stop. Maggie wasn't up at the cabin once we started the Esperanza thing. If she wanted to drop something at the cabin, she would have had to mail it."

Lindsay was shaking her head, smiling. "So while Esperanza's men are trashing your house, certain that she left the incriminating evidence there, it's safe in a little mailbox."

"Exactly."

"Which is where we're going as soon as you dispose of the tail," Lindsay finished for him.

"Don't let me forget to thank Oscar when we get back. This baby's gonna leave that hay wagon in the dust." Mitchell took one more look behind him. "Ready?"

"No." Lindsay met his look of exasperation with a shrug. "But don't wait for me."

His lips curling into a wolfish grin, Mitchell reached down and grabbed the stick shift. They were approaching a crossroads, where the other road headed back into the mountains. Checking the oncoming car one more time and gauging the distance to the next intersection, he threw the car into second. The engine whined. The Mustang rocked with power. Mitchell swung through the corner and hit the gas, and left Lindsay thinking of how the ships in science fiction movies hit light speed.

They swooped over the mountain roads, the little car growling like a cat, Lindsay holding on to the window frame for dear life and Mitchell working the car like a fine instrument. Lindsay saw the color leave his face as they dipped and soared across the high passes, saw the perspiration break out on his forehead. He never lost his purpose, though. His eyes kept swiveling on the road ahead to the rearview mirror. He worked silently, mechanically, his actions economical and quick.

In the end, speed and familiarity won over determination. Within a half hour, Mitchell pulled the Mustang into Gabe's back lot and killed the engine. Ten minutes later, the Mustang was cooling off in Gabe's barn, and Mitchell and Lindsay headed to the post office in Gabe's Chevy truck.

"There's a question we haven't answered yet," Lindsay suggested, thinking that no woman of childbearing age should be subjected to the shock system on the truck.

Looking more relaxed than before, Mitchell glanced over. "There are a lot of questions we haven't answered yet. Which one in particular bothers you?"

"Their trashing your house." Lindsay held her purse in one hand and the window with the other, this time out of necessity. She was afraid she'd bounce out onto the road if she let go. "How did they know?"

"I'm not sure I want to find out," Mitchell answered quietly.

That wasn't the answer Lindsay had wanted. She'd been hoping for bugs or tracking devices or maybe psychics, but Mitchell wasn't going to give her any.

"Why," he went on, "didn't Maggie use one of our regular drops? We had the one the task force always used, and then we set up one of our own. Why didn't she trust either one?''

"Well, Esperanza's pretty powerful," Lindsay demurred. "And nobody knew about your cabin."

Mitchell looked at her, and Lindsay knew that he wasn't any happier about the train of thought than she. "Nobody except the task force."

The post office probably didn't look any different than it had when it had been built in 1932. A clapboard building decorated in presidential portraits and Wanted posters, it boasted ten private boxes, and a postman who Lindsay was sure had been working that first day in 1932. The inimitable Ernie, she assumed.

The minute the little man saw Mitchell, he started nodding, jabbing a finger in Mitchell's direction in a gesture that Lindsay assumed meant something equivalent to "About time you showed up." Without saying a word of greeting, he disappeared into the back room.

Lindsay grinned. "You're well thought of everywhere you go."

Mitchell actually grinned back. "My fan club grows daily."

When Ernie returned, it was with an armful of mail. He didn't look very happy about it, either.

"Got a bag?" he asked in a voice that would have frightened vultures.

"Just the one I drove in with, Ernie," Mitchell teased.

Suddenly the tight old face split in a huge grin. Lindsay wasn't sure she liked the joke at all, but Ernie clearly thought it was a scream.

"Been waitin' for you to show up," he acknowledged, dumping the pile into Mitchell's arms. "Gabe said you'd been by. Figured it wouldn't take you long to remember you had some unfinished business here. Got some sweet-smellin' mail in there," he chuckled, and winked at Lindsay.

"Fabric softener samples, no doubt," she tossed back.

The little man almost had a seizure. Mitchell rolled his eyes and gave Lindsay a shove in the direction of the truck

"Nice meeting you," she called as he shouldered her out the door.

"Pleasure's mine, miss!" Ernie yelled back. "Tell your friends hello when you see 'em, Mitch."

Halfway out the door, Mitchell brought both of them to a halt.

"Friends?"

Ernie nodded. "Guy named Bob. Stopped by for directions to your place. Shook my hand. Nice fella."

"Was he alone?"

Ernie shook his head. "Two other guys in suits. Little chrome-head and a big black guy. They are friends, aren't they?"

Mitchell exchanged looks with Lindsay. "Yeah," he answered Ernie, with less conviction than he would have a few hours before. "They're friends. Thanks, Ernie."

"So, what do we do?" Lindsay asked back in the truck.

Mitchell just sat staring out the window, the mail still in his hands. "I don't know," he admitted.

"If Bob's with them, it's okay."

Mitchell fixed her with a glare. "Do we know that?"

"Yes!" Lindsay backed off a little, trying to distance her feelings about Bob from the rest. "The force is Bob's baby. He wouldn't do anything to jeopardize it."

"And everybody else lives, breathes and eats the law up there. So if we have a leak, who is it?"

"How do we even know we have a leak?" she demanded. "There could be some explanation for this we don't even know yet. There might be a tap on the phone lines, or a tracking device, or—"

"It could be that sunspots are transmitting vital information to Esperanza's house," Mitchell retorted without much patience. "I kind of doubt it, McDonough."

"So, what do we do?"

He began rifling through the mail, dropping some items, tossing others to Lindsay, ripping open the suspicious ones. About halfway down the pile, he came to a manila envelope. Mitchell stopped, his hand suspended above it, his breath caught in his chest. Lindsay saw him go pale again. The handwriting on the front was Maggie's.

"Here," he said, throwing it into her lap. "Hold this till we get someplace a little more private." He dropped the rest of the mail into the back and started the truck.

The envelope felt very heavy in Lindsay's hands, like her purse did with a gun in it. Something small slid around in the package when she tilted it, and something else crackled. She desperately wanted to open it up, but one look at the cold determination on Mitchell's face deterred her.

"Oh, my God." Bob Peterson let the door swing open as he pulled off his sunglasses. He didn't believe what he saw at first. It didn't look any better in the real light of day. He crinkled his nose. It was beginning to smell in here. Behind him Al echoed his oath as he, too, stepped into Mitchell's living room.

"Mitchell! Mitchell, are you here?"

"I told you," Oscar said, pulling his .357 out to search the rooms. "My car ain't here, he ain't here. He doesn't want me any madder at him than I am."

"But where is he?" Al asked, following Oscar's example with less temerity. "Where would they have gone?"

"I don't know," Bob mused. "My guess is they got here, saw this and took off."

"I don't blame 'em," Oscar said. "Wow." He'd just taken a peek at the workroom. Flipping off the light, he closed the destruction in again.

"I wonder if they found it," Bob reflected.

"From the looks of it," Al answered, "nobody found it. God, I can't imagine what Mitchell did when he saw this."

Al's words seemed to wake Bob. "Which is why we have to get after him. He has Lindsay with him. I don't want any surprises."

The three men met again at the front door, satisfied that except for a gathering horde of flies the house was empty.

"Where to now?" Oscar asked, holstering his gun and retrieving the car keys.

"I don't know. Let's head back to the post office and see if that old guy has some ideas."

"Oh, my God." Lindsay sat at the picnic table across from Mitchell in the little clearing, a sheet of paper in her hand. "How could Wilson possibly have gotten this?"

Mitchell looked up from where he was paging through Perez's diary. "From the inside."

Lindsay stared at the paper again, a copy of meeting minutes that outlined the task force game plan for crushing the Esperanza empire. Top secret, recorded only once, it was a document kept in Bob Peterson's office safe. This copy had been in the envelope Maggie had left for Mitchell.

She hadn't left any notes, anything explaining why she'd decided to send Mitchell the evidence, or why she'd sent it to the cabin. The only items in the envelope, when Mitchell had ripped it open and turned it out onto the cedar table, had been the black book and the copied minutes. The book was all it would take to nail Esperanza, and the paper all that was needed to prove that a leak existed in the elite task force.

Lindsay felt as if someone had punched her in the stomach. It wasn't as if she worked for a big, impersonal organization. She knew everyone in the task force. She knew their families. Even though she didn't spend her time off with them, she respected and liked them. The idea that one of them had sold out sickened her.

"How?" she wondered, her voice stricken.

Mitchell looked up. "Who knows? This isn't the easiest business to be in."

"Thanks, Mitchell," she countered dryly. "I can do without the lectures. I don't need to work the field to know how hard it is out there. But don't you feel...I don't know, violated?"

He couldn't help but smile. "Watch out, Doctor," he warned. "You're beginning to sound more and more like an agent."

Lindsay couldn't quite bring herself to smile back. "Mitchell, what do we do?"

"We smoke him out," he told her, reaching for the paper she held. "We nail Esperanza and his pigeon at the same time."

"How?"

Mitchell shrugged. "The usual method is to give the suspected person bogus information and catch him when he acts on it."

"Him."

Mitchell looked up and Lindsay saw betrayal in his eyes. She saw the anger of a man who had believed in a friend. Trust was important in Mitchell's world. It was sometimes all he had, the knowledge that there were some guys he could rely on. One of those guys had just sold him out.

Reaching over, he took the minutes from Lindsay's hand and held it up before her. "Where did this come from?"

Lindsay held his gaze. "Bob's safe."

"And who did we tell we were coming up here?"

"That doesn't mean a thing. Anybody could have listened in on that line."

Mitchell shook his head impatiently. The sun skittered through his hair and warmed his face. He looked so handsome outdoors in the afternoon light, as if, somehow, he shouldn't be found anywhere else. If Lindsay had walked up to the picnic table at this very minute, she would have thought he was taking a long lunch hour, just going through some business out in the open. Somehow this conversation shouldn't be taking place here. Mitchell shouldn't be accusing one of his oldest friends—or talking of treachery. Not in the sunlight, in the mountains.

"Who could have gotten into Bob's safe?" he demanded.

"Mitchell," Lindsay argued, leaning closer. "All of us have been in that safe at one time or another."

"With Bob there watching us."

Her instincts brought her to her feet. "It can't be Bob!"

Mitchell followed her. "It can't be any of them," he countered, never losing her gaze as he collected their evidence. "But it is. If it isn't Bob, he can help us. If it is, we have to go out of the task force."

Giving Lindsay one last look begging understanding, Mitchell turned back toward the car.

"Mitchell," she persisted, even more lost in this morass than he. "It can't be Bob. I *know* him."

Mitchell stopped. He didn't face her. "You *know* all of us. You're the one who hired us, remember? You teamed us and watched over us with that damn textbook of yours. Who else do you think it can be, expert?"

But Lindsay couldn't come up with anybody. She stood behind him, silent, shaking with frustration. He was right, of course. She had hired everyone. If anyone should have spotted a weak link, it should have been herself. She racked her memory for a clue, for a hint as to who might be desperate enough or callous enough to sell out his friends. The breeze sighed through the pines and a jay swooped to the table and perched, his head cocked to watch the people. Lindsay kept her eyes on Mitchell's back. She had to admit that she had no names for him. Nothing.

"So, what do we do?" she asked once again, defeated by the enormity of the situation.

Mitchell turned on her, his eyes even brighter, his knuckles white around the envelope. "*We* don't do anything," he said, towering over her. "I put you someplace safe and I check Bob out. After that I'll have a better idea of who I can take this all to."

"Don't be ridiculous," Lindsay retorted. "You can't do this alone. You have to have help."

"Not yours, I don't."

"Then whose?" she countered, hand on hip, the other holding on to her purse. "Al's? He has a family to support. Maybe he needs help with those car payments. Or Brent. He's hip deep in a divorce. Money again. Or Oscar. He was good in New York, but you probably know what that city can do to a cop, Mitchell. How do we *really* know he's clean? It could even be me. How do you know I didn't use a phone when I was alone? Want me to go on?''

"I want you to tell me where I can take you that they won't find you.''

"No! I'm the only person you can trust right now.''

"I can trust me,'' he countered. "And that's who's gonna do this. You're going underground.''

Lindsay took a step closer, her chin to his chest, her eyes sparkling with fury, her head back to challenge him. "Damn it, Mitchell, you're not making sense. Why not let me help? You taught me how to shoot the damn gun. You dragged me up here. Why are you dropping me now?''

"Because we're getting too close. From here it's a damn minefield, Lindsay, and you don't know how to walk it.''

"It hasn't been a walk in the woods to this point, either!'' she shouted, knowing he should take her with him, knowing damn well that if he were alone, he would take chances he shouldn't. "What's the matter? Don't you think I can keep my cool? I kept my cool when you were a raving maniac, Mitchell. Or is it that you don't trust me? Is that it? Do you really not trust me?''

"I don't want anything to happen to you!'' he shouted, just as furious as she. The jay took off in a flutter.

"You don't want anything to happen to me?'' she shrilled. "Isn't it a little late for that? I don't have a chair left to sit on, Mitchell! I've been accused of not knowing enough to spot a bad apple. I've been uprooted and shot at and attacked in a car. Short of the rack and thumbscrews, I can't think of anything much that will make my day worse!''

"No!'' he retorted. "No! You're not going with me, and that's all there is to it!''

"Why?''

He turned back to the car, refusing to answer. Lindsay followed. She grabbed his arm to make him stop.

"Why?''

Mitchell stopped, whirled on her, his face contorted with rage. She'd gone too far. "Because I'm falling in love with you, damn it!''

His words slammed into Lindsay's chest. She wanted so much to believe him. She wanted to stop him and make him prove it right here. But after their conversation in the car, she couldn't. It was just too pat. Just because he'd come to her twice when he'd needed her, it didn't add up to undying devotion. All it meant was that she had been the one nearby, and Lindsay had had enough of that kind of affection in her life already.

"Don't give me that," she snapped. "If you're going to lie, at least make it a good one."

"What do you mean?"

"I mean I'm not that stupid. You wouldn't love me if I were the last woman in Denver. Give me the real reason, Mitchell, or I don't move."

"I told you!" he argued, taking hold of her other arm. "I love you!"

"You do not! You're trying to get me away from you so you can do something stupid. Well, it won't work." She could have done without the tears in her eyes. They didn't help her argument any.

"Damn you, McDonough," Mitchell snarled, gripping her so tightly he hurt. "You are the most stubborn woman I've ever met."

"It'd probably serve you right if you did love me," she retorted. "You deserve somebody more stubborn than you."

"It probably would," he agreed, the volume of his voice falling curiously. He caught her gaze, the green of his eyes flinty and sharp, the sun dappling the depths. His grasp was like a vise. His jaw was tighter than it had been the moment he'd discovered the ruin in his house.

Lindsay faltered. She couldn't understand why her knees should melt, just because Mitchell was staring at her like that. She couldn't imagine why she wasn't breaking free and getting back to the car before he made an untenable situation worse. She went very still. When he dipped his head to hers, she didn't realize that she had already lifted hers to meet him.

"It probably would," Mitchell murmured again and kissed her.

Fine agent she'd make, Lindsay thought distractedly. The minute she felt Mitchell's arms around her, she dropped her purse. She vaguely heard the clunk as the gun hit the ground. It didn't seem to matter, though. She couldn't seem to think past Mitchell's onslaught on her senses. His mouth, demanding and hard, his hand tangling in her hair, his arms so tight around her that she couldn't breathe. She thought she heard the wind rise, but it was only her own blood rushing past her ears. Lindsay thought she felt the ground give way. She wrapped herself around Mitchell, knowing only he could keep her upright, only he could hold her together. The sun melted through her, glowing in her belly and coursing through her arteries. The wind swept her, steeling her strength, and, she knew, her argument.

"So," Mitchell growled a few minutes later, his head still over hers, his arms still holding her close. "Will you please just behave like a good girl and hide for a day or two?"

Lindsay tried to retrieve her outrage from the remains of her emotions. "Don't patronize me, Mitchell."

He pulled away, holding her at arm's length, his expression thunderous. "Don't flatter yourself, McDonough. Now are you going to behave, or do I have to tie you hand and foot?"

Lindsay couldn't help a sly smile. "I heard you were like that."

Mitchell laughed, a surprised bark that didn't alleviate his concern. "I mean it, Lindsay."

Lindsay took a long breath, her attention on a scattering of pinecones at her feet. When she lifted her gaze to Mitchell, she did her best to rein in her impatience. "I know just the place. You get us over the mountains, and then give me the wheel. It's also someplace you might be safe, so don't say no if I tell you to get some sleep."

"You'll stay there?"

"Only if you report in as regularly as if I were the office." Pulling out of his grasp, she held out her hand, her expression level and serious. "Deal?"

Mitchell smiled. Shaking his head, he took her hand. "Deal. Now let's get the hell out of here before I say something else stupid."

Quirking an eyebrow at him, Lindsay picked up her bag and followed him up the hill. Oh, well, she thought, things could be worse. He could tell me he loved me and then admit that *he's* the leak.

Chapter 13

The door was opened by a bigger man than Mitchell. He took one look at Lindsay standing on his porch and gave way to an awesome scowl.

"Well, where have you been?"

"Who's he?" Mitchell demanded, not liking the man's golden good looks or the fact that he seemed to have such a hold on Lindsay.

The man sized him up. "Who the hell are *you*?"

"I'm Special Agent—"

Caught in the middle of what was beginning to look very much like two hounds making territory, Lindsay began to laugh. "Oh, for heaven's sake, settle down, you two. Alex, let us in so I can explain. And so I can have something to *eat*. I'm starved."

She didn't wait for further invitation before shouldering her way past the man in the doorway. Mitchell was slower to follow.

"Alex?" He frowned, tapping his memory for the name. A quick scan revealed some facts he hadn't taken the time to evaluate before. The man had Lindsay's amber eyes, and he had used a brusque familiarity when talking to Lindsay that Mitchell recognized from his own family. Taking advantage of the fact that Alex had turned away, Mitchell brushed his way past and stepped inside.

"Damn it, Lindsay, why didn't you tell me?"

Without bothering to stop on her way to the kitchen, Lindsay laughed again. "Pure meanness."

It wasn't really, though. It was a test. A silly little test that had no place in their present situation. She should have told him right out that Alex lived in town. She could very well have even filled him in on her planned destination. But since Mitchell had stolidly refused to elaborate on his rather suspicious declaration out on that mountain, Lindsay had seen no reason to tell him that the other man in her life was her big brother.

Big being the operative term. It had really been funny to see the look on Mitchell's face when the two of them had come face-to-face.

"Lindsay," Alex growled as he followed hot on Mitchell's heels, "who the hell is this guy? And where have you been? I've been trying to get you for days. Mom and Phil have been calling me, all crazy because you weren't home, and they didn't know where you'd gone."

"I left a message with your service," she answered, already busy looking through his cabinets. "I was at Mitchell's most of the time . . . Oh, by the way, Alex, this is Jason Mitchell. He's on the task force with me. Mitchell, this is my brother Alex. If it weren't for him, you wouldn't have Lindsay McDonough to push around. He talked me into applying at the task force."

Alex immediately swung on Mitchell. "*You're* the guy who's been harassing her?"

Mitchell bristled. "It's been mutual, believe me."

"It's okay, Alex," she assured him with just a hint of sarcasm. "He says he loves me now."

"After a week at his place?" Alex scowled. "I'm sure."

Lindsay found herself grinning. Backing out of the cabinet, she went for the refrigerator. "Alex, you really have to do something about your food supply. Do you think we could put a pizza under expenses, Mitchell?"

"We've already claimed both houses, a car and a Jeep," he answered, easing around her brother and joining her at the refrigerator. "Why didn't you *tell* me about him?"

Lindsay looked over to see Alex still considering both of them without much charity. He was really formidable when he got mad. All that time in football, she imagined. He had shoulders like bridge abutments and a chest that could bounce concrete. It still amazed her how gentle he had been with her, handling her as if she'd been a newborn baby.

"I did," she answered with wide-eyed simplicity. "I told you he was my brother, and that he was a C.P.A."

"You didn't tell me he was Paul Bunyan."

She chuckled. "What did I tell you about those preconceptions, Mitchell? I just forgot to tell you that his last name was Thorne."

That did it. The last memory clicked in. Alexander Thorne, Denver Broncos, All-Pro fullback, retired by injury at the ripe old age of thirty-four. Mitchell had watched him every autumn for twelve years.

He turned to Lindsay's brother with an outstretched hand. "My apologies. She never told me about you."

"She did," Lindsay argued diffidently.

Alex took Mitchell's hand, although he wasn't quite ready to pass judgment. "She sure told me about you. I guess she didn't tell me everything, though."

Mitchell scowled. "She has a way of doing that."

Lindsay interrupted before they got too chummy. "He has some MuShi pork in here, Mitchell. Are you game?"

Explanations, after a fashion, were served up over food. Mitchell was the one who told Alex what Lindsay had been doing at his cabin. Lindsay would have skirted around it. She was amazed at how frankly Mitchell dealt with it. She was also gratified at how easily Alex accepted it. The words exchanged between the two on the subject were sparse, but it seemed to be more than enough for them to understand each other. By the time they got to coffee and cookies, Alex was listening quietly to an abbreviated account of the present crisis, his forehead creased just a little, as if he didn't want to miss a word of what was happening.

"There's a snag," he admitted, absentmindedly tapping a finger against his coffee cup. "I have to be out of town in about an hour and a half. It's a trip I've been putting off for over two weeks now, and the company's in big trouble. They're on a deadline, and I don't have anybody else to send. Are you going to be able to stay here with Lindsay?"

"Twenty minutes ago, that was a problem," Lindsay offered dryly.

"It'll still be a problem if he's anything less than a gentleman with you," Alex assured her.

Thinking back to the screaming matches they'd already had, the threats and charges, Lindsay couldn't help but laugh.

"He wouldn't think of it," Mitchell assured Alex, glaring meaningfully at Lindsay. Then he turned back to Alex. "The problem is that I won't be able to be here all the time. I have to follow this problem through to its end. Which is why I wanted her safely out of the way."

Alex nodded. "I appreciate that. I have some friends from the team I can have come over, if that'll work."

Mitchell was shaking his head. "I don't want any more people involved than I have to. We're not talking about people who play by any rules here. Still and all..."

"I have a gun," Lindsay reminded him. "And I can call the police if I hear prowlers."

"You have a gun?" Alex demanded.

Lindsay grinned. Some things didn't change. Big brothers were never quite ready for their little sisters to grow up. To have her armed on top of it must be even worse.

Mitchell wished he could have thought of one person he knew well enough to trust. The problem was that his only friends in the area worked for the force. There just wasn't anybody available on short notice.

"Never mind," Alex said with a sudden shake of his head. "What am I thinking of? This is my sister. Forget the company. If you can stay here for just a while I'll go get it settled. Then I won't set foot out of the house until you've taken care of your business."

"Don't forget to stop by the store while you're out," Lindsay suggested.

Alex reached over to rumple her hair. "Isn't there anything else you think about?"

Mitchell's wondering gaze was on Lindsay's hair, now pleasantly tangled. "She lets you do that?" he demanded.

Alex looked over without much comprehension.

Lindsay was way ahead of him. "I wouldn't try it, Mitchell," she warned. "Alex is my brother. He's also bigger than you are."

Mitchell grinned. "I'm bigger than you."

Lindsay grinned back meaningfully. "I have a gun. Leave my hair alone."

"Is there a semilucid explanation for all this?" Alex finally asked.

Lindsay shook her head. "Not really. Go save the company."

Alex grabbed a briefcase and keys and let himself out through the garage. As soon as he was gone, Mitchell began to pace. Lindsay sat at the kitchen table and watched, wishing she could be of more help, wishing she could figure out some way of making him stay. The bad guys were out there, and they wanted him. And Mitchell was going to wade right into them without backup or protection. Lindsay was just beginning to get used to the idea that she might be falling in love with him. She didn't want to entertain the possibility that she might lose him within the same day.

"Sit down," she commanded, casting around for some way to help.

"I think better on my feet."

"Oh, off your brain, huh?"

Mitchell turned a scowl on her as he passed. "As sweet and supportive as ever, I see."

"Don't expect me to change just because you start making rash claims in the love department, Mitchell."

He came to a stop before her so that he could look down on her. "Claims I can always rescind."

For some reason Lindsay thought of the morning he'd come out of the shower to find her in his bedroom. He had

stood over her the same way, powerful and mesmerizing, the
light skittering off his eyes and revealing the potent sexuality there. She also remembered that later she'd thought that
he hadn't forfeited any of that sexuality by donning clothes.
She'd been right. He was crowding her space again, setting
up a static dance across her skin as she brushed against him.
His touch set off sparks, even through two sets of clothes.

"Go right ahead and take it back," she challenged, lov-
ing to see contest flare in his eyes. "I knew you would. Make
any promise to get me here and then revert to form."

"You're not going to goad it out of me, McDonough,"
he warned, laughter in his voice.

Lindsay eased a hand forward. "Goad what out of you,
Mitchell?"

"Don't be cute, McDonough. I'm not going to say it
again. I shouldn't have said it once."

"You've got that right. You're going to go to hell for lying
to a widow." Her fingers reached his leg, then started
stroking just behind his knee. She saw him stiffen and
smiled anew. "Problems, Mitchell?"

He yanked her to her feet. "Nothing a good spanking
wouldn't cure."

Lindsay met his glare with a bold smile, daring him,
fighting him—keeping him from walking out that door any
way she could. "Too kinky for me, Mitchell. What about
something really radical, like candles and music?"

"For what?" he demanded through clenched teeth. He
had her by the arms, but sensitive areas were much too accessible to her hands. To Mitchell's delight and chagrin, she
was making full use of her mobility. "Damn it, stop that."

"Why?" she asked, eyes wide once again.

"Because your brother would reduce me to fine powder
if he knew what I was contemplating right now."

Lindsay gave her head a slow shake so that her hair swept
across her cheek. "He only said you had to be a gentleman
with me. Would a gentleman disappoint a lady?"

"What?" His vocal chords seemed to be tightening.

It didn't escape Lindsay's attention that her pulse rate had
exceeded several speed limits, or that her knees had once

again been reduced to jelly. She knew what she was doing. This reaffirmation of life seemed like some kind of protection against death. She wanted Mitchell to remember her when he walked that tightrope and remember that she was waiting back here for him, no matter what the two of them finally thrashed out in their personal affairs department. Still she couldn't help but think that if she were going to offer such a gift, she should be able to enjoy it, too. Both to her relief and her consternation, she was. Oh, she was.

Mitchell lowered a threatening glare on her. "He said he was only going for a while."

Lindsay just smiled. "His office is on the other side of town."

"Oh."

She edged closer. "And it's rush hour."

"True."

"His car's unreliable."

Mitchell held her back. "I have some calls I have to make."

"Phone works all night."

"So do I." His words were more of a reluctant admission than a boast.

Lindsay wormed her way right back into his arms. "Want to see my bedroom?"

"Kitchens are nice." His hands lifted her blouse.

"Bedrooms are better."

"Why?"

"Isn't that a stupid question?"

"Not *that* why." He kept her still, his head bent over hers, his arms holding her to him even as he challenged her. "Why do you want this? It seems to me that just this morning you were telling me no more."

That stopped Lindsay, her arms caught within Mitchell's, her head at his shoulder, his hands the ones making forays now. She didn't want to answer, to move, to break the spell his fingers were creating along the edges of her breast. She just wanted to pretend that they were going to make love, and then fall asleep and wake tomorrow over coffee and bacon like they had before.

"Because suddenly it's important," she finally admitted in a very small voice.

"Tell me why," he murmured against her hair. "Tell me why it's important."

"Now that's a stupid question," she managed breathlessly.

"I still want an answer."

She closed her eyes, shaken by the fire his fingers were lighting. Her own hands had stilled, seeking purchase, a way to balance herself against Mitchell's touch. "Because you're leaving in a while to go play games with Esperanza," she said. "You have no backup you can trust, and you won't let me come along. And I don't like it."

"What else?" he demanded softly, gathering her close.

"Nothing."

"Come on, McDonough. What else?"

"All right," she snapped and pulled away. "All right, damn it, I'm falling in love with you, too. Are you happy?"

"My," he teased, reaching a hand out to her cheek. "Aren't we romantic?"

Lindsay leaned into his touch, wishing her admission didn't hurt quite so much, wishing she weren't steeling herself for rejection. "As romantic as you."

"What do you suggest we do about it?"

Lindsay closed her eyes for a moment to seek her courage. She didn't want the words, didn't want the truth this close. "We get through this, Mitchell. You and I."

"And then?"

She had to smile at him. "And then we go to our corners and come out fighting."

Mitchell smiled back, and for the first time Lindsay saw just how gentle his eyes could be. She let his gaze absorb her, falling into that soft green sea like a bird seeking nourishment.

"And until then?" he asked, pulling her back to him again.

"We make the most of our time until Alex gets home."

Bending down, Mitchell swept her into his arms. "Want to show me your bedroom now?"

Lindsay smiled. "Thought you'd never ask."

Lindsay heard the garage door open and edged back out of bed. Mitchell still slept, sprawled over the double bed as if he'd fallen, his hair in his eyes, his face young and relaxed. Lindsay hated to wake him. Slipping back into her clothes, she wondered just how long she could put it off. He did need the sleep, after all. How could he be expected to function, as tired as he obviously was? Especially after such strenuous activity. She smiled at the thought and tiptoed out the door.

Alex wasn't fooled for a minute. Dropping grocery bags onto the kitchen counter, he drew a bead on Lindsay as she entered from the hallway.

"Where is he?"

"Sleeping," she allowed, poking into the nearest bag to search for nourishment. "He hasn't been able to get a lot in the last few days."

Alex snorted. "I bet."

Lindsay couldn't help but chuckle. "If I want guilt and self-righteous indignation, Alex, I'll call Mom. From you I need a strong shoulder."

"What you need is a little restraint."

"Restraint?" she echoed. "I've been restrained for six years. Heck, Alex, I was restrained while I was married. I think I like this better."

"But you're not used to it, baby," he objected, leaning closer to her. "I mean, this is the guy you haven't been able to stomach for the last four years. What makes him Mr. Perfect inside a week?"

"A brain transplant couldn't make him Mr. Perfect," Lindsay retorted. "But I have found that he's a lot more tender and compassionate and strong than I thought. And he sparks something in me that's been missing."

Alex snorted again.

"Knock it off, pal," she suggested, cracking open a box of cereal. "You won't have a thing to say to me until I marry a centerfold with the IQ of lettuce. Then we can compare notes."

"Low blow," Alex grumbled. —

"But true. Tell me one thing you and your ex, the lovely Bambi, have in common."

"Her name was Barbi, not Bambi, and that's not relevant."

"And don't give me that 'It's my duty as a big brother' garbage."

"You two yell like that all the time?"

Lindsay and Alex turned to see Mitchell padding down the hall in bare feet, buttoning his shirt.

"I thought you were going to get some sleep," Lindsay accused.

"I did," Mitchell informed her, pouring himself some water. "Almost three hours. That's more than I've managed most nights in the last three weeks."

"You weren't going one-on-one with Esperanza most nights," Lindsay argued, her food forgotten for the ache in her chest. She was going to cry again, she just knew it. Damn Jason Mitchell. He was setting up totally unpredictable reactions in her she wanted no part of. She didn't want to cry for him. She didn't want to ache. She wanted to slip back into that bed and into his arms and sleep away the rest of the night.

Turning away from the sink, Mitchell once again took Lindsay by the arms. "You behave for Alex so I know you're all right."

Lindsay sought a reprieve in his eyes. She found none. "Let me come along."

Mitchell shook his head. "No. I've done this kind of thing before, Lindsay. I'll be okay. You just stay put till you hear from me."

The tears came, filling Lindsay's eyes and sliding down her cheeks. "Damn you, Mitchell, you go and get yourself killed, don't come running to me."

"You'll make a great mother," he assured her with a grin as he gathered her to him.

"You'll call on the hour?"

"I'll call."

Lindsay held on tighter, suddenly afraid to let him go. "Take me with you."

Lifting her chin with his finger, Mitchell smiled at her. Lindsay had never seen such tenderness before, such a bittersweet refusal. "I'll come get you as soon as it's over," he promised, his thumb circling her cheek, his eyes encompassing hers with their warmth. "Only me. It won't be long. I promise."

There was so much Lindsay wanted to say. But all she could do was smile and lift her own finger to his lips and nod. "I'll be here."

"You know something?" he asked her, excluding the rest of the world with his eyes and his hands. "There was something I could never figure out. It was about your clothes. If you used your suits and glasses as a way of, you know, distancing yourself, why come to my cabin in jeans and tennies and braids? I think I know. I think you thought you were safe with me. You thought that I wouldn't get too close to you no matter what you were like, so for the first time in four years, you were yourself. Bad mistake, McDonough. Bad mistake."

"Why's that, Mitchell?" she asked, barely breathing.

"'Cause it turns out I'm the one you should have been afraid of the most." Bending to steal a kiss, he offered her one more smile. "See you later."

Lindsay watched in silence until he reached the hall. "See you later, Mitchell."

"What was that about clothes?" Alex asked as the door shut.

Lindsay waved the matter off as she dived back into her cereal. "Oh, some stupid theory of his. He thinks that I distance myself from people, and I do it by the image I assume at work."

"He'd never seen you in jeans before?"

"No," she answered, still not facing him. "Why should he?"

"Because he's right. When you're in that upwardly mobile uniform you wear, you're as much fun as winter in Greenland."

"Thanks, Alex," she retorted. "I needed that."

"It's not really your fault. Does Mitchell know anything about Patrick?"

She nodded. "Did you know that his father was an alcoholic?" Her voice sounded small even to her, tight with the tears she had suppressed, strained with the fear that had sparked from ember to blaze with the shutting of that door.

Next to her, her brother wrapped a comforting arm around her shoulder and drew her close. "Then I'd say he knows you pretty well."

"Yeah," she agreed with a funny little sob. "He does, damn it. I should never let him back in that door."

Alex shook his head. "You should never let him out of your sight again."

Turning her face into her big brother's shoulder, Lindsay finally cried.

What had ever happened to all-night diners? Mitchell wondered. They used to be interchangeable, from the worn linoleum and tattered stools that marched along under the counter to the centerpiece of stale donuts. It had been comforting somehow, as if no matter how bad you felt, the place always looked worse.

Now he had to contend with ferns and pseudo-wood paneling and No Smoking areas. Even the clientele was a disappointment, high school dates and yuppie bowling leagues. How could you possibly nurse a hangover and get information in a place like this?

Then again, it really wasn't that late yet. Maybe the true denizens didn't come out for a while. The perky young hostess led him to a booth, handed him a laminated menu and asked if he would like some coffee. When he said beer, she nodded and said his waitress would handle that. Hostesses only did coffee. Maybe Mitchell would get a job like that.

He checked his watch. Time to roust out Bob. Time to set this all in motion and ferret out the mole. He wished he could get rid of that acid eating at his chest, that decay of trust. He had spent the time since he'd left Lindsay going over the most likely candidates for squealer of the year. He'd come up with everybody. And nobody. Everybody had needs of some kind or another. Bills, kids to raise, wives to pay off, mortgages. But nobody would sell out their friends. He knew that. He knew every member on that team, and knew it.

So who was it?

"Good evening, do you know what you want?"

Yeah, Mitchell thought looking up at her. I want to be back in that little condo on the edge of town with Lindsay. I want this all over with. I want to find out that it was a mistake. Nobody was selling out their friends.

"Beer," he said instead.

While she was gone, he made his phone call.

It was going to be easier than he had thought. When he called Bob's home, Moira said that Bob was still at the office. Mitchell thanked her and dialed again. The phone was picked up on the second ring.

"Where the hell are you?" Bob demanded—Bob, who had never raised his voice to Mitchell in the ten years he'd known him.

Mitchell rubbed at his eyes. "I'm here. Why are you still at the office?"

"Mitchell, damn it, you get yourself in here. We need to talk."

"I know we do," Mitchell agreed. "But I'm afraid it's going to have to be on my terms, Bob."

"What are you talking about? Mitchell, I have half this force out trying to find you. After I saw your house, I was afraid you would try and get even for it. This is a team project, Mitchell. You come in and share the load."

"Who all is out looking?"

"What?"

"What agents?"

"Are you kidding? Everybody who was in the office when we got back. They all figured they wanted to help you put this thing to bed."

Mitchell nodded to himself. "Well, go ahead and call 'em all back in. I'm okay. I'll be in in the morning."

"Lindsay..."

"Is fine. I'll bring her in later."

"Are you okay?"

"Yeah." He nodded again, eyes shut, his chest closing off. "I'm okay. I found it. Maggie mailed it to me at the cabin."

"But your cabin was Tinker-Toys, Mitchell. How could they have missed it?"

"They missed it because the postmaster was holding my mail for me. We picked it up and headed back in."

"Is it what we need?"

"Oh, yeah. Yeah, it has everything. Names, dates, amounts, contracts. Enough to make Esperanza one very unhappy man. There was something else."

"What's that?"

"Something about the task force. I think you'd better see it."

There was a pause, and then Bob's voice came back on the line. He didn't sound as excited anymore. "What about the task force?"

"Something Maggie found. She had it in the packet. I have the original with me. I left a copy at the front desk of the *Denver Chronicle* to be opened in the event—"

"What are you talking about, Mitchell? What about the task force?"

"I'll show you in the morning. Right now I'm going to bed."

"Mitchell!"

"Six o'clock, Bob." Mitchell forced a laugh. "You know the funny part? Esperanza's going to be madder about this little bit of information about the task force than you are."

Not waiting for Bob to talk him out of it, Mitchell hung up. Now it was started, the seed of doubt planted. He checked his watch. Only eleven. He would call Lindsay, drink his beer and coffee and head down to stake out the *Chronicle*. Whoever was on Esperanza's payroll had no choice but to get that evidence. He couldn't chance appearing on an incriminating list somewhere. He could get Mitchell in the morning when he came in. But he couldn't let the extra evidence against him slip through his fingers. Especially the way Mitchell had set it up.

A squealer might hope he would get some mercy from a court system. At least some apathy. It was a different matter with Esperanza. If, as Mitchell had insinuated, the evidence would make Esperanza mad at his man, there wouldn't be anything as convenient as an appeal system to hope for. So whoever the leak was couldn't count on sending Esperanza's heavyweights to pick it up. He had to do it himself. And he had to do it soon.

Mitchell slipped another quarter into the slot.

"Hello?"

Mitchell almost found a smile for her. "You don't sound sleepy at all."

"I keep telling you, Mitchell. You don't know anything about me. I usually don't go to bed until at least one. What do you have so far?"

"Fifty cents' worth of phone calls. How about you?"

He could hear her sigh. "Vanishing patience, thanks. Are you okay?"

"No. I'm being held captive. I just thought I'd call before they tied me up with silk scarves and began to have their way with me."

One of the bowling team chose that moment to seek out the rest rooms. She never glanced at Mitchell as she passed, but at his words, she began to hesitate. Mitchell grinned.

"Well, have a good time," Lindsay answered, which made Mitchell grin even more.

"I intend to," he assured her. "One of them has the most wonderfully styled blue hair. I'm thinking of asking her to marry me."

That did it. The lady bolted into the bathroom as if her heels were on fire and her perfectly coiffed blue hair threatened. Mitchell found himself laughing, when moments before he had wanted to drive off a bridge.

"Thanks, McDonough," he said. "You made my day."

Lindsay sounded a bit bemused. "If you say so, Mitchell."

"I'm watching the *Chronicle* building, just so you know. Talk to you in an hour?"

"You're not going to tell me anything else?"

"Nope. Good night."

He hung up on her, as well. The beer was waiting for him back at his table. Mitchell eyed it without interest. Thinking about the hours he was going to have to spend outside the *Chronicle* building warding off street people and hookers, he shrugged and sat down to drink. Might as well take his nourishment where he could get it.

One of the benefits of choosing the *Chronicle* was that it boasted a telephone booth a half block away, so that Mitchell could make his calls without losing sight of the front door. He had asked one of the security guards to snap a picture of anybody who came to pick up the package, just in case, but he wanted to be there. He wanted to nail his friend on the spot with the goods.

Mitchell lifted the top of his Styrofoam cup and blew the steam off his coffee. It was dark tonight, the wind whipping the litter off the streets like small white birds and tugging at the signs. The few trees in this part of town rustled and moaned.

Another storm, he thought. Wonderful. It seemed as though he had never been through a summer with so many storms. He stood beyond the puddle of light thrown off by the street lamp, his eyes on the well-lighted front entrance—the only entrance open until the trucks began heading out from the loading dock at about four—certainly the only way for someone to gain access to the front desk.

He called Lindsay at twelve and then at one. She sounded no less alert, no less worried, even though she bantered and argued with him as she had done before.

Mitchell couldn't believe it. For the first time in his career, he actually looked forward to calling in. He waited to hear her voice, to replenish himself with the sound of her. He kept his eyes on the building and let his mind stray to the bed they'd shared that afternoon.

Mitchell had never had to pine for women. He'd never wanted to, either, come to think of it. No one had ever incited such a heat in him or created such a calm. There had never been a woman in his life who had so insidiously slipped in beneath his defenses to lay him bare. There just hadn't been one voice he'd waited to hear, or a laugh he'd wanted to share.

Lindsay challenged him and goaded him and stirred him to life, and Mitchell couldn't remember that happening before, either. He couldn't remember ever caring enough to form an image of a woman in his mind to carry with him like an amulet to ward off evil and restore health. Damn it if he didn't with McDonough, though.

By two, the wind had risen even more, whining through the alley and whipping at his clothes. Most of the people had disappeared from the streets and traffic had died. Mitchell pushed away from the wall, stretching his back and wishing he had another cup of coffee. This kind of thing was so much easier with a team. They could have at least commandeered a room somewhere across the street to set up the telescope and camera and call out for pizza and coffee. As it was, he was tired, sore and hungry. And, by the looks of it, he wasn't going anywhere soon.

Stepping over to the phone booth, he dropped in a quarter. He still had his eyes on the door, watching empty concrete and marble and wishing for someone—anyone—to show up so he could get out of there.

He dialed Alex's number.

After five rings. Mitchell checked his watch. It *was* two. Maybe she'd fallen asleep, after all. Seven rings, then eight—his stomach was knotting up. Come on, Lindsay, answer the phone.

There was a click. Mitchell breathed a sigh of relief.

"Hello?"

He didn't recognize the voice. "Who's this?"

"This is Sergeant Faulkner. Who's this?"

Mitchell grabbed hold of the phone for support. The world was spinning. His chest had caught fire. "Sergeant? Police?" he demanded. "What are you doing there?"

"Can I ask who's calling, please?"

"What's your badge number?"

"Now, just a minute—"

"Your badge number, quick. What is it?"

"Three-seven-two-oh-four. Now, who the hell is this?"

"I'm Special Agent Mitchell," he answered, struggling to keep his voice even, to keep the terror at bay. God, Lindsay, what happened? "I work at the task force with Ms. McDonough."

"Who? There's nobody here by that name."

"No young woman? Late twenties, dark blond hair, light brown eyes? Five-five, a hundred ten pounds."

"No, sir. Nobody. If you'd like to come over..."

"What about her brother? Alex Thorne."

"Like I said, if you'd rather come over."

Mitchell knew that speech. He tried to gulp air into tortured lungs and nodded blindly. He'd lost sight of the *Chronicle* door and suddenly didn't care. He had to find Lindsay.

Mitchell didn't assure the sergeant that he was on his way. He just dropped the phone and ran. The receiver swung in a lazy arc, a tinny voice calling from it. Beyond, there were footsteps and the front door of the *Chronicle* wheezed open. But Mitchell was already gone.

Chapter 14

Mitchell swung into the driveway and pulled to a stop behind the crime scene wagon. There were four police cars and an ambulance scattered over the street, and bathrobed neighbors clustered across the lawn. Mitchell pulled himself out of the car and reached for his badge. Three police were on him before his hand reached his pocket.

"Is Faulkner here?" he demanded, wading through them with upraised hands.

"Inside. Why?"

Mitchell flipped open the leather holder for the leader in the group, the one most likely to pull the gun he was fondling. "I called. Special Agent Mitchell. This is task force business, so I need to talk to him."

Shoulders eased all around him. The team leader nodded and smiled, and motioned him on in.

"Thanks," Mitchell acknowledged.

He tried to put on his professional face, impassive and aloof. Calculating. Inside he was a seething mass of anxiety. He didn't want to go in that house—didn't want to know what he would find. Lindsay was gone and the ambulance was here. And Faulkner wouldn't talk to him on the phone.

What had happened to Lindsay? Where was she? The idea that Esperanza might have his hands on her terrified him. He couldn't even court the idea that she might be dead.

And Alex. God, you wouldn't think somebody that big could be vulnerable. The responsibility gnawed at Mitchell like a rat. He paused at the foot of the porch, casting a cautious eye through the open door and raked a hand through his hair. Then, taking a gulp of air that had to substitute for courage, he stepped inside.

Faulkner was black, almost as big as Oscar, with the beginnings of a belly and a father's eyes. He turned at Mitchell's appearance and approached.

"Can I help you?" he asked in a quiet voice, flipping his notebook closed. His uniform stretched taut across his shoulders. His hat rested on the only upright end table.

The room was a mess, but it wasn't an Esperanza-orchestrated mess. Mitchell saw the aftermath of a fight, nothing more. Over by the couch a medical examiner's tarp covered a large form on the floor. A dark red stain spread across the fawn carpeting beneath it.

"Sergeant Faulkner?" Mitchell asked, trying to keep his eyes from the body, his hand out to the policeman. "I'm Mitchell." With his other hand, he once again displayed the badge that gained him such easy access.

The sergeant quickly scanned the badge, nodded and clasped Mitchell's hand in greeting. "Sorry about this," he said. "We got the call about 0145 hours and responded within five minutes. By then, I'm afraid it was all over."

"The brother?" Mitchell asked hesitantly. "Alex?"

Faulkner motioned over his shoulder. "Kitchen. The paramedics are with him."

Mitchell felt himself slump with relief. "He's alive?"

Faulkner actually smiled. "Be tough to kill something that big. He's got a couple of slugs in his belly. Enough to keep him down, but not out."

"Can I talk to him?"

"Sure. Listen, about the woman. He came to and told us. She's alive. Evidently she was taken. She got the guy over there before she left, though. Her brother says she wounded a few others, too."

Mitchell couldn't help a weak grin. "She does have a temper. Oh, by the way, Faulkner, can I ask a favor? Can you keep a lid on this for a few hours? We're right in the middle of something, and if word of this leaks out, it'll ruin everything."

"You sure?" the sergeant asked. "We might be able to help find your friend."

"I'm sure. All I need is till about 0800. But I'll keep your name for the showdown, if you don't mind."

For the first time, Faulkner let loose with a real smile. "Be my pleasure."

Mitchell nodded his thanks and walked on into the little kitchen.

The floor space was pretty much taken up by the two paramedics, their equipment and Alex. Mitchell noticed that his feet hung over the edge of the stretcher. Pity the paramedics who had to roll him out.

Mitchell didn't like the pallor of Alex's skin. He looked washed out already, his eyes half open as he watched the paramedics working with the IVs and radio.

"I let 'em get her," he croaked when he caught sight of Mitchell.

The paramedics looked up from where they crouched. Mitchell negotiated his way between them and bent down by Lindsay's brother.

"No, you didn't," he said, a hand on his arm. "I let 'em get her. I didn't think your address would be in her file. Whoever I'm following pulled it out and went for it on a chance. I'm sorry, Alex. I didn't mean for this to happen."

Alex huffed in indignation. "The day I can't take...care of myself."

"Guns are a little different than linesmen," Mitchell reminded him. "Did they say anything?"

Alex shot a look at the men at his elbow. Mitchell turned to consider them. The IVs were taped and running, the radio packed for transport, the tackle box closed. They were ready to move.

"Give me just a minute with him, huh?"

The guy with the gold badge gave him a considering look, passed it to Alex, then nodded and motioned to his partner. The two of them backed into the living room and Mitchell settled into the extra space.

Alex turned his head, intent on his message. "He said you would hear from him. He . . . he has a trade to make."

"What did he look like?"

Alex closed his eyes for a minute. It seemed as if the energy were seeping out of him. Mitchell saw his chest rise and fall in short, gasping breaths. He knew the feeling. Mitchell had hurt that much before. He understood the effort it took to stay in control.

"Short, thin. Hispanic. He didn't have an accent. Brown eyes, thin mouth."

"Scars?"

Another pause. Alex opened his eyes again, surprised. "Acne. Bad acne scars. He's maybe forty. Know him?"

Mitchell nodded, a hand to his forehead to rub at the throb that had ignited at the name. "Paul Colombo. I should have recognized his signature. He's Esperanza's personal hit squad."

Alex just shook his head, his eyes closing again.

"Take it easy," Mitchell said, giving Alex one last pat on the arm before getting to his feet. "When I get Lindsay back, we'll be in to see you."

Alex couldn't even get his eyes open. "You make sure you do."

"Mitchell?"

Mitchell turned to see Faulkner in the doorway, flanked by the paramedics. Mitchell motioned the two men in and followed the sergeant out the door.

"Call for you. Want to take it here or the bedroom?"

Mitchell stiffened. He hadn't even heard the ring. Trying not to be too obvious, he shrugged. "The bedroom, thanks."

He took it in Alex's room, standing so that he could see across the hall into the darkened room where he and Lindsay had made love. The bedclothes were still tumbled. He was sure if he went in there he could smell her, wildflowers blooming in the darkness. Mitchell steeled himself against the fire in his chest, the desperation that was welling in him, and picked up the phone.

"Mitchell? I'm sorry—"

"Lindsay?" He grabbed the receiver tighter, stunned by the sound of her voice, shaken by the fear he heard.

"Ready to deal, lawman?" Colombo. Mitchell knew the voice. Cold as death with eyes to match.

"What do you want?" Mitchell asked, struggling to keep his voice indifferent.

Colombo chuckled. "Question is, what do *you* want? We have a multioption plan. Either keep the book and find your lady friend in several trash bags, or give us the book and get her back. Would you like what's behind door number one or door number two, Mitchell?"

"When and where?"

Another chuckle, this time of satisfaction. "Funny. I thought you'd say that. She's *real* pretty, isn't she? Just enough of a spitfire to make it interesting."

Mitchell closed his eyes, concentrating on slowing down his breathing. Colombo was goading him, testing for soft spots. If Mitchell revealed Lindsay as his one weak spot, they would hurt her just to get back at him.

"I wouldn't try anything with her," he said instead, praying he could control the rage that seared him. All he wanted right now was his hands around Colombo's throat. He'd pay for touching Lindsay. "What she did to your friend in the house here isn't half of what she tried to do to me when I got fresh."

"No luck, huh, Mitchell? Too bad. I bet it bothered you."

"My ego healed fine, thanks. Now, where do you want to meet?"

"You guess, my friend. Someplace you spent some time just a little while ago. From what I understand, you liked it so much you didn't even want to get down. They had to carry you off, huh? Not like your partner.''

Mitchell went cold. Icy fingers clamped around his gut and wouldn't let loose. No. No, he couldn't. He squeezed his eyes shut, praying. They couldn't expect him to go up there again. Mitchell lifted a shaking hand to his face.

"Mitchell? Are you still there? I'm waiting for an answer, man. The deal go down or not?''

His fingers pressed hard against his eyes, Mitchell pulled action out of chaos. "I want him there."

"He don't go nowhere.''

"If he wants the book, he'll be there.''

There was a pause, a murmuring in the background. "An hour, Mitchell. We'll be waiting.''

Mitchell needed to warn Lindsay. To settle her and reassure himself before going up. "Let me talk to her again.''

Colombo's voice dripped sarcasm. "Oh, now, what for?''

"For nothing more than your slimy life, Colombo. You hang up without letting me talk to her, and no matter what else happens, you're pigeon bait.''

He knew Lindsay was on the phone before she spoke. Just that realization squeezed him, blocking his breath and hammering at his chest. He couldn't live through this nightmare again. He couldn't do it. And this time he would top that building to see Lindsay in the wind, the storm battering her and setting her eyes alight.

"I was right,'' he growled, pulling up his reserves of calm to soothe her.

"Right about what?''

God, her voice sounded so small, so very thin, as if she were losing energy like Alex. Mitchell saw her that way, her life seeping away before he could stop it, and it tortured him.

"I do love you, damn it. I didn't know until you decided to take a walk.''

"I'll have to do it more often.''

"Alex is okay. Are you?''

A pause, a gathering of strength. "Yes, I'm sorry, Mitchell.''

He wanted to reassure her, to force life back in her voice, but Colombo took the phone. Mitchell heard Lindsay go and felt as if he'd just seen Maggie fall again.

"Listen, friend," Colombo said. "You know to come alone. We see one blue suit anywhere around that building, she does the big swan dive. Am I understood?"

Unconsciously Mitchell nodded. "Yeah."

"An hour, then, Mitchell. I'm looking forward to it."

Faulkner was waiting for him when he made it back out into the living room. "Are you sure you don't want some help?" the sergeant asked.

He had listened in. Mitchell could see it in the gentle reproach in his eyes. Mitchell should have been furious. Any other time he would have had a serious talk about the sergeant's bad habits and transient nature of his badge. Any other time. Checking his watch this time, he nodded.

"Yeah, you can do me a favor. Call Max in security at the *Chronicle*. See if anybody came to pick up my package. If it's anybody besides a forty-five-year-old Caucasian male with gray hair and brown eyes, five-eleven, one-ninety, call Bob Peterson at the task force. Fill him in. Nobody else, understand? And make sure the line's clean. If you tell him just what you heard, he'll know what to do."

"And if Peterson's the one who shows up at the desk?"

"Then," Mitchell sighed, pulling out his gun to check the load one more time. "We're all in trouble, Faulkner."

Look up. See what's waiting for you.

Mitchell looked up. Nothing had changed. The skeleton reared against the sky, a deadly black cluster of geometrics that ate the light and spat it out from its top, where the storms lived. Lightning flickered up from the mountains, splitting the sky, anticipating the thunder. The wind tore at his clothes, funneling through the empty alleys and collecting at his feet. Mitchell felt its cold fingers clutch his belly, where the fear lived. He was looking up into his own nightmare.

The night shuddered around him and the dread ate away his purpose. His stomach heaved. His hands were slick with sweat. He couldn't do this. He couldn't go back up there.

When he lifted his wrist to check his watch, Mitchell realized that he was shaking. Scared, sick and shaking like a man with d.t.'s, just because he had to leave the ground.

Because he had to leave the ground to face Esperanza up in a stormy sky, where the walls were open and the floor threatened to drop away. He lifted his head to take another look and immediately lowered it. His stomach tumbled again. He would fall backward if he looked up again. Fall forever, his body tumbling and floating like street trash in the wind. He couldn't face that height again, but he had to. Lindsay was up there, and the only thing worse than facing his nightmare would be losing her and creating a new one. There was no turning back.

The elevator waited for him, just like before, the once-bright paint on the wire cage chipped and scraped. Mitchell stepped into it and wrapped his fingers around the strands of yellow. The wind gusted around the base of the building, flapping at plastic tarps and moaning through canyons of steel and concrete. Mitchell closed his eyes. He tightened his grip, and took a deep breath. Took another one. Still it didn't settle his stomach or stop the sweats. He couldn't get rid of the feeling that it was Maggie moaning to him. Accusing him, warning him. Mitchell listened to her, then opened his eyes.

It didn't change. It didn't get better. The night still trembled with the approaching storm. The building still stood, treacherous and dark. And Lindsay still waited, afraid, wondering, watching for him. Mitchell steeled himself against all of it and punched the button.

The car jerked upward. Mitchell did his best to keep his eyes open. He wanted to face the open floors, but he fell back against the grille. He wanted to face the night, but every time the lightning shivered, it laid bare the disappearing earth.

Concentrate on Lindsay, he thought, turning a little so he could see the passing stories. Think about how you're going to save her. If they were using the building, they knew about his acrophobia. And if they knew, they wouldn't expect any action out of him.

Twelve stories in the air, Mitchell laughed, a short, sharp sound swept away by the wind. It had sure happened that way once. He couldn't let it again. Whatever else went on up there, he had to get Lindsay safely back down this elevator.

Lindsay.

He pulled her to him, picturing her in the wild darkness, her eyes flashing at him in indignation, her voice sharp and clear as she challenged him. Her hands, so soft when he had hurt so badly, when she had dragged the pain out by the force of her conviction and propelled it into the light. She'd fought him toe-to-toe for his recovery, never giving an inch, never giving up. She would be waiting up there for him now, back as straight as a sword and eyes as hot as fire. She would watch for him and worry, knowing as well as he what it would cost him to mount that beast again. And she would be afraid.

In his mind Mitchell pictured her pallor, the rigid lines of her features as she battled her terror, and it ignited a pain fiercer than the fear that blocked his throat. He saw that her eyes were on the elevator shaft, waiting to see if he would arrive, hoping he wouldn't have to, knowing he would. It was with that image so vivid in his mind that it paled the lightning, that Mitchell braced himself. He kept her there before him, larger than the night, the floors that mounted beneath him, larger even than the empty sky that threatened.

Mitchell looked up then, his fingers wound tight into the mesh. Only a few more floors. He reached in for his gun and checked it and checked for more clips. Then, still holding on to the metal, he bent to check his sock. He wouldn't have much time. He sure as hell wouldn't have a second chance.

Hang on Lindsay. Hang on. I'll be there.

The cage groaned around him. The wind tugged at him like an impatient child. Mitchell lifted a shaking arm and wiped the sweat from his eyes. He turned to face the front, his hand still anchoring him. He tried to get his breath in the thin air and to get his heart to slow its race to the sky.

Mitchell saw light creeping over the edge of the top floor. The thick slab of concrete edged past the opening. Thunder slammed into the building, shaking it. Lightning danced around its edges, and Mitchell flinched. The storm had broken.

He saw Esperanza first. He looked like a melting snowman, all matter and no form, a grotesque shadow in the shifting light. The drug czar commanded the center of the group and kept a circle of space around him. His men collected at its edges.

Mitchell scanned them as the car lurched to a stop. He tried to let go and couldn't. The ground still shook beneath him. The building swayed in the wind, tarps flapping and raindrops chattering against the concrete like automatic weapons.

"Come on out, Mitchell," Colombo called, stepping forward. "I know how much you enjoy these little late-night gatherings."

He was a ghost in the night, moving as stealthily as a cat. Four other men were grouped to Colombo's right. The ones Mitchell could see well stood loosely, their hands within close range of their guns.

Mitchell couldn't get enough air. A wave of dizziness and an awful sense of unreality rocked him. Where did the nightmare end and reality start? Who would he find at the floor's edge, Lindsay or Maggie? Why had he thought it would be better this time? Why had he thought he could manage it? He took a slow, deep breath to placate his screaming lungs and pulled his hand free of the bars.

"Where is she?" His voice sounded strained, even to his ears.

"Say, Mitchell," Colombo goaded. "You don't look so good. Something you ate, maybe?"

Mitchell refused to address him. Keeping his eyes steadily on Esperanza, he repeated his question. "Where is she?"

After a moment spent contemplating the storm, Esperanza gave a short wave of the hand. Colombo immediately moved around a beam to where equipment had been stacked. He disappeared behind the pile and into the darkness. Mitchell watched him go and wondered whom he would bring out.

He didn't bring Lindsay back with him. He brought Al.

Mitchell saw his friend and felt a shudder of recognition go through him. Not Al. God, not Al.

"Thought we'd give you a little present," Colombo sang out, shoving Al to the floor. "We know you wanted your snitch. Since we won't be needing him anymore, we'll be happy to take care of him for you."

Mitchell couldn't take his eyes from his friend. He felt disoriented, as if he were seeing the wrong person on the floor.

"Why?" he asked automatically.

"Oh, simple," Colombo said obligingly. "See, it turns out that your friend Al here, he found out that a certain agent he knew had got hold of some information Mr. Esperanza wanted. And do you know he was going to get it without letting Mr. Esperanza know? Seems there was something in there about him he didn't want Mr. Esperanza to see."

"No, there wasn't," Mitchell said.

Al stiffened. Straightening a little, still on his knees, he raised stricken eyes to Mitchell.

"I wanted to smoke out the snitch," Mitchell told him, his voice unaccountably sad. "You should know the trick, Al. You and I used it on the Ferron case three years ago."

The storm gathered strength around them, battering the mountains and city alike, shaking the sky. Mitchell shivered with its fury. It seemed to suck the life from Al even as he watched, reducing him to a shell. Mitchell wiped at his forehead again.

"Why, Al?"

"I didn't want to, Mitch. You gotta believe me."

Oddly enough, Mitchell did. He remembered the times Al had appeared at the cabin, bearing chicken soup, eyes clumsily concerned, hands never quite still. He had stayed as long as he could each time, trying his best to make a difference when he didn't know how, really only wanting to help.

"Then why? You set Maggie up. You set me up."

"I told you to stay in the cabin!" his friend retorted, his face contorted with anguish. "If only you would have stayed there, it would have been okay. This would have all been over and you wouldn't have had to face this again."

"He's right," Colombo agreed from where he leaned against the pillar. "You wouldn't. And you look so bad. All sweaty and green. You really don't like it way up off the ground like this, Mitchell? I guess it's a real long way down, though, huh?"

"Esperanza," Mitchell snapped, glad of Colombo's presence. He incited a rage that ate away the nausea. If only he could feel as if both his feet were on the floor. He couldn't quite see, either, except for the slashing lightning, the faraway earth, the ghosts of nearby skyscrapers. He couldn't hear very well past the bellow of the thunder. "Have him bring her out here or you don't get it."

He never turned away from Colombo to get his answer. Esperanza must have made the move, because his henchman scowled and pulled himself upright. Reaching around behind him, he dragged Lindsay out the same way he had Al. She stayed on her feet, though.

They had taped her mouth. Mitchell could see the slash of it across her face. He blinked, trying to clear his eyes. She stood on her own. It didn't look as though she'd been hurt. She was trembling, but her head was high. Mitchell wanted to run to her.

The fire grew in his chest, the white-hot taste of fury and fear. Nothing could happen to her. He had to stop this somehow before she was hurt. Without realizing it, he took a step closer.

His move was some kind of signal. The ring of men closed around Esperanza. Guns appeared. Colombo grabbed a handful of Lindsay's hair and yanked her backward. Mitchell saw the pain lance her features, saw the fear she'd been hiding from him. He stopped, his hand out. Too late, he saw what they meant to do.

Colombo dragged her to the very edge, where the wind battered at her and the rain soaked her. Lindsay stiffened, cowered from the emptiness behind her. Colombo lifted a gun to her head and smiled.

Two feet from the elevator, standing on concrete that still seemed to tilt and sway, too far away to help, Mitchell froze. His heart died in him.

"No!"

He wasn't going to reach her, after all.

Chapter 15

He was here.

Mitchell had come.

Somewhere in the back of her mind, Lindsay heard the thunder. She saw how the lightning swept over the shadows and angles of the open concrete floor. She smelled the rain and ozone. But the storm didn't seem to concern her. Even when the crackle and fizz of electricity leaped at her, she didn't think to notice. Mitchell had come to get her, and that was all that mattered.

That man Colombo held her up only by her hair. He had a gun shoved into her neck, slowly stroking it against her, so she knew how much he was going to enjoy killing her. Her heart hammered in her ears and crowded her chest. Her throat burned. The wind was so cold at her back.

Lindsay was shaking. The edge was at her feet, right in the middle of her heels so that she couldn't quite keep her balance. She knew what waited beyond the edge of her shoe, and it paralyzed her. Colombo had been taunting her for hours, now, it seemed, telling her she would pay for killing his friend, that he was going to take great pleasure in thinking of ways to satisfy his sense of justice. He had stroked that gun along her neck, back and forth, telling her over and over again how Mitchell would never show up to save her from him.

Hours, first in that smelly black car of his, crumpled on the floor of the back seat, and then here. And all the time Colombo had taunted her with his gun and his certainty. Mitchell wouldn't come. He would let her die like his partner had. He would let her fall.

But he had come.

He'd walked right through his nightmares to save her, and Lindsay knew then that Mitchell hadn't lied. He loved her.

Lindsay felt the desperation bubble up in her, building like sobs in her chest. She had to let Mitchell know somehow what Colombo had in store for him. He'd told her in the car, on the elevator, up on the echoing, cavernous building as they had waited for the others. He would see Mitchell dead, no matter what it took. Even if he came, even if he proved his courage, Colombo would kill him. Her heels exposed to the storm, Lindsay still found that most of her fear was for Mitchell.

No matter what, she kept him in sight. He was like an anchor against the brutal wind, against the tremor in Colombo's hand. As long as Lindsay could see him, she'd be all right. He had come for her, and he would show her how they could get out. He had to. He had to think faster than she, faster than Colombo, or they wouldn't get back off that building, and Lindsay couldn't believe that would happen, no matter what Colombo had been whispering into her ear.

Mitchell.

He stood so far away, more than forty feet, his hand stretched out to her, his eyes cavernous in the light. She could see the sheen of sweat on his forehead, the unnatural way he stood, as if he couldn't get his balance, either. God, Mitchell, please, she begged silently, sudden tears stinging her eyes. Get me off here. Don't let them drop me.

Lindsay caught Mitchell's gaze. Even across the shadow-strewn distance she saw him stiffen and focus on her, as if no one else stood between them. He let his hand drop back to his side. Straightening, lifting his head a little, he let his shoulders ease.

It's okay, he was saying, we'll get through this. Lindsay understood it as well as if she had heard his voice. He would pull her away from that edge and get them down, and no one would stop him. Lindsay believed him, locked into him, drew courage from him like water from a deep well. Colombo didn't ease his hold. The storm still plucked at her with impatient fingers. But Lindsay was able to gather all the determination in her and offer it back to Mitchell with a smile.

He smiled back and she realized how much she loved him.

One of Esperanza's henchmen stepped up to Mitchell and patted him down. The man came away with the Beretta and resumed his place, the gun now in his own belt. Mitchell never took his eyes from Lindsay. He concentrated his focus, his energy was concentrated on her, supporting, soothing, easing. He had to let her know that they would make it, if she'd just pay attention and follow his lead. If she'd just trust him.

Now, Mitchell thought, surprised by the faint whispers of hope the smile in her eyes ignited in him, I just have to get us both out of here.

Stay with me, Lindsay. Help me get us down. He saw how fragile her courage was and understood. All courage was. He had to step back onto the thirty-ninth floor to really believe that.

"Now then, Mr. Mitchell," Esperanza said in a voice that mimicked the whine of the wind. "You have something to give me. After you do that, I will return what's yours."

Shifting his gaze a little to the left, Mitchell reached into his jacket pocket. The four guns were immediately leveled on him again. He allowed a careful smile and slid an envelope free with two fingers. He felt Lindsay's eyes on him. He moved slowly to give her time.

Colombo knew what Mitchell was doing. He jerked Lindsay's head back a little. His gun dug into her neck. Mitchell saw her flail for balance, saw her eyes go wide.

"All right," Mitchell immediately conceded, his eyes solidly on Esperanza, his chest too tight for air. "Here it is. Tell your pet monkey to let go of my friend or I send this sailing off into space."

Esperanza nodded. Colombo eased his grip by millimeters, bringing Lindsay a little closer to security.

Mitchell nodded. He lifted the envelope between himself and Esperanza, trying to think faster than the fat man, faster than the psychopath at the edge of the building. Trying to think, period, when the world still gyrated around him in time with the lightning flashes. "Since I'm here, mind my asking some questions?" He plunged on when no one immediately raised a gun. "Why was I safe as long as I stayed in my cabin?"

"Simple generosity." Esperanza wheezed in delight. "After all, your government's been so good to us. Since you suffered so much after you . . . interrupted what was to have been my last transaction, I decided to let you off if you'd just stay quiet until I rescheduled the deal and emigrated with my accumulated . . . proceeds." He shrugged, the fat wobbling as he moved. "Why make more trouble, when all I wanted was to live out my life out of reach of American law?"

Mitchell fingered the envelope, doing his best to ignore the sweat that trickled down his back. Lindsay's terror bit through him like lightning, urging him to action. Instead, he waited. "And I screwed all that up, huh?"

Esperanza remained unflustered. "Not yet."

Mitchell nodded. "I see. If I give you this and then ignore you for the next few days, you'll hand over the lady and let us off the building."

"I'll even throw in your friend down there," Esperanza offered with a small wave of the hand.

Al. Mitchell had actually almost forgotten about him. He was huddled beyond the ring of men like a penitent before the gates of heaven. Like Lindsay, his eyes were on Mitchell.

"Something to think about, isn't it, Mitchell?" Colombo called out. "Back on terra firma. No more sweats, no more shakes. You could take the lady here to live in Florida, where you wouldn't ever have to go above sea level again.''

Mitchell saw the gleam of Colombo's smile, the lazy arc his gun traced on Lindsay's neck. The rain swept around them in a veil, silhouetting them against the storm. Keep it up, he thought. Come on, Colombo, say something else. Stoke the fury until it blanks out the chills and dizziness. Mitchell lifted a hand to his forehead and wiped, emphasizing his weakness for Colombo's benefit—keeping his eyes on Lindsay, so she would understand.

"The envelope, Mr. Mitchell," Esperanza insisted.

It wasn't much of a chance. Lindsay was still balanced on the edge, held on only by her hair. Mitchell still had four guns and Esperanza to get past. But he knew his chances of getting off that floor alive if he did nothing. If he could get Lindsay to move, maybe he could help. Maybe he could keep her safe, as he'd promised.

He stepped a little closer to Esperanza. The guy with the gun stood to the fat man's left, his flat black eyes never wavering from Mitchell.

"One thing," Mitchell demurred, pulling the envelope back just as he was about to hand it over. "I had the chance to read this, and you were right. Perez was very thorough." Swinging his gaze from Esperanza to Colombo and then letting it flick briefly across Lindsay, Mitchell gave the envelope a little shake. "*Very* thorough. I thought that if you didn't mind, I'd take the satisfaction of telling you one part of this myself. Kind of a favor for a favor, you know?"

Esperanza wasn't impressed. Mitchell didn't care. It wasn't Esperanza's attention he really wanted. He shot Lindsay one more look and saw her grow wary. Good.

God, please let it break the right way. Let her be ready.

"Turns out," Mitchell went steadily on, his eyes back on the man in front of him, "that you had bigger problems than this. And we weren't the only ones with a snitch. Your friend Perez was working with somebody in your small circle of friends to hand you over to us on a platter, so that the Wilsons could take the action all to themselves."

He had Esperanza's interest. The porcine eyes narrowed even more. "What friend?"

Everybody was listening now, straining past the rumble of thunder and the whine of the wind. Mitchell smiled. He lifted the envelope a little and turned to face Colombo. "Your friend Paul over there."

"What!"

It was just the reaction he'd wanted. Colombo instinctively moved to protect himself. He lurched toward Esperanza, dragging Lindsay away from the edge of the floor. Suddenly lightning slashed at the building, blinding them all. Mitchell saw Lindsay beginning to turn and he made his move.

Everyone was still moving toward Colombo when Mitchell pulled the .38 from his sock. He swung it around. Lindsay lifted a knee hard into Colombo and he screamed. She dropped and rolled. Four guns came up. Five. Mitchell shot Colombo and watched him swing against a girder, his gun clattering to the cement.

One of the guns went off. Mitchell lunged for Esperanza. The big man couldn't move very fast. He had relied on his men and Mitchell's fear of heights to protect him. It hadn't occurred to him that Mitchell could be compelled by something even stronger.

Mitchell caught him turning for the elevator. Wrapping his arm around Esperanza's neck, he pulled him back. The man who had shot suddenly toppled, crying out, his gun flying loose. The other three saw what Mitchell had done and froze.

"If you'd like to see yourself reach old age," Mitchell murmured in Esperanza's ear, "I'd suggest that you tell them to donate those guns to the government."

"Put them down," Esperanza squeaked, the feel of a .38 against his ear evidently as convincing as Mitchell's logic.

Three automatics hit the concrete. Mitchell saw that the fourth man was still trying to get back up for more action. He nudged Esperanza, who started barking orders. His employee sat right back down where he was and lifted his hands.

It had been Al who had disabled the fourth man, the man who'd done the shooting. Mitchell saw him struggle to his feet. Mitchell was all set to see to Al's welfare when he looked beyond to check on Lindsay.

She lay on the floor beyond, curled on her side, her back to him, her hair in her face. Colombo sprawled no more than a few feet from her. Mitchell's stomach plummeted. His heart stopped. Lindsay wasn't moving.

"Lindsay!"

He almost let go of Esperanza. If Al hadn't been right there, he would have dragged his hostage all the way across the floor. As it was, Al was at his side before Mitch could move.

"I'll hold them," Al said, holding out his hand.

Mitchell looked down to see purpose in the agent's eyes, redemption. Al must know he would never find his way back, after what he'd done, but that didn't mean he would stop helping Mitchell.

Mitchell handed him the gun. He couldn't find the words for his friend, and didn't try. It was up to Al now. Mitchell had to get to Lindsay.

"Hey," he whispered, his voice shaking as badly as his hands as he crouched over her. "McDonough. Are you okay?"

She didn't answer. Mitchell reached out to brush her hair back. She was warm, and he could see that she was breathing.

"Lindsay?"

Her eyes were open. Staring. Mitchell followed their line of sight and saw Colombo there, dead and glaring, and he turned Lindsay to him.

"It's okay, honey," he soothed, pulling her into his arms. "It's all over now. I have you."

Lindsay didn't respond, as if his voice didn't break through her shock. Mitchell untied her hands and gently peeled the tape from her mouth. He knelt down and pulled her against his chest, where she would know she was safe, where she could hear the beating of his heart against her.

Mitchell was surprised to find that his eyes were stinging, and his throat ached. His shaking got worse instead of better as he crushed her to him, finally sure that she was all right.

"You came," she whispered. "You came."

The wonder in her voice pierced Mitchell with its sweetness. The certainty claimed him. She'd known he would do it, even when he hadn't.

"Of course I came," he answered with a smile only she saw. "I told you. I love you."

Lindsay smiled back finally, her eyes brightening with relief and exhilaration. "I think I believe you this time, Mitchell."

Mitchell pulled her tighter, sure that he'd never felt such a surge of life in himself before. "You'd better, McDonough. I'm going to be around for a while."

"Me, too," she whispered, even more awed than before. "I love you, too."

"Barbecues," Mitchell declared with a snort, flipping a steak with his spatula. "How suburban."

"Domesticity of the worst kind," Lindsay agreed from where she was setting out the plates on the picnic table.

He nodded, without bothering to see that she was grinning. "It's all your fault, you know."

"I bought a picnic table, Mitchell," she countered. "I didn't chain you to it."

"You chained me to *you*, McDonough," he retorted with a wave of the spatula in her direction. "You married me."

Lindsay scowled at him with hands on hips. "You're right. It was underhanded of me. I should have told you no for the fifteenth time so you could keep badgering me. Silly me, I figured that if I finally said yes, you'd stop sulking."

"I do not sulk."

"Pout, then. Of course, I guess that's better than whining, which is what you're doing right now."

It seemed that the steaks were going to have to fend for themselves. The spatula hit the grill with a clang and

Mitchell whirled on Lindsay. Shrieking in mock terror, she took off for the back door of the cabin.

"Nice to see that wedded bliss hasn't dimmed any," Alex drawled from his spot popping beans at the kitchen table as the two slammed into the house.

"You're bigger than he is!" Lindsay accused on her way by. "Stop him!"

Alex watched Mitchell thunder by scant feet behind her and shook his head. "Heck no. He's got a gun. Besides, I like him better than you."

The front door banged open and silence returned to the house. From her position by the sink, Mitchell's mother considered Alex with lifted eyebrows. "Are they always like this?"

"Nah," Alex disagreed. "Usually they're really lively."

Ellen Mitchell gave a grin and shook her head. "I have to admit that I never thought I'd see Jason this way in my life. He was always such a...oh, I don't know. He was never a little boy."

Alex nodded. "Well, he met the woman who was never a little girl, and it looks like they're making up for lost time."

She nodded, a mother's nod of decision, of acceptance. "Then it's a good thing she found Jason. I think they're good for each other."

Alex had to grin. There was still a lot of howling and shouting going on outside. "If they don't kill each other first."

"Just who do you think you are?" Lindsay demanded, caught tight in Mitchell's grasp. They'd made it as far as the front yard.

Mitchell dragged her to him, panting from exertion. "Your husband. Remember? For better, for worse, for foul mouth, for morning temper...."

Lindsay won that round with a well-placed kick that landed them both in the tall meadow grass. "It's all your fault," she accused just as breathlessly, wriggling in his grasp. "I told you not to wake me before seven."

"I thought you meant you'd be grumpy." He laughed, pushing the tangle of hair from her forehead. "Not a wolf woman." She was beautiful today, all sunlight and spice, her cheeks sun-tinted and her hair bleached out. Mitchell especially liked the way her jeans cupped her bottom and traced the line of her legs.

Lindsay bucked against him again, howling in indignation. It wasn't much of a trick for Mitchell to keep her down. "Wolf woman, huh?" she snarled, eyes narrowed but suspiciously bright. "Is that what you think of me? Of your wife of four months?"

"Every morning." He laughed again, battling flailing arms to pepper her face with kisses. "You try explaining teeth marks to *your* mother."

"You'll have bigger things to explain than that," she panted, twisting her head to miss the barrage.

"What?" he countered. "It isn't a full moon already, is it? You're not going to be howling? We won't find small neighborhood animals missing?"

"You're going to find some vital parts missing, Mitchell."

Mitchell grinned. "Try me, McDonough."

Lindsay made a strategic move and succeeded in provoking a delighted groan from her husband. "I'd say I have matters firmly in hand," she said, giggling.

"I'm at your mercy," he admitted, even though his hands had found their own trail to follow. "So, what do I have to explain? Besides physical exhaustion at thirty-five."

"If you can't keep up with me, Mitchell," she taunted, feasting on the taste of his skin, "maybe I'd better find a younger model."

"You do," he warned, smiling at the delicious little gasp he'd surprised from her, "and I'll be forced to drag you back here again. By force."

"Brute."

"Yes, ma'am."

"It'd be your own fault then if you couldn't give your mother an answer, when she asked where her grandchildren were."

Mitchell didn't listen very well. His attention was taken up by the silken fullness of her breasts. "What?"

"Stop playing and listen!" she insisted. "I've been waiting for the right minute to tell you."

"I will not," he retorted, dipping to taste one nipple through cotton and lace. It felt marvelous, firm and full. "And if it's so important, why wait till I have you prone in a field?"

"Because it's the only way I can get your attention."

Mitchell had to chuckle. "Well, you have it."

"Grandchildren," Lindsay prodded, lifting his head to face her. This really wasn't the way she'd wanted to tell him, at all. But with all the relatives and houseguests over the last few days, it seemed to be the only time they had to themselves. And this kind of news shouldn't wait.

"A wonderful idea," he agreed, dropping his eyes again. "We should have some of our own someday."

"Not someday," she retorted, pushing him away. "Now."

It took him a second. "Now?" he demanded. "How can we have grandchildren now?"

"We can't," Lindsay whispered, her voice hesitant with news that could never be given at the right or wrong time. "Your mother."

She never heard the car pull up. The first thing Lindsay knew, a group of people stood at the edge of the driveway watching.

"Nice to see you two are getting along better," Bob said equably, a bowl of potato salad in his hands.

"What!" Mitchell demanded of his wife, pulling her closer.

"Hello, Bob," Lindsay replied without moving. "Moira, Brent, Oscar. Glad you could come. Go on in. We'll be there in a minute."

"Fat chance," Oscar snorted delightedly.

"It doesn't look like it did the last time we were here, I hope," Bob remarked.

"Cleaned up and repainted," Lindsay assured him. "You'll be getting the bill."

"Fine," he agreed with a sage nod. "Fine. I talked to Al today, by the way. He sends his congratulations. He's in minimum security, you know."

"I'm glad," Lindsay nodded, sincerely pleased. Al's mistake had been to try to protect his daughter when she had started to sell drugs to support her habit. Once Esperanza had found out, he'd had Al on the hook. Al's turning state's witness had garnered him a light sentence. "Tell him I'll deliver my next news personally."

"Lindsay!" Mitchell warned. "You were going to tell me first."

Lindsay smiled up at her friends. "Excuse us, won't you?"

"No problem." Brent grinned. "Call if you need anybody to pick up the pieces."

"That," Mitchell answered without looking away from the amused challenge in his wife's eyes, "is a distinct possibility."

The screen door had whispered shut before either of them moved again.

"I'm getting cramped," Lindsay complained. "Mind if we sit up?"

"Yes," Mitchell argued, holding her on her back. "If I let you up, you'll torture me for another twenty minutes. I'd like to get this over with before the rest of the guests show up."

"Your fault." She smiled up at him, brushing his hair back from his forehead. "If you had let me talk right away, I wouldn't have taken so long."

"So talk," he growled. "What grandchildren?"

"Your mother's," she answered evenly, the smile still in place. "I told you."

Mitchell suddenly went very quiet. "How?"

Lindsay laughed, delighted by his perplexity. "Oh, the usual way, I'm sure."

"I suppose you think that's my fault, too?" he demanded, although his voice was suspiciously tender.

"If it isn't," she assured him, "then I've been cleaning up the wrong cabin all these months. Congratulations, Mitchell. You're going to be a daddy."

Mitchell started awake. His heart was beating hard and his breath seemed caught in his chest. A dream. It had been a dream.

He turned to check the other side of the bed. She was there, so softly asleep that she looked like a nymph caught in a beam of moonlight, her hair spilling over the pillow in a golden shower, her pink-tinged face tucked into her pillow, her lips parted just a little in sleep.

It hadn't been a dream. It had really happened. Lindsay had told him that afternoon, holding his future up to him out in a field of wildflowers and aspen, breaking his heart with the beauty of her gift, with the boundless joy in her eyes.

A child. He was going to be a father. Mitchell sat slowly up in bed, careful not to wake Lindsay. He looked around the room that had so recently been his prison, and wondered at its changes. More than the decor. More than just his escape from the nightmares, though Maggie had finally been put back into his memory, where she wanted to be.

The difference in this room was in the lady who lay next to him, the lady who had given him the gift of hope and in return stolen his heart. On the wall across from their bed hung the cross-stitching Lindsay had promised him. Mitchell could read Pliny's words even in the dark. *Hope is the dream of the waking man.*

Mitchell smiled. The dreams finally of the sleeping man, too, he realized, looking down on his wife.

"Mitchell," she murmured, still half asleep, nestled against him. "Are you all right?"

She had given him back his peace. His dreams. She had bestowed happiness upon him like a fine, nourishing rain and promised to stay to watch it grow in him. Yes, Mitchell thought with new contentment. I'm all right. For the first time in my life. I'm really all right.

"I'm fine," he assured her, slipping back beneath the covers to draw her into his arms. "I was dreaming."

Lindsay snuggled closer, her head on his shoulder, her arm against his chest. "Good," she whispered, hearing the wonder in his voice. "You deserve it." Sighing a little, she smiled. "Ozzie and Harriet never had it so good."

Mitchell opened his eyes. "What?"

She patted him on the chest. "Nothing. I love you."

"And I," he said softly, thinking of his dream and smiling back, "love you."

* * * * *

Silhouette Desire ®

1989
IS THE YEAR
OF THE MAN!

What makes a romance? A special man, of course, and Silhouette Desire celebrates that fact with *twelve* of them! From Mr. January to Mr. December, every month has a tribute to the Silhouette Desire hero—our **MAN OF THE MONTH!**

Sexy, macho, charming, irritating . . . irresistible! Nothing can stop these men from sweeping you away. Created by some of your favorite authors, each man is custom-made for pleasure—*reading* pleasure—so don't miss a single one.

Mr. January is Blake Donavan in RELUCTANT FATHER by Diana Palmer
Mr. February is Hank Branson in THE GENTLEMAN INSISTS by Joan Hohl
Mr. March is Carson Tanner in NIGHT OF THE HUNTER by Jennifer Greene
Mr. April is Slater McCall in A DANGEROUS KIND OF MAN by Naomi Horton
Mr. May is Luke Harmon in VENGEANCE IS MINE by Lucy Gordon
Mr. June is Quinn McNamara in IRRESISTIBLE by Annette Broadrick

And that's only the half of it—
so get out there and find your man!

Silhouette Desire's

MAN OF THE MONTH . . .

Silhouette Intimate Moments®

COMING
NEXT MONTH

#277 IN A REBEL'S ARMS—Barbara Faith

Southern belle Caroline Winwood had come to San Germaine to find her father, but discovered danger and deception instead. Nothing was as it seemed, and when mysterious Major Christoffe Santini came to her rescue, she suspected the passion he aroused might very well be the deadliest peril of all.

#278 THE REAL THING—Lucy Hamilton

Jessie's world had been turned upside down, and only one man could make it right—FBI agent Sam King. He wasn't the perfect knight in shining armor, but Jessie knew he was the man of her dreams. Yet, with danger lurking around every corner, turning dreams into reality soon became a race against time.

#279 WATER FROM THE MOON—
Terese Ramin

Tragedy had once torn Casie and Cameron apart; now it brought them together again. But this time, in the unstable country of Zaragoza, Casie was responsible for Cam's life, not his love. Only if she could best the odds and foil his kidnapping, would she ever again win his heart.

#280 CHANGE OF HEART—Maura Seger

Gerry's boat company was sinking, and only world-class sailor Jake Austin could save it by winning an upcoming race. But five years ago this man, who hadn't believed in love, had won her heart. Gerry now found herself hoping for a victory that had nothing to do with the contest.

AVAILABLE THIS MONTH: